BY HER SIGHT

THE UNITAM REALM SERIES

BOOK ONE

SUNNY HART

Published by Sunny Hart
In USA

Edited by Insomniac Editing Services

Cover by Cauldron Press

Created with Vellum

AUTHOR'S NOTE

This book is a Reverse Harem romance where the heroine will not have to choose between any of her men. It will feature a FMMM relationship and is recommended for 18+ due to mature content.

DESCRIPTION

In the Unitam Realm, power determines where you belong.

Blind, orphaned witch Claire has spent her entire life wondering where she belonged.

She's grown up in a small coven on the outskirts of the Unitam Realm. While the teasing about her blindness hurts, the ridicule the coven members give her about her orphan status cuts deeper. What kind of disappointment do you have to be to have your parents abandon you?

When the semi-sentient Academy sends her an acceptance letter, she's sure it's a mistake. If she doesn't belong at Windshire, she surely won't belong at the Academy. But what does she have to lose?

As she navigates new friends, intense classes, and professors who seem to be split on whether she will pass or fail, her power starts to unravel inside of her, leaving Claire with more questions about her parents and where she belongs.

And why does the Stonemont Triad (Desmond, the charming wizard, Everett, the silent Gryphon, and Malcolm, the grumbly Dragon) want to get to know a low-level witch like her?"

This is a slow-burn HEA RH and the first book in the series. Slight cliffhanger at the end.

CHAPTER 1

One step forward. One step sideways. Half turn. Claire knelt at a fresh row, hands digging into the dirt, searching for the next prize to add to her basket. The sun was warm against her skin, its rays licking at her exposed forearms. The skirt she wore was sure to be stained with the cool mud that pressed against her knees, but she would take care of that this afternoon when she moved on to the laundry. There was something soothing about working in the garden, her hands encased in the cool soil, hunting for the potatoes that Mary would add to dinner later.

The afternoon breeze danced along the back of her neck, lifting the sweaty hairs there that spilled out from the high bun she had coaxed her curly hair into. The breeze felt wonderful against her flushed skin. She felt the tremble of the earth off to her left, and the subsequent air shift indicated someone was approaching.

The Windshire Coven members called her blind, but Claire didn't feel like that was correct. While she couldn't see color or make out details, the shadows that she could see formed rough shapes of the world around her. In addition, her other senses were much more in tune with the world. She could not describe it, although no one had ever asked her to, but it was almost like she could feel the vibrations or disturbances in the air and earth allowing her to sense when something in her environment moved.

After living most of her life at the orphanage on the outskirts of the Windshire Coven, she could navigate her little world easily. Claire couldn't tell you how she came to live at the orphanage. To listen to Mother Kemp's story, five-year-old Claire was found wandering in the woods on the outskirts of the Windshire Coven nearly 20 years ago.

They sent missives out to the surrounding covens and shifter communities, but no one stepped forward to claim the child. A magic reading confirmed that the child was born a witch, although an extremely weak one. Claire often wondered if that's why she was abandoned.

In the Unitam Realm, power ruled and the most powerful were usually pure of blood. At first her lack of power didn't bother her but the other children of the compound grew cruel as they got older, teasing Claire that she was born of an affair and when she showed such little magic, she was discarded. Other children teased her about her freaky eyes, almost a milky white they were so pale blue. At least that's the color the adults told her. Claire could accept the teasing about being blind as that was something she couldn't help. However, the teasing remarks about how she was abandoned and would never belong cut so much deeper.

Claire was never one to wallow, though. Or at least she tried not to. Instead, she shrugged off the loneliness and focused on the good things. Her life was a simple one. She rarely left the orphanage grounds, but the house had plenty to keep her busy. Mother Kemp was the warden of the orphans and insisted that all the orphans earn their keep. Claire tended to a simple list of chores that Mother Kemp assigned and spent her evenings with a reading spell, devouring the orphanage's small collection of books. It was a good life, if not a simple one. She should not ask for more.

Yet as she hoisted the basket of potatoes up onto her hip, her back straining in the effort, she found herself immersed in the all too familiar daydream where she was meant for more than this orphanage, that she belonged somewhere, with someone.

The smell of starch wrinkled her nose. She turned and caught the shadows forming a figure. "Yes, Mother Kemp?" She asked.

"Are you almost done here?" Mother Kemp's voice was emotionless. In all her years here, Claire would never accuse her of being a mother figure. Sometimes, in her daydreams, Claire wondered what her own mother was like. Was it because she was loving or cruel that she gave Claire up? Was she dead because no one would knowingly abandon a five-year-old?.

"Just these last two rows," she replied.

"Drop the basket off in the kitchen when you're finished and then you need to head to the village to pick up the standing order from the bakery," Mother Kemp instructed, "Mary isn't feeling well."

Claire took a step back, questions swirling in her brain. Before she could ask any of them, Mother Kemp had left.

Claire finished the last two rows almost on autopilot. Mother Kemp never asked her to go to the village anymore. Before her 18th birthday, Claire had made infrequent trips to the village that usually resulted in the children of the coven teasing her or playing cruel tricks on the blind girl.

Her 18th birthday had been one of the last times she had been in the village. It was the day of her coming of age ceremony with some other coven children. Eighteen was supposed to be a big year for witches with their coming of age ceremony dictating their place in the coven. Witches and wizards with lots of magical power tended to get higher placement in the covens as they were more useful to the coven leaders. The best of them even applied to the Academy outside the Capitol city, Regis, for a chance to learn from the greatest and maybe one day work for the Council.

Claire's coming of age ceremony, though, had been a humiliating event. The scrying bowl that the coven elders used to determine the power level of the young witches had barely rippled. The coven elder had announced that Claire had little to no magic and was going to be inconsequential to the success of the coven. Claire's cheeks still heated and her stomach clenched in knots as she thought about the jeers from her peers and the whispers from the adults of the coven.

It was like declaring open season on Claire for the children of the coven. If someone was going to be inconsequential to the coven's success then that made her fair game for all the taunts, teasing and pranks the coven children could come up with. After a nasty prank a few years after her coming of age ceremony left Claire stranded in the woods for several hours, Mother Kemp stopped asking her to go to the village. She hadn't been to the village in nearly three years now, something that was apparently changing today. The nerves had Claire's hands shaking slightly as she resumed her task.

Finally, at the end of the last row, Claire dusted off her skirt the best she could and then placed the basket of potatoes in the wooden chest outside the kitchen building. The scent of stew wafted out the door, and Claire decided to check and see if Mary needed anything else before Claire headed to the village. And put off going into the village a little while longer.

"Mary," Claire said from the open doorway, trying to find the cook in the room.

"By the fireplace, child." Mary called all the children at the orphanage 'child' while they were here. Claire often wondered if that helped Mary keep her distance.

"I was about to head into the village for the bread like

Mother Kemp asked and wanted to check on you. Mother Kemp said you weren't feeling well?"

Mary was an elderly hedge witch that was widowed and childless. She didn't live at the orphanage, instead she had a small cottage not far away, but she had been working at the orphanage as its cook for as long as Claire had been there.

"I'm fine, child, my knee is just acting up. Wasn't going to make the walk to the bakery. Sit and eat a small bowl before you go."

Claire walked three steps into the room and then held her hand out, finding the edge of one of the wooden chairs around the big table in the center of the room. She sat softly as Mary ladled some stew into a bowl and slid it across the table to Claire.

Claire cupped the bowl with her hands, momentarily enjoying the warmth on her palms before she traced the rim with a finger tip until her finger caught the spoon Mary had set in the bowl. Raising a spoonful to her mouth, she blew on it softly while Mary stirred the pot. The sound of the ladle clanging against the large metal pot was a familiar sound in the kitchen. Stew was easy to serve multiple children and took fewer resources than other meals.

The familiar sounds and smells of the kitchen and the taste of the stew settled Claire's stomach and nerves. It had been three years, surely that was long enough for the coven children to forget about Claire. It would be an easy trip to help Mary.

Like always, Mary was not in a talkative mood, and Claire quickly finished her bowl of stew. Rising from the table, she took the four steps to the small wash basin against one wall of the room. She dunked the bowl and spoon in the small bucket of soapy water Mary kept there and rinsed it before placing it on the drying rack above the basin.

"I'm off to the village now," Claire tried to keep her voice light even as her stomach pitted.

Mary just grunted an affirmative and Claire exited the kitchen building. Luckily for Claire, there was a fence that ran down the road from the orphanage to the village outskirts. It was an old stone fence, and the sun-warmed stone felt lovely under her fingertips as she followed the wall.

She lifted her face to the sun, her steps as sure and steady as the stone wall next to her. On the worst days, when loneliness ate away at her emotions and tears slipped down her cheeks at the aching to belong somewhere, nature had always helped Claire. The warmth of the sun, the coolness of the breeze, the steadiness of the earth, the calmness of the water. These elements were her only friends even if they didn't want to work with Claire's magic.

In Unitam, most magic users were proficient at one or two elements. The more powerful magic users were proficient at two elements with the rare magic user proficient at three elements. Usually the more powerful magic users developed a mastery with one of their elements. A magic user with just one element might develop a mastery of it but that was rare as well. Windshire Coven typically produced magic users that had a wind proficiency although other elements were welcome as well.

All too soon, Claire heard the sounds of the bustling village. Shouts from the coven members as they greeted each other, children laughing, and the bustle and clanging that seemed to always be going on while the village's affairs were attended to. Even though Windshire was on the outskirts of the witches' region, it always seemed to be busy. Traders used the road Claire was currently on to reach the village from the Capitol and back again.

For a few minutes, it seemed like Claire was going to make it to the baker without being accosted, but those hopes soon turned to dust.

"Oh look, it's the blind freak." Melanie was one of the

witches that was at the same coming of age ceremony as Claire was. She was the granddaughter of one of the coven elders and one of the most powerful magic children with a wind proficiency. She had applied to the Academy but was denied. The coven still treated her like royalty for even being able to apply.

"Melanie," Claire acknowledged politely, hoping that time had softened Melanie's cruel streak.

That always seemed to be Claire's downfall, her belief that others could be better.

"Ew, don't speak to her," Anna, one of Melanie's friends, joined her, "I can't believe they let you out of the orphanage."

Claire tried to keep walking, but the girls' shadows moved to block her way, "Excuse me," she said politely but her insides were churning. Why couldn't they just leave her alone?

There was a moment's pause, and then the girls moved out of the way. Claire let out a soft sigh of relief before she felt a powerful gust of wind hit her in the back. She fell to her hands and knees, right into a puddle that had definitely not been there before. Melanie's and Anna's laughter faded as they left Claire there.

Claire supposed she should be grateful that Melanie had only used her wind magic combined with Anna's water magic. Or at least she tried to be grateful as she stood up, her skirt drenched and her hands muddy. Claire wiped her hands on the back of her skirt, fighting back tears. She didn't belong here.

Claire kept her head down as she hurried to the village bakery. The bell on the door jingled as Claire entered the bakery. She waited while Donna finished up with a customer. The customer gave Claire a wide berth as she exited, sniffing dramatically like Claire stunk.

"What in the realm happened to you?" Donna asked her.

"Tripped," Claire murmured, "Mother Kemp sent me to get the bread order."

"Mary's knee acting up again?" Donna asked as she bustled

behind the counter, her shadow moving back and forth as she packaged up the order.

"Yes," Claire whispered. Donna had always been neutral towards her but Claire was still fighting down her nerves after her last coven encounter.

Thankfully, Claire didn't encounter anyone else as she hurried back to the orphanage. Her wet skirt was becoming uncomfortable and Claire knew she would need to wash it before tonight or the mud would set in.

"What took you so long, child?" Mary asked as she entered the kitchen, "I needed this bread thirty minutes ago."

"Sorry, Mary," Claire murmured, "I was held up in the village."

Claire could feel Mary's gaze assessing her dirty clothing. "Well, you'll have no time to clean up because of your tardiness. Mother Kemp is requesting to see you in her office. You have a letter."

Claire stilled until Mary snapped at her for dawdling, breaking her out of her shock. She never got mail. The only people she knew were other orphans. Even when the orphans were adopted or aged out, Claire had never grown close enough to any of them to correspond. And no one in the coven would send her letters. They preferred to give insults, either whispered behind their hands or delivered to her face.

She dropped the basket of bread on the table and exited the kitchen. Crossing the courtyard, she entered the main building and hurried down the familiar hallway. Arriving at Mother Kemp's office, she lifted her hand and rapped three times.

"Enter." Mother Kemp's strong voice called.

Claire opened the door, the metal knob turning easy in her grip. "Come in and close the door." Mother Kemp said.

Claire softly shut the door behind her, turned and took three steps to the center of the room, folding herself into one of the two chairs in front of Mother Kemp's desk. "I have a letter?" She questioned.

Even blind, Claire could feel the weight of Mother Kemp's stare. "Yes. An offer letter. From the Academy."

Claire's mouth dropped open for a second before she closed it quickly. The Academy was for magic users like witches and shifters, usually reserved for the more powerful magic users. It was an education beyond what a coven or community could offer and only for the best and brightest, like Melanie and Anna. Not a low level witch like Claire.

"There must be some kind of mistake." Claire stammered.

"There is no mistake. You leave tomorrow. The Academy will provide transportation."

"But, what about the cost? My life here? I barely have any magic." Claire's mind was racing.

She could hear Mother Kemp shift forward as the smell of starch grew stronger. "While it is an unusual circumstance, every so often, the Academy chooses a select few students to receive a full scholarship."

Now Claire had even more questions. However, it looked like Mother Kemp was not inclined to give more answers, sitting back in her chair. "I would suggest you pack anything you wish to bring and say your goodbyes tonight. The carriage will be here first thing in the morning according to the letter."

Numbly, Claire rose to her feet and took the letter that Mother Kemp gave her. She left the office, thoughts swirling. There were no goodbyes to say as the other orphans avoided the blind girl. And clearly Mother Kemp had said her version of a goodbye. She could say goodbye to Mary in the morning and see if there was any bread left over for the trip.

Moving past the entrance hallway, she climbed the stairs to her attic room. As the eldest orphan, Claire was given her own room. She climbed the creaky old stairs to the stuffy room. It was small, barely enough room for the single bed and a small shelf that held Claire's meager collection of clothing and other belongings.

From under the small bed, she pulled a canvas satchel she had rescued from the trash and gave a good cleaning to. She folded her spare clothes neatly and stuffed them in the bottom of the bag. She followed it with her ink and quill set and a bound parchment book. She felt the worn cover of a book graze her fingertips. One of her favorite fairy tales. She spent many a night lost in these familiar fairy tales. After a moment, she shoved that in her bag as well, feeling a slight bit of guilt over taking it from the orphanage's small library but with all the changes coming her way, a bit of familiarity might be what she needed.

Finishing packing, she sat down on the corner of her bed. For the last time, she took in the smells of the familiar drafty room. The sharp scent of the soap she used to scrub the floorboards and the slightly musty smell she could never quite get out. The fresh scent of the forest coming through the sole drafty window.

For the last two decades of her life, this place had been home. Now, she was about to leave that because a sentient building offered her admission to the most prestigious school in the realm. Admission only offered to students who became great. Mother Kemp said there was no mistake but Claire couldn't help but feel like there was.

She had barely any magic, nothing to offer the world. She remembered the cruel taunts of the other children of the coven and knew that the students of the Academy would be just as bad if not worse when they discovered she was a fraud. She didn't belong in the coven but what if she belonged even less at the Academy? Worried thoughts raced through her mind until she felt a slight headache come on.

Placing a hand on her forehead and her other on her stomach, Claire forced herself to take a few deep breaths. She couldn't see how she belonged at the Academy but right now it was a better choice than Windshire. Multiple covens had children who attended the Academy. Maybe Claire could find one who would take pity on her and allow her to join their coven as a hedge witch.

Feeling slightly better with the new plan and with nothing left to pack, she curled up on the bed. Pulling the light blanket over her body, she fell into a restless sleep, her dreams filled with shadowy figures that jumped out at her at every turn.

CHAPTER 2

The next morning, Claire was sitting out on the front steps of the orphanage, her bag placed carefully on her feet. She held a small sack in one hand with a roll and some dried meat. In the other hand, the Academy's invitation was firmly in her grasp. The journey to the Academy would take a few hours by carriage.

While outwardly she appeared calm, internally Claire was a bundle of nerves. This was the only home she had ever known even if most days it didn't feel like she belonged. The familiarity of it was soothing and now she was going to throw it all away? For what? An invitation to the Academy that was probably a mistake?

The bright day caused shadows to dance everywhere around the courtyard and she took in the familiar outlines of the fence and small rose bushes she had lovingly cared for. Who was going to look after them now? Maybe Claire once the Academy realized it made a mistake and sent her back. Or maybe that job would fall to someone else, a small voice inside her thought. Maybe she never belonged here because she was always meant to belong somewhere else, like the Academy?

Claire shook off those thoughts. 'What was done was done' was what Mother Kemp liked to say. She was going to the Academy and she was going to make the best of it. Claire was glad for the bright day though. It would be easier to 'see' the approaching carriage. The brighter the day, the more she 'saw' with the shadows although she could still only see about five paces away. On cloudy days or in dark rooms, the shape of the shadows was still visible but harder to make out. In those dimmer settings, it limited her shadow vision to three paces. Today, while her entire vision was a solid nothing, the shadows appeared as darker objects in her 'vision'. It was not a completely accurate system though so Claire usually relied on her other senses as well.

Like now, she could hear the creak of wheels coming down the lane to the left. The thuds of horses' hooves beat a rhythmic pattern as the jingle of harnesses filled her ear drums. As the sounds got louder, she could make out the shadow outline of a carriage pulled by two horses. Two shadowy figures sat in the driver's seat and two more horses and riders flanked the carriage.

She stayed seated, wishing Mother Kemp was outside helping introduce her, but she had been called away to a meeting in the coven.

The carriage rolled to a stop outside the fence. One shadow from the driver's seat got down while one horseman dismounted. The shadows drew closer and Claire rose to her feet.

"Well, this is certainly unexpected," one shadow drawled as the scent of spearmint filled her nostrils. The bitter sweetness made Claire draw in a sharp breath. The deepness of his voice confirmed at least one figure was a man.

She reached out a hand, unsure of how to address the comment. Instead she simply said, "I'm Claire. I'm assuming the Academy sent you?"

The shadowy figure who first spoke stepped closer and grasped her hand. Tingles spread from where their hands connected and for a moment it seemed like the shadows lightened so she could vaguely make out how tall he was. He towered over her slight frame. His skin was smooth with calluses on his fingertips. A musician maybe?

The silence hung between them as he drew in a long breath. Did he just sniff her? With her focus on him, she failed to notice the other shadowy figure had moved closer. "Introduce yourself, Desmond, or let the girl go."

Claire couldn't see it but she could feel the heat of the glare that Desmond must have shot the other man. That seemed to be another side effect of her senses, it was almost like she could feel emotions sometime.

"Now you're the one being rude, Everett," Desmond chided, "I was just taking a moment to admire this little beauty before us."

Claire felt the heat rush to her cheeks. Desmond gave her hand one last squeeze before releasing it. The tingles vanished immediately making Claire almost miss them. She shifted towards the other man and held out her hand, "Pleased to meet you, Everett," she said softly, the etiquette lessons the orphanage had drilled into them forced her actions. She would rather flee back into the orphanage. These men were dangerously close to overwhelming her. She'd never experienced these feelings before from touching any of the others here in the coven.

The hand that grasped her this time had callouses on the palms. Instead of tingles, coolness seemed to radiate from their joined palms, sending the sensation up her forearm. He dropped his hand faster than Desmond did and she cursed herself for mourning the loss. What was happening? She really needed to get out more, she thought and then almost snorted at the thought. She was about to 'get out' more than she ever had.

"Pleasure," his tenor voice replied.

"Fascinating." Desmond purred next to them, the glee in his voice was clear. "This trip just got more interesting."

Claire frowned. "What do you mean?"

"Don't mind him," Everett said, "he doesn't get outside his workroom much and seems to forget how to behave in the outside world."

Oh that makes sense, Claire thought, worried that they might have been teasing her. She smiled brightly at Desmond, ignoring the intakes of breath from both of them. "You and I can navigate the outside world together. This is my first time leaving the coven."

"Is that so, little witch?" Desmond murmured, "In that case, let's begin the adventure."

A shadow suddenly edged her 'vision' and Claire startled backwards, her heel catching on the step behind her. Before she could fall, Desmond grasped her elbow, startling her again and making her drop her bag of food. "I'm sorry," she apologized, cheeks flaming. She gestured awkwardly to her eyes, "Um, Mother Kemp always said it was obvious, but I, uh, actually can't see and you caught me off guard,"

She might not be able to see but she definitely felt the look pass between the two men.

"Our apologies, little witch," Desmond said, "you seemed to see us when we approached."

"Oh, that's because my other senses are better to make up for the lack of sight. It's quite common, I'm told. I could hear the carriage and then I could smell you when you approached." It was so much easier to explain it as a complete lack of sight rather than trying to explain the shadows.

"I told you, you should have bathed before you came," Desmond teased Everett.

A light thud made Claire think Everett had hit Desmond in retaliation for the teasing so she hurried to explain, "Oh um it's not a bad smell," she said, "Everett smells like the forest after the rain and Desmond smells like spearmint."

The weight of their gaze made her think she said something wrong. "Interesting," Everett said so softly that she wasn't sure she was supposed to hear it.

Everett's shadow reached down for her bag much more slowly. Claire reached a hand out for Desmond's elbow. Desmond led her to the carriage and helped her into one of the bench seats before placing her bag next to her.

"One moment, little witch," he said, giving her hand a quick squeeze before closing the door. She buried her face in her hands as soon as he did. How embarrassing! She clearly hadn't interacted with enough people to know what was and wasn't normal. The pit in her stomach that had been there since last night grew bigger as she thought about how much worse it would be at the Academy. How much more out of place she would be

Her ears perked up at the sound of voices outside the door. Without her enhanced hearing, she might have missed the words. "Malcolm is going to be so upset he missed out on this," she could hear the gloating in Desmond's tone.

"Out of all the places, an inconsequential coven on the outskirts of the region was not what we imagined." Everett's dry tone came through the door.

Claire frowned. They had been searching for her? That doesn't make sense. She's a low-level witch and they are clearly Academy guards of some sort. Maybe teachers? No, teachers wouldn't escort students. They had to be guards. Maybe they were just talking about the drive to get here. The Windshire Coven was a lower level coven compared to most. The less power a coven or community had the farther away from the Capitol they were located. A concept that always puzzled her because don't the weaker always live closer to the protection?

The door broke her musings. The fresh smell of forest, and

she wasn't sure, but also some kind of spice filled the carriage as Everett took a seat across from her. As soon as he sat, the carriage lurched forward into motion as the driver clucked to the horses.

"Can I see your invitation, Claire?" Everett asked.

Claire smoothed out the paper before handing it over reluctantly. While it was just a piece of paper, she almost felt protective over it as the words gave her a path out of the coven.

Everett gingerly took it from her almost sensing her reluctance. The rustle of paper sounds as he unfolded it, a sharp breath as he read the words. "You're Academy-chosen?" His voice was sharp.

She shrank back into the seat slightly, "That's what Mother Kemp said." She saw an opportunity to get more answers, "I don't really know what that means though?"

Thankfully, Everett explained, "The Academy is a sentient structure. It adapts to the needs of the teachers and student body. Rumors say it was constructed by the Fae and the Elves long ago before the Great War. The Academy stays neutral and quiet for most of the time during the application process but occasionally helps choose students if the Headmaster needs help with a decision." It seemed like he wanted to say more but stopped himself

Now Claire had even more questions. The first one seemed most important. "You said the Academy will help the Headmaster choose between two applicants. But what if the student never applied?"

"You never applied?" Everett's question was sharp.

Claire shook her head, "I'm a low-level, blind, orphaned witch who's never left the coven before today and I rarely leave the orphanage grounds. Why on earth would I apply?" The frustration and the fear of the unknown sharpened her words.

The cushions squeaked as Everett must have leaned back, "Could someone have applied for you?"

Claire shook her head again. "I don't think so? Mother Kemp would have let me know if she did, I think?"

"Someone must have applied for you." Everett reasoned, "and you just didn't know about it. The Academy is sentient but it's never initiated an acceptance letter by itself before. It mainly focuses on the grounds and buildings."

Claire nodded her agreement although she was certain no one would have bothered to apply for her. She interacted with very few people at the coven. Most stayed away as if they could catch blindness or as if she could steal their magic.

"The students at the Academy are usually more advanced in their magic. Are you saying you're a low-level witch compared to others in Windshire Coven or low-level compared to the rest of the kingdom?"

Claire shrugged, "I haven't really interacted with or learned about the rest of the kingdom so I really have no comparison. If you're asking what I can do, I've mastered some basic spells but nothing much else. I can't manipulate wind like most of the other Windshire witches and wizards can do but I'm assuming that's because of my orphan status."

Everett's scent got stronger as the cushions creaked again. He must be leaning forward. "Your parents weren't Windshire Coven members."

"No," Claire shook her head. "I was found wandering the forest at five years old. No one claimed me from local covens or communities so Windshire took me in at the orphanage. I don't know who my parents are."

"So why are you so certain you are a low-level witch?" Everett challenged.

Claire shrugged, "Probably because when the elders tested me, that's what they declared."

She did not add that the testing has been a public affair like most were when children reached eighteen. The burn of humiliation as the elders declared her practically useless with magic and the jeers of the other children and some adults still rang in her ears. She shifted uncomfortably wishing Everett would drop the questioning. She didn't need to be reminded how out of place she felt and would continue to feel.

"Interesting." Everett mused, "the Academy doesn't break centuries of protocols for a low-level witch."

"Maybe it was a mistake?" That would make sense for Claire. A glitch in the system.

"Maybe." Everett said, his tone suggesting he wasn't convinced. "Here," he handed the paper back to her.

She folded it and slipped it inside her dress pocket carefully. "You should rest," he suggested, "it's a long drive to the Academy. I'm going to ride out with Desmond for a bit."

Claire nodded as he tapped the wall of the carriage. The movement stopped as he opened the door and hopped out, closing the door behind him. After a few seconds, the carriage moved forward again and the murmur of voices started. There was too much noise from the carriage to hear the voices but Claire closed her eyes as her cheeks burned. Great. Just great. She wasn't even at the Academy yet and she was already a freak compared to the rest of the students. With her eyes still closed, the movement of the carriage started rocking her to sleep. She surrendered hoping when she woke up, this would all be just a dream.

* * *

"SHE SAID WHAT?" Desmond questioned Everett.

"She said she never applied to the Academy. That she simply got the letter."

Desmond's mind raced at the knowledge. He loved knowledge. Malcolm and Everett teased him about being a bookworm but Desmond knew that knowledge was power. He didn't enjoy missing pieces, but he did like solving puzzles. And the brown curly haired woman with the palest blue eyes he had ever seen in the carriage in front of them was most definitely a puzzle.

"That shouldn't be possible," he murmured more to himself than to Everett.

Everett heard him anyway with his enhanced hearing. "I know." Everett's mouth was in a tight line, clearly not happy with the knowledge.

"What did you tell her?" Desmond questioned.

"That someone must have applied for her without her knowledge. That's the only way I could explain the Academy breaking centuries of protocols."

"Good," Desmond nodded. "I'll reinforce that story when we get to the Academy. The fewer people who know the better. I'm sure Headmaster Dorian agrees or he would have said something to us when he sent us to retrieve her."

Everett just grunted. Clearly in agreement but his gryphon must be riding him hard. Desmond couldn't even imagine how Malcolm would be reacting right now. The temperamental dragon shifter was quite dramatic.

The third member of their Triad, Malcolm has been called home by his family and therefore unable to join the other two on their journey. Probably for the best, Desmond mused, Claire was already skittish, no need to throw a moody, possessive dragon into the mix. Especially one that just found his mate and learned that the sentient Academy, known for picking champions, had just singled her out. Nope, that information was better shared after they got to the Academy and preferably well away from Claire although Desmond felt a pang in his chest at her being away from his side.

His Triad had been looking for their mate for over a decade now. The Council pushed a few females in their early years but Malcolm could throw a tantrum if necessary. Well, they all could, Desmond thought. After a spectacular tantrum of almost blowing up the Council member's summer home, it relieved the

Triad of the pressure of a forced mating. However, they were still scrutinized by the Council which could pose a problem if the Council got wind of Claire although being at the Academy provided their Triad a measure of protection.

His Triad had stayed at the Academy past their graduation date intentionally. The Academy offered mastery programs which allowed them to continue their education and provided a small measure of protection from the Council as Headmaster Dorian was fiercely protective over his school and grounds. Everett had taken up a leadership position in the Academy guard while Desmond taught an alchemy class. Malcolm taught a combat class, which suited the surly dragon. Besides the education and protection, one of their reasons for staying was the theory that their mate would surely be a powerful witch or shifter and therefore would pass through the Academy walls at some point.

Usually, power attracts power, and the Academy was the place powerful children went to learn. Never in a million years would Desmond expected to find their mate in a lesser known Coven on the outskirts of the region. Or for her to claim to be a low-level witch.

An enigma indeed.

As the miles fell away Desmond felt his excitement and worry grow. Excitement about learning more of his mate and worry about what she would face at the Academy. Desmond exchanged glances with Everett, the message clear between them, no harm would come to their mate.

CHAPTER 3

Claire jostled awake as the carriage rolled to a stop. Rubbing her heavy eyelids, she yawned before stretching her arms to the ceiling. Her fingers hit the velvet-covered ceiling before her arms fully extended and she brought them back down to her lap.

The door opened, letting some light into the darker shadows of the carriage. "Good afternoon, milady," Desmond's cheery voice sounded way too pleasant for such a long journey. "We have arrived at the Academy. I'm going to grab your bag and then help you down from the carriage."

Claire nodded, throat tight at his simple words. Whether or not he knew it, he was one of the first people to acknowledge her blindness but not treat her like an invalid with his offer to help. She felt her bag lift from her feet and then reached a hand out. Placing it in his grip, she felt the familiar tingles from their contact as he helped her from the carriage. Letting go of her hand, he placed it in his elbow as he moved her away from the carriage.

She saw a shadow step up to her right side. "Did you have a good rest?" Everett's voice was gentle for how deep it was.

Oh gosh, she had slept the whole way. "Yes, I'm sorry for being a terrible travel companion."

Desmond scoffed, "You were lovely. Now you know who is a terrible travel companion? Malcolm. He is a terrible travel companion. Always complaining because of his ridiculous standards."

"Who is Malcolm?" Claire asked timidly, wishing she could take the words back as the weight of both men's eyes landed on her.

"He's the third member of our Triad." Everett answered her, "and really the biggest drama award goes to Desmond."

Desmond scoffed but before he could respond, Claire broke in, "Your Triad?" That was a term she had heard a few times in the Windshire Coven but rarely.

"It's kind of like a group." Desmond said, "you'll learn more about Triads here."

Claire sensed he was leaving some information out but chose not to press. He didn't have to give her the answer.

"Right," Desmond said, "Let us get you to the Headmaster's office so you can meet Headmaster Dorian and get your welcome package. It will have all sorts of useful items like your class schedule and room key."

"You've got about fifteen steps up in six paces," Everett murmured from her right elbow as Desmond moved them forward. She turned her head in his direction and sent him a soft smile as the shadow outline of the steps became visible.

Ignoring his intake of breath, instead she asked, "Can you tell me about the layout of the Academy?"

"Of course!" Desmond exclaimed. Claire had a feeling of their Triad, he was the jokester. "We are about to climb the stairs of the main administrative building. This building houses the Headmaster's office and the other teacher's offices, the dining hall and the library. The Headmaster's office is in the center of the building, the teacher's offices and library will be on the left or east wing of the building and the dining hall is on the right or west wing of the building.

"Straight out the back of this building is the courtyard. It's large, about a hundred paces wide and two hundred paces long. There are four dormitory buildings on the east side all in a row. The closest dorm building to the administrative building is Dorm Building 1 and then 2, 3, 4 follow afterwards. On the west side of the courtyard, there are two class buildings. Finally, at the back of the courtyard is the combat arena that backs into the forest."

Desmond placed a hand over hers on his elbow as Everett opened the doors to the administrative building, "While the forest isn't off limits for students, it backs up into forbidden land so I wouldn't advise going out that way. The boundary line isn't easy to recognize."

Claire nodded, "Thank you for the warning. If it's difficult to recognize, why have it so close to where the students are?"

Everett answered this time, "It didn't used to be forbidden land, it used to be Elvish land, but after the war and the Elves' disappearance, there have been sightings of strange creatures of magic. The guards patrol the area but it's best to not tempt fate."

Claire nodded about to ask another question when Desmond's cheery voice broke in, "On that depressing note, little witch, wait right here with Everett while I duck into the Headmaster's office and see if he's ready for us."

"Ready for us?" Claire asked but Desmond had already slipped away. She turned to Everett, "Are you both coming with me? I'm sure you have other more important things to do after you had to waste an entire day escorting me here."

"Never wasted." Everett practically growled, and Claire took a half step back. She could hear Everett's deep breath as he calmed himself. "No student is ever a wasted trip. It's part of our jobs to be here to welcome new students. I am in the Academy's guard and Desmond teaches an alchemy class here while he finishes his mastery program."

Claire deflated internally a bit. Of course, they were only being so nice and polite because it was their job too. She forced a smile, "Well I'm glad it's part of your job because it's definitely helped having someone knowledgeable of the Academy along."

There was a silence like Everett was trying to find the words to respond but it was broken when Desmond opened the door in front of them. "The Headmaster is ready for you, little witch."

Claire reached out her hand and Desmond took it, tugging her gently through the doorway into the unfamiliar office. He led her six paces in and then placed her hand on the arm of the chair. A shadow of a desk in front of her and a figure behind it was barely formed in the noticeably darker room. She figured the Headmaster kept the light low for what one girl at the orphanage called 'dramatic effect' and as Claire folded her shaking hands in her lap, she had to admit it was working.

"Hello, Claire Windshire. Welcome to the Academy." The Headmaster's voice was a deep bass, spoken with authority but not with the frigidness of Mother Kemp's. "I'm Headmaster Dorian."

"Pleasure to meet you," Claire was proud when her voice came out clear. "I'm sorry but I have a lot of questions."

The Headmaster let out a deep chuckle that was surprisingly warm, "I'm sure you do. It's not every day someone applies on a student's behalf without the student's knowledge."

Claire leaned forward, "So it was a mistake then?"

"Not in the way you are probably thinking, Claire. While yes, someone applied on your behalf, and, before you ask, I am not sure who did so yet but I am working to find out, the Academy did grant you admission. And the Academy never makes mistakes."

"I thought it was rare for the Academy to do that."

"Yes," Headmaster Dorian agreed, "how much do you know about the Academy?"

Claire was unsure of what Desmond had told the Headmaster so she was blunt. "To put it frankly, Headmaster, I'm an orphan witch from Windshire who has never left the coven and rarely left the orphanage gates. No one has any idea who my parents were and at the coming of age ceremony the elders found little to no natural magic ability inside me. So I am really trying to understand why I am sitting here in front of you."

There was a pause while the Headmaster was looking at Everett or Desmond and Claire fought her impatience. Sure she dreamed of a better life and a place to belong but right now her attic room back at the orphanage was sounding like the best place for her.

The Headmaster ignored her rant and started explaining, "The Academy is a building built not only of stone but of magic. Ages ago when the Unitam Realm organized and the different races recognized the benefit in sharing knowledge rather than staying secluded, they each gave up part of their land to form the Capitol City and elected one member from each race to serve upon the council. One member from the dragons, the shifters, the Fae, the Elves, and the Witches.

"When the need for the Academy arose, the Elves offered an additional part of their land, swearing that it would remain independent of all the races and the Council's authority. This is the land that the Academy rests on now.

"Now the Fae and the Elves were master architects and together with stone from the Dragon Mountains, they constructed the buildings of this Academy. Whether knowingly or unknowingly, as they built they imbued the Academy with some of their magic, giving it sentience.

"The Academy has used its sentience to protect its students, like during the Great War that only ended two decades ago for example. It has also served as a sounding board for Headmasters like me when deciding on who to offer admission. That happened in your case, Claire."

"How often does that happen? The Academy making admission decisions?"

"Rarely." The Headmaster admitted.

"Then why are you all so sure the Academy didn't make a mistake?"

"The Academy doesn't make mistakes." The Headmaster was firm. "If it offers you admission, it must see something in you that you do not see yourself. The question is whether you want to stay and discover what that is. Neither I nor the Academy will force you to stay. The choice is yours."

There was rustling behind Claire like Desmond and Everett were restless at his words. She hadn't realized she had a choice to leave. She had assumed it was a done deal. She could either return to the coven. To the orphanage and the simple life she had there. That would be more familiar. Easier. But also more monotonous. Or she could stay here. And have the adventure she always reads about and find somewhere other than Windshire to belong.

She raised her head from her hands. "I'm assuming Desmond told you I am blind." She said softly, "How many blind students have you had here?"

"None during my tenure as Headmaster," Headmaster Dorian said. "However, that doesn't mean you will not be successful here. I am assuming you have mastered the spells of having a text be read to you and a quill to write for you?"

Claire nodded.

"Good. That will take care of most of your homework. I will inform the teachers that you will need to use that spell in their classrooms to take notes but the work will be on your own merit."

He paused and pulled a drawer out on his desk. Taking out something, she heard rustling as it slid across the desk. "This is your welcome packet," her fingers extended until she caught the corner of the thick envelope, "It contains your class schedule, information on the classes and your room key. Your room key is spelled to you like the other students' are spelled to them. Meals are included and I will have someone show you the dining hall. Students receive a small weekly stipend that can be spent on trips to the Capitol once the privilege is earned. Uniforms are required for class day but you may wear what you want on your time off. The Academy provides uniforms and will be in your room."

He slid something else across the desk, "This appeared in my drawer this morning, courtesy of the Academy. It is a guidance orb. Simply say the location you want to go on campus and it will guide you in that direction, it will warm when you are on the right path and cool if you are not heading in the correct direction.

"Additionally, I am assigning you a student mentor, Holly Brandlevine."

"Oh, I don't want to trouble anyone," Claire protested, unwilling to saddle another person with her responsibility.

"Holly volunteered for the position." The Headmaster said. "She is an excellent student and frequently mentors younger students. You will be in excellent hands with her."

As if talking about her summoned her, a knock came on the door. "Come in." Headmaster Dorian said.

The door opened, and a cheery voice called out. "Hi, Headmaster Dorian, Everett, Cousin."

Cousin? Were she and Desmond related?

The footsteps approached and stopped by Claire. "You must be Claire."

Claire turned her head. While the new shadowy figure was significantly shorter than the other men were, her exuberance took up the space her height did not. "Pleased to meet you."

Claire offered her hand and strong but slender fingers took hers, giving them a light squeeze.

"Are they done boring you with all the administrative protocols?" Holly asked.

"Oh, it's not been boring," Claire protested, not wanting to get off on the wrong foot with the Headmaster.

Headmaster Dorian chuckled, "It's alright, Claire, you don't have to cover for me. I am well aware of Holly's distaste for all things administrative. I think we've about finished here. Holly, I trust you'll give Claire the tour and show her to her dormitory?"

"Of course, Headmaster, anything that doesn't involve paperwork."

"Naturally. Claire, if you have questions, my door is always open."

"Thank you, sir." Claire nodded respectfully. She rose from the chair and turned towards Holly, holding a hand out, "And thank you for offering to be my guide."

"Oh, absolutely!" Holly said, taking her hand and placing it in her elbow like Desmond had. "When I heard you had to suffer through these two brutes escorting you, I knew I had to offer a friendly face."

"You only wish your face was as beautiful as mine." Desmond retorted as the girls neared the door.

"I don't have to wish," Holly said haughtily, "I already know it is. Are we going to suffer your presence along the tour?"

"I'm afraid we have some more to discuss with the Headmaster."

Claire could feel his gaze on her, and she offered a small smile. "Thank you both for escorting me here."

"Trust me when I say it was our pleasure, little witch. But fear not, we shall meet again."

When Holly laughed, Claire let out a small giggle as well at Desmond's dramatics.

Before the men could respond, Holly tugged them out the

door. "If we don't leave now he'll never quit," she giggled, "my cousin definitely has a knack for dramatics."

"He doesn't seem that bad," Claire didn't know why she felt the need to defend him, she barely knew him.

"That's because you haven't seen him when he gets on a roll. Once he's in character, he's impossible to break out. Although, it has led to some hilarious moments."

"Anyway, enough about my cousin, tell me about you?"

"Oh I'm really not that interesting. I'm from Windshire Coven and just got my Academy invitation yesterday."

"What's your magic proficiency?"

Claire ducked her head. This was it. The test to see if the Academy students are going to be just as cruel as the Windshire children were when they learned she didn't have magic. Claire almost couldn't force the words out. "Um, I don't have one."

"So you've mastered more than one?"

"No," Claire had a brief hesitation as she wondered if she should broadcast her situation but nothing about Holly's energy felt like Melanie's or Anna's . And if Headmaster Dorian trusted Holly, then Claire should too.

She tugged Holly to a stop. "How much has Headmaster Dorian told you about my situation?"

For not the first time in her life, Claire wished she could see the face across from her. "Not much. Only that you were a new student who needed help adjusting to the Academy."

Claire blew out a breath. "Okay, I'm just going to lay this out there and trust that you won't try to use it against me. I have little to no magic and until today I had never left the Windshire Coven and rarely left the gates of the orphanage where I grew up."

Holly paused, deciphering the information as Claire waited, her muscles tense.

Holly must have felt Claire's body tighten up and she squeezed Claire's hand on her elbow. "I've got you. I can catch you up on not only life here at the Academy but anything you might have missed in Unitam.

"Why would you help me?" There had to be a catch. If there wasn't a catch, Holly had to be the nicest person Claire had ever encountered.

"Because every student deserves to be helped. You were accepted into the Academy and so you deserve the experience."

Claire nodded. She didn't fully trust Holly yet but her intentions seemed good.

"Now it's my turn to ask a question." Holly said. "Why did you accept the Academy's invitation of admission?"

Claire paused. "To be honest, I'm not sure. My entire life I dreamed of a life beyond the orphanage walls and while I don't entirely believe I belong here, I also don't want to turn down the opportunity to be here. Even if it means I'm only here for a short time and I go back to the coven or go somewhere else. I'll always have these memories."

"For some reason I don't think you will be back at the coven anytime soon. But enough serious talk. Let's proceed to your dormitory and I'll give you a quick tour on the way there."

Claire took Holly's arm again as Holly pushed open the door to the courtyard. "The Headmaster's office is in the middle of the administrative building. Two hallways run on either side of it and lead out to the courtyard. We are now on the landing and about to go down some stairs." She paused briefly at the top of the stairs while Claire found the first step with her foot.

"Was my cousin completely useless or did he explain the layout?"

"He explained the layout. There are four dormitory buildings to our left, two class buildings to our right, and the combat arena is straight ahead.

"Excellent. Now the courtyard is one of my favorite places. There's a few fountains, some benches and lots of tables and shady trees to study under."

"It sounds lovely." Claire smiled as she thought about the two of them studying together.

Holly squeezed her hand, "It really is. Now Headmaster Dorian sent me a copy of your schedule and you'll have two classes in the morning, lunch, two classes in the afternoon and then combat training. I'll be available to walk you to your classes as mine are all close by. Should I not be available, I'll make sure you know your classroom number and your guidance orb should take you straight there.

"The four dormitories are in a line on the left side of the courtyard as we are facing now. Dorm building 4, closest to the Combat Arena and the forest is reserved for mastery students and Triad suites. Dorm Building 3 is reserved for upperclassmen singles. Dorm Building 1 is reserved for lower classmen singles. We are in Dorm Building 2 which is reserved for females."

"Your cousin said he was part of a Triad?"

"Yes, Desmond, Everett, and Malcolm make up the Stonemont Triad. Desmond is a wizard, Everett is a gryphon, and Malcolm is a dragon. They are one of the most powerful Triads in the Realm, so the Council watches them closely. That's part of the reason they've extended their time with the Academy."

Claire wanted to ask more questions, but they were already approaching the doors to her dormitory.

"You are in a room on the third floor." Holly informed her as they entered. "I'm on the fourth floor and just a summons away if you need me."

They climbed the two flights of stairs rather quickly and Holly guided her down the left hallway. "You are the eighth or last door here on the left. It's past dinner time but I can go down to the dining hall with you after you get settled in?"

"No, I'll be fine," Claire patted her bag, "I have a bit of food from the journey and I'm not that hungry anyway."

"Ok. Would you like help settling in?"

"No, thank you, you've been beyond helpful."

Holly squeezed her hand and her steps slowed as they approached the eighth door. "Well, I'm only a summoning stone away. I'll come get you in the morning for breakfast. Oh! I almost forgot, we have bells here so you'll always know what time it is."

"Thank you," Claire said gratefully, not even thinking that she would have to know the time for classes. Windshire Coven didn't have bells, and Claire had estimated time based on the number of chores she had in a day.

She dug out the room key from the envelope the Headmaster had given her and pressed the key to the door. With a click, the door opened and Claire let go of Holly's arm. "Thank you again."

"You are very welcome, Claire. I will see you in the morning!"

Claire heaved a sigh after she shut the door to her room. So many thoughts and questions swirled in her mind, almost giving her a headache with their racing. She shoved the whirlwind down into a deep corner and took a few deep breaths to clear her head. One step at a time.

And the first step was to familiarize herself with her room. She slung her bag over her shoulder to rest on her right hip. Using her left hand, she started at the frame of the door. Taking careful measured steps with her fingers on the smooth stone wall with her fingers slightly in front of her body, she took three steps before she met the next wall.

Pivoting a quarter turn, she took two steps before her fingers hit a wooden surface. One step to the side and one step forward and her fingers confirmed this was a chest of drawers. Crouching and using her hands to paint a picture, she found four drawers.

Straightening again, she took another step forward and then

a step sideways. Two more steps and her feet knocked against what must be the frame of the bed. Two steps sideways and she explored the bed against the corner of the room. The mattress and blankets were soft under her fingertips and she resisted the urge to sit down, knowing she would not have the motivation to stand back up.

Starting again at the head of the bed, she pivoted another quarter of the turn. Less than a half step and the stone wall turned into glass as she felt the warmth of the sun come through the window. Another two steps and her feet came into contact with a chair and desk placed in the opposite corner of the room. Books were stacked on a shelf above the desk. Four books for four classes, she guessed. Combat class wouldn't have a book.

Two steps to the right of the desk was another door. Pushing it open, she explored the small but private bathroom. She wasn't used to privacy. The orphanage bathrooms were communal for the children. Only Mother Kemp had a private bathroom.

Exiting the bathroom, she made it one more step before hitting another smaller door. It opened to a small closet that she explored quickly before closing it and taking one more step to come back to the first wall. One step to the side and her fingers ran across the door she started at. She put her back to the door and leaned heavily against it, letting out a deep sigh. In the distance, the bell chimed seven times. Claire was very grateful for the bell as that would allow her to keep time accurately.

She pushed away from the door and walked carefully to her bed. Placing her bag down, she unpacked the few changes of clothes. Stepping to the dresser, she opened one drawer and frowned when her hands met the fabric already folded in them. These must be the uniforms the Headmaster was talking about. The clothes seemed to be organized by drawer, shirts on the top, pants and skirts folded in the second, loose more comfortable clothes in the third which Claire guessed were for combat class. Her face flamed when the fourth drawer contained undergarments and soft sleepwear. All the clothes seemed to be made from high-quality material. Claire sat heavily back on her heels before rising to her feet. She repacked her clothes from the orphanage into her bag and shoved it under the bed.

Taking some of the more casual clothes from the third drawer, she placed them on the bed to change into later. She took the other items from her bag, the fairytale book, her ink and quill set, and her bound parchment and laid them on the desk. She reached up around her neck and unclamped the chain with the guidance orb. She carefully laid it next to her ink and quill set.

Grabbing the clothes from the bed, she ducked into the bathroom. Figuring out the shower knobs took a bit of time as she wasn't sure which was which. She finally managed to get the water to a nice warm temperature and quickly stripped. As the water ran over her, a wave of exhaustion hit her as the events of the day finally took their toll. For nearly 20 years the orphanage had been her home and although her routine was a simple one, it represented normalcy. Now her routine had been ripped from her by an invitation from a sentient Academy. She let out a harsh laugh, wondering, not for the first time, why her?

A second wave of exhaustion hit and she quickly finished up. Drying off with a towel hanging outside the shower, she quickly donned the loose shirt and pants set. Stumbling slightly out of the bathroom, she pulled back the covers and tumbled down into the bed. She groaned at the softness of the mattress that formed to her body. She would just take a quick nap and then get up and do some reading before her first day of class tomorrow.

CHAPTER 4

She did not, in fact, just take a quick nap.

Claire groaned as the bright morning sun warmed her face. Opening her eyelids slightly, she snapped them back shut at the contrasting shadows. Wait, why was the sun shining on her face? It had been hitting the desk earlier? The bell chimed seven times and she groaned at the realization. She had slept the rest of the evening and all night apparently.

Blearily, she pulled herself out of bed, stumbling into her chest before her brain caught up to her mental map of the room. She grabbed a shirt out of the top drawer and wavered between the pants and skirts in the second drawer. She grabbed a pair of pants deciding to play it safe on the first day.

To her pleasant surprise, a cup holding a toothbrush and toothpaste sat on the corner of the sink in the bathroom. She quickly brushed her teeth and splashed cold water on her face, waking her mind up even more. She dressed quickly, guessing that Holly was on her way to get her.

She turned to her desk, fingers catching on a strap on the back of her chair. A new satchel was at the end of the strap. She could get onboard with a sentient Academy building. "Thank you," she whispered, feeling silly about talking to the walls but not wanting to be disrespectful. She packed all four books in the satchel as well as her quill and ink set and parchment book.

Grabbing the guidance orb, she clasped the chain around her neck and ran her thumb over the smooth surface of the sphere. She had a feeling that these were rarer then she thought so she double checked that the chain was secure one more time as a knock sounded on her door.

Claire stepped the six paces to her door and her fingers found the cool metal knob. Twisting it in her grip she pulled the door open.

"Good morning!" Holly's familiar cheerful voice emanated from the shadow figure before her. "How did you sleep?"

"Very well, thank you." Claire murmured at a lower octave. Some people were morning people naturally and it seemed Holly was one of them.

"Great! Do you have your room key?"

Claire patted her pants pocket and realized she did not have her room key. "No, I almost forgot it." She turned and walked three paces back into her room and then one pace sideways to the dresser where she remembered placing it last night. Her fingers closed around the metal key and she shoved it into her pocket before retracing her steps.

"Damn girl," Holly said as she reached her, "you didn't stumble into anything?"

Claire blushed. "No, I've gotten pretty good at creating a mental map of where things are in my head and I spent some time last night doing that." She omitted the part this morning where she had stumbled into the dresser before remembering the mental map.

"That's super cool. So are your other senses enhanced as well? My grandfather lost his vision in battle but he could always hear the grandkids sneaking into the cookie jar my grandmother kept in the kitchen."

"A bit. I don't know if they are cookie-catching good though."

The girls shared a laugh as they made their way down the staircases and out into the courtyard. Claire kept her hand on Holly's arm but maintained a bit of distance. She needed to start getting familiar with the landscape.

Once out of the building, Claire could hear the chatter of other students as they all made their way to the dining hall. As if sensing her thoughts, Holly leaned closer. "All students share the same breakfast and dinner and lunch is staggered depending on your class schedule."

"How many students are there?"

"Around two hundred and fifty students."

Claire nodded. It made sense that the number was so small. The Academy was exclusive after all. The familiar twinge in her stomach reminded Claire just how out of place she was here.

The chatter around them got louder as the students jostled closer together before the dining hall's doors. Claire could feel a few curious looks on her but no one approached her yet. "Have classes already started?" She murmured the question to Holly.

"No, today is everyone's first day."

Claire breathed a sigh of relief. At least she wouldn't stand out too badly then.

Once inside, Holly tugged her to the left and down the wall of windows to the back corner. "I'll introduce you to my friends and our table so you always have a place to sit."

With all of the people and tables in the room, the shadows lumped together making it impossible for Claire to distinguish the layout of the room. Where did they go to get food?

The noise quieted as they moved farther from the entrance. Holly stopped before a large shadow in the corner, the lack of light making it harder but not impossible to distinguish the shape of a table and three figures sitting around it.

"Everyone, this is Claire, she's a brand new student and my

friend so help me make her feel welcome. Claire, this is Bethany, Cody, and Zack. And so Cody doesn't stick his foot in his mouth like he's prone to do," Holly teased, "yes, Claire is blind."

While Claire wasn't exactly comfortable with Holly saying it so bluntly, she had long gotten used to people introducing her as blind. Hopefully one day that wouldn't become her only identifying feature.

Claire gave a small smile and a nod to the table. "Pleased to meet all of you. I hope you don't mind if I join you for breakfast?"

"Cute as a button and she has manners?" A female voice who must be Bethany came from the table. "She can stay forever and we can kick Cody out."

"Hey!" A rough voice from the far edge of the table protested, "I forget to say good morning to you one time and all of a sudden I am an animal?"

"You're a wolf, so yes." Bethany shot back.

"Shifter." Cody growled.

"Children," a tenor voice who must be Zack chided, "we want Claire to like sitting here, not be scared off by your bickering."

His shadow figure got up from the table and approached. "Claire, it's a pleasure to meet you. Holly is the best person to know here and has saved all of our butts a time or two."

Holly brushed it off, "We all have to take care of each other. Now let's sit and get some food before Claire's first day of classes. Claire, it's a bench seat around a circular table so I'll put your hand on the table so you know where the edge is."

Holly threaded her fingers over the back of Claire's hand, like a reverse hand hold, and placed them on the edge of the table. Claire grabbed it and stepped over the bench seat and settled in it. Lifting her satchel over her head, she placed it in between her feet.

"We've already ordered," Bethany, who must be sitting to Holly's left, pushed something towards Holly.

"We use this orb to place our order and then food kind of appears on the table courtesy of the Academy's magic."

"Holly," Cody whined, "You ruined the surprise. It's always fun to watch first timer's faces when the food appears in front of them."

"She can't see, you moron, so she's not going to jump like the others have been." Bethany shot at him.

As the two started bickering, the scent of wildflowers grew stronger from her right as Zack leaned over. "Ignore those two," he said, "Bethany's a feline shifter and Cody's a wolf shifter so the term fighting like cats and dogs fits."

Claire smiled and turned her head towards him, "And what are you? Or is that not a polite question to ask."

Zack said, "I'm a witch. Fire is my proficiency and hopefully my mastery. What about you?"

"Witch." Claire said carefully, "Proficiency unknown."

When Holly squeezed her left elbow lightly, Claire knew she must have made the right decision in describing herself. "Here," Holly broke in, "Let's order. What do you want for breakfast?"

Claire thought about the tasteless grits or oatmeal they usually had at the orphanage and figured the fancy Academy wouldn't have that here. "What are my options?"

"Well you can get whatever you want, but I usually get bacon and eggs with a side of fruit."

"That sounds wonderful." Claire said.

"Here give me your hand and you can feel the orb's magic but I'll order for you the first time."

Holly took her hand and placed it on a square box. "Two orders of bacon and eggs with a side of fruit."

Claire added a silent please as the orb heated beneath their hands then cooled again.

Holly released her hand and Claire brought it back to her lap. "It usually takes a few minutes to appear."

"So what classes do you have, Claire?" Bethany stopped arguing with Cody.

"Um," Claire reached down and dug her schedule out of her satchel, "I haven't had a chance to look yet."

"May I?" Zack asked and Claire nodded. He tugged the paper out of her hands and read off her schedule. "First class from 8:30-9:45 is Runes with Professor Andrea Brandlevine."

"Brandlevine?" Claire turned to Holly.

"Oh you'll love Professor Andy." Holly said. "No relation but when we are at the Academy, everyone takes their community's or coven's name. I think she actually might be a distant relative but she is really cool. She's an earth witch like me and a great professor. You'll be in good hands."

Claire nodded feeling her body relax that at least one of her classes wouldn't be terrible. "What's next?" She asked Zack.

"Let's see, from 10:00 to 11:15 you have History of the Realm with Professor Henry Storm."

"Oh he's a neat guy." Cody broke in. "He was a warrior during the Great War and lost his entire Triad and his Fourth to the war. Losing a Triad should have killed him too but he was such a strong warrior that he was able to survive. He's tough but fair and a good teacher. I'm in that class with you."

"Ok, next you have lunch from 11:30-12:30. Holly and Bethany have lunch with you. After lunch you have Spells and Potions with Professor Benton."

Cody groaned and the sound of flesh hitting flesh came afterwards. "Don't scare her, you moron." Bethany chided.

"What?" Cody said defensively, "the man's an arrogant ass!"

To break up the impending argument, Zack broke in, "He's not the most pleasant of professors. He thinks rather highly of himself as he's a second cousin to a Council Member but he's not out to get his students."

"No, but he does have his favorites." Holly said. "It'll be fine though. We can help as we all went through Spells and Potions last year."

Claire nodded although her stomach squeezed. She guessed it was too much to ask to have all good professors.

"Moving on, after Spells and Potions you have Herbology with Professor Helene. She's a bit prickly but if you do the work and take care of the plants you'll be fine. She's a wealth of information as she's part Dryad." Zack informed her.

"I'll have that class with you," Bethany said, "We can study together."

"Finally, you have Combat Class with me!" Holly said. "Professor Malcolm is a bit of a drill sergeant but he's one of the best warriors the Realm has right now."

"Malcolm? Like the third member of Desmond's Triad?" Claire asked.

"You know Desmond?" Bethany questioned.

Claire nodded, "He and Everett escorted me to the Academy yesterday. They mentioned a Malcolm just not that he was a professor."

"The one and the same." Holly confirmed. "Desmond helps assistant teach occasionally but he's in his mastery program mainly. Everett is a leader in the Academy Guard."

"They patrol the forest, right?"

"Yes but the forest is off limits to students." Zack warned.

"I remember from yesterday." Claire nodded, "Believe me, I have no intention of going exploring."

A slight pop sounded and Claire jumped a bit in her seat.

"How did you know the food appeared?" Cody asked. "You jumped like the rest of them?"

"There was a noise." Claire said.

"I didn't hear a noise," Holly said, "maybe it's because your other senses are better."

"Maybe," Claire felt a little self-conscious that she had heard the noise when the two shifters at the table had not. "It's hard to distinguish a lot of the noises in here." She said as she felt for her fork from the side of the plate. "Can one of you paint me a mental picture of the room in case I need to navigate it without Holly?"

"Sure, we can all do that." Bethany said.

Holly leaned in close and whispered, "Your bacon is at the left side of your plate, your eggs are on the right side. Your fruit bowl is to the top left of your plate and your water glass is to the top right."

Bethany started speaking so Claire squeezed Holly's arm under the table in thanks.

"The dining hall is exactly how it sounds. A large open room with no walls sectioning off the space. The Headmaster says it's supposed to encourage mingling of the students but most group together. There are about 60 round tables in ten rows of six tables. Lower classmen usually eat at the back of the room and upperclassmen and mastery students eat closer to the door you came in. The kitchens are through the walls behind us. Large windows from floor to ceiling line both sides of the walls and in the evening there are six large chandeliers that light the hall."

"To get to our table, just enter through the door and follow the wall to your left. It's about fourteen paces to the side wall and then it's about forty paces or eight windows to our humble little corner."

"Thank you," Claire said, "that was very helpful."

"Do you have mental maps for everywhere?" Cody asked as Claire took a bite of the fluffiest egg she had ever tasted. Eggs were a treat at the orphanage and only for when the chickens had an excellent laying season and the surplus eggs weren't needed to sell to the coven.

Claire nodded as she chewed and swallowed quickly, "Yes, especially if I need to navigate by myself. At home, there often wasn't anyone available to guide me but once I've been somewhere once, I'm usually good at creating the mental map to go back."

"And where is home?" Bethany asked.

"Windshire Coven." Claire replied, quickly taking a bite of bacon to avoid further questions. It didn't work.

"I don't think we've ever had a witch from Windshire before," Zack said. "How did your parents take the news?"

Claire cleared her throat, "Um I wouldn't know, I've never met them. I'm an orphan."

As it usually did, the question shut up the table. "And you all say that I'm the one that sticks my foot in my mouth." Cody broke the tense silence.

Claire let out a small laugh. "It's okay. It's obviously not a comfortable topic but it's hard to miss someone you've never had."

"Still, I'm sorry." Zack said.

Claire nodded at him, accepting his apology as the table fell silent again. This time it wasn't from her.

"Cousin," Holly's voice lacked its usual cheery beat but was still friendly, "to what do we owe the pleasure?"

"What, I can't check in on my cousin?" Although Desmond's voice was cheery it held a sharp undertone. Almost a challenge. No one else seemed to react so maybe Claire was just imagining it.

Holly's tone was even, "Not if you usually don't and not unless you want to draw unwanted attention. You can keep an eye on me while being more discreet. You know there are eyes and ears everywhere here."

Claire wasn't sure if they were talking about Holly anymore but Desmond must have conceded. "Fair points, I'll take my leave now. Have a good day ladies and gentlemen."

Claire felt his eyes on her for a second longer than was probably appropriate and once he left, the lingering smell of spearmint still filled her nostrils.

"Sorry about that," Holly apologized to the table, "I'm pretty sure my mom asked him to keep an extra eye on me."

While the rest of the table seemed to accept her explanation, something about it rang false for Claire. It seemed like Desmond was there to check up on her and Holly told him that there were too many eyes. But why would other people care? Was she not supposed to talk to Desmond outside of him bringing her to the Academy?

Holly broke into her musings by laying a hand on her shoulder. "We better get you over to class before the rush happens."

Claire grabbed her satchel from under her seat and stood up from the table. "Thank you all for letting me sit with you and all the information about the hall and classes."

"No need to thank us," Zack said.

"That's right," Cody broke in, "we're friends now and you're stuck with us. Ouch, Bethany!"

"No one wants to be stuck with you." Bethany scolded.

Holly tugged her away as the pair started to argue again. "If we sit there and listen to them we will be here all day."

"Do they really not like each other?" They walked down the wall of windows, the morning sun hitting Claire with each window they passed.

Holly laughed, "I have my suspicions that they more than like each other but neither wants to admit it."

"Is it because Cody is in a Triad?"

"No, not every student is selected for a Triad. Cody is a pack alpha's son and Bethany is a pride leader's daughter. Their territories run next to each other so they kind of grew up together as the two clans have a neutral peace but cats and wolves tend to not get along. And usually species don't mix."

"Well that seems silly. If they like each other, why can't they be together?"

"Well it's not a hard and fast rule. Triads are usually mixed species as the overarching rule is that power breeds power but if you aren't in a Triad then the rules are a little stricter."

They were crossing the courtyard now and Holly changed the subject. "Okay we exited the dining hall and Runes is in Class Building One, the class building closest to the dining hall."

"Class Building One?"

Holly laughed, "Creative, I know. All of the prestige of the Academy for a boring name. Legend has it that each of the buildings was named by the Fae and Elves that built them but the names were a closely guarded secret."

They paused in the middle of the path. "I want to test your guidance orb." Holly said. "Just in case I can't be here. You should be able to hold it and say *'inveniet'* Runes Classroom."

Claire reached a hand up to the orb resting on her chest. "*Inveniet* Runes Classroom."

Immediately the orb warmed under her finger tips and she took a step forward. It warmed slightly again. She knew the building was to her right but she tried taking a step to her left and the orb instantly cooled. She smiled.

"That's wicked neat." Holly breathed. "Guidance orbs are rare so I've never seen one in action before. Let's try it out. Hold my arm still but let the orb guide you."

Claire started down the path to her right, feeling the orb warm. The shadows darkened as the building rose up in front of them. They reached the building and Claire brought a hand up to the door. Running her hand down the seam of the door, she found the knob and twisted it.

Entering the building, she felt a tug to the left and followed the hallway down about twenty paces until the orb heated and buzzed once. "Is this it?"

"Yes! I'm glad it worked. I'll always try and be here but just in case I'm not, it's good to know it'll get you to where you need to go. Come on, we still have about ten minutes before classes start so I'll introduce you to Professor Andrea."

Holly pushed open the door to the classroom. "Holly," a warm, earthy voice came from the front of the room, "it's good to see you. This must be Claire, the Headmaster told me you were going to be joining my class."

"Pleasure to meet you," Claire said as Holly tugged her up to the front of the room. How much and what did the Headmaster tell the teachers?

They stopped at the front of the room and the shadowy figure rose from the raised desk and stepped down towards them. A warm hand took Claire's "I'm Professor Andrea but most of my students call me Professor Andy. I've got your desk right up here."

Claire let go of Holly's arm and followed the Professor to the right side of the room. "Each desk stands on its own with a chair. There's a hook on the right side of the desk for you to hang your bag."

"You're in good hands with Professor Andy," Holly said. "I'm going to head to class as it's in the next building."

Claire nodded, shoving down the small pang in her stomach. The others had spoken highly of Professor Andy but for her entire life Claire had relied on the familiar and her familiar person at the Academy was walking out the door.

She sat down at the desk Professor Andy indicated and the professor settled into the seat next to her, "Now the Headmaster said you would be using the writing spell to take notes. Unfortunately in Runes, you can't use that spell because the magic of the spell might activate the runes and I want to prevent an accidental explosion." The professor laughed and Claire let out a small laugh with her. Less from her words and more from the contagion of the professor's laugh. It was as warm as her voice and seemed to fill you up.

"So I took the liberty of collecting the etchings of the runes from the student library and the librarian bound them in a book for you to use. Below each rune is a section describing the runes which I'll be covering in class. You can use a reading spell on that section without any problems."

"Thank you." Claire was truly grateful. "I'm sorry to cause so many problems before the class has even started."

"Nonsense. It's my job as a professor to ensure the success of every student in the school. Not every professor believes in the same philosophy but the Headmaster seems to think you are destined for great things and after meeting you, I'm inclined to believe him."

Claire wanted to ask more but students started entering the classroom. Professor Andy stood and greeted them as Claire familiarized herself with her desk.

She hung her bag on the hook, grateful that this was the side of the desk closest to the wall and thus preventing someone from getting into her bag without her knowledge. Not that she thought Professor Andy would allow that but it had been a common trick of the children at the coven to try and pickpocket her bag. Claire had gotten very good at sensing them but part of preventing it was making it difficult to access her things.

After retrieving her parchment book, ink, and quill, she secured the bag closed and placed the items on her desk. Fingers brushing the surface as she created a mental map of the small desk, her fingers brushed a book. This must be the rune book that the professor was describing. She pulled it closer to her and opened it, letting her fingers run down the page. Different etchings caught her fingers, the etchings rougher and slightly raised from the parchment. She shut the book as the professor called the class to order.

Professor Andy was warm yet professional as she took attendance and settled the conversations around the room. She started the class by giving an overview of runes. Runes came from the ancient magical language and served as a channel to see one's magic into. Professor Andy often described the runes as tools as she spoke emphasizing the importance of using the tool correctly and for its own purpose.

When sending magic through the runes, Professor Andy described the feeling of pulling your magic up from your well and pouring a little bit into the rune at a time until you felt the rune activate. Claire knew she would struggle with that part. Whenever she used spells before, she never felt like she had a well to pull from. It just seemed to come from her body and she had to tug it forcefully to get it to let go to do the spell. Especially if the spell was new to her.

Throughout the class, Claire could feel different pairs of eyes on her and wondered how much the other students knew. Mother Kemp always told Claire her eyes were a dead giveaway, describing them as a very pale shade of blue. The children at the coven called them creepy and dead-looking. About as far from normal as Claire could get.

Professor Andy ended class by describing the four runes designed to call the four elements and told the class to practice drawing them out on paper tonight in preparation for practicing them tomorrow. When she dismissed the class, Claire waited in her seat as the students all shuffled towards the door. Holly said she would be here but Claire wasn't sure if she was supposed to wait for her in the classroom or in the hallway.

Running footsteps sounded from the hallway as someone slowed outside the classroom door and entered. "Mr. Clawmoon," Professor Andy said dryly, "Are you running in the halls again,"

"Sorry, Professor," it was Cody from the cafeteria, "Holly was running late and asked if I would take Claire to our next class as we are in it together."

"Is that alright with you, Claire?" Professor Andy asked.

"Yes, Professor, Cody is a friend." Claire smiled at the obvious protective tone in the professor's voice.

"Well go on then. Don't want to be late."

Cody made his way down the aisle towards her as Claire swept a hand over her desk, making sure she had packed everything up. Satisfied she hadn't forgotten anything, she turned and reached out a hand. Grabbing hold of Cody's elbow, she started down the aisle with him. "Thank you, Professor." She called over her shoulder.

"You're very welcome. Make sure you draw out your runes by hand for tomorrow."

As they exited the classroom, Cody spoke, "Luckily, our history class is in this building one story up. We'll take the stairs at the end of the hall."

Claire kept up with Cody's brisk pace as they continued down the hall and pushed through a set of doors. While they were still inside, the space echoed with the sound of students' chatter and footsteps and Claire guessed the staircases were causing the echo.

Cody tugged on her elbow and they headed to the right. "There's ten steps, a landing and then another ten steps," he explained.

Claire nodded, "Thank you for taking me. I'm sorry you had to run."

"You could hear that?"

Claire nodded again.

"Damn, your hearing is practically as good as a shifter's."

"Thank you?"

"Oh it's a good thing." Cody was quick to explain, hearing the question in her voice. "Shifters have the best hearing in the realm."

They entered the history classroom and Cody tugged her up to the front of the room. "Professor Storm? My name is Cody Clawmoon and this is Claire Windshire."

"Ah Claire, the Headmaster let me know you would need to use a writing spell in my class?" His voice was melodic but not necessarily warm like Professor Andy's had been.

"Yes, Sir." Claire lowered her head.

"I don't think you'll need it much today as we are just going to cover the syllabus and distribute the text books but you are welcome to use it whenever you need and that includes your required assignments."

"Thank you, Sir."

"Now Cody, your reputation precedes you. Are you going to continue your antics in my classroom?"

Claire was curious when Cody let out a laugh, "I'll do my level best, Sir, but nothing that would disrupt Claire."

"Good."

The professor must have dismissed him as Cody led Claire back to the back left of the room. "Here, the desks are identical in every classroom but you sit in this one against the wall and I'll sit in the one directly to your left."

Claire folded into her seat and hung her bag on the hook. As she dug out her things, she asked Cody, "What was the Professor talking about up there?"

Cody chuckled, "I'm a bit of a prankster or trouble starter and ran some good ones last year. All in old fun though, I don't do anything to humiliate anyone. I think my favorite prank last year was setting spelled frogs loose in Herbology. Except they didn't 'ribbit' they squawked like a chicken."

Claire smiled. Her heart had dropped a little bit as the children of the coven liked to humiliate her and call them pranks when questioned by adults.

"Good morning, Class," Professor Storm's voice echoed a bit in the room. Unlike in Professor Andy's class where the conversations gradually quieted, the students in this class fell silent in the next breath. Claire found herself sitting up a bit straighter at the response this man seemed to command from the room.

Professor Storm launched into the description of the syllabus and the semester layout. There were four major sections of history in the Realm that this class would provide an overview for. Students could choose to dive deeper into the sections in classes in future semesters. The four sections this class would cover were the Beginnings of the Realm, the First Alliance, the Building of the Realm, and the Great War. There would be four major papers on each of the sections and shorter weekly discussion question papers. The professor began to pass out books and Cody handed her one before passing the stack back.

"Are there any questions?" Professor Storm asked from the front of the room as most of the books had been passed out.

Someone must have raised their hand as a student from the front row called out, "Is it true you fought in the Great War."

"Yes, my Triad and I fought for the Realm. Any questions about the class?"

This student was persistent though, "Will you tell us about it?"

"When we get to the section on the Great War." The Professor seemed uncomfortable with the questions and Claire remembered that he had lost his Triad during the war. That must be the cause of his discomfort.

"If there are no more questions about class, then you can be dismissed early for the period. Don't expect this as a regular thing though. All other classes will go the full time."

The students rushed out the door barely letting him finish. Claire and Cody waited till the rush and then headed towards the door, "Thank you, Professor," Claire called out as they were exiting.

"You're very welcome. Enjoy the rest of your day, you two."

Once they were in the staircase, Claire asked, "You said at breakfast that he had lost his Triad in the Great War?"

"Yes and his Fourth. It's a miracle he survived. Speaks to just how strong of a warrior he is."

"His Fourth? Sorry, there are no Triads in Windshire."

"Fourth is the term for the woman that is matched with the

Triad. Like a mate for shifters or a bonded for witches. Fourths are usually also incredibly powerful and make the Triad complete. Professor Storm was part of one of the earlier Triads. Their Fourth was a witch, I think? Triads and Fourths go through a bonding process similar to a shifter's mating process and usually the death of a Fourth or Triad member means the rest will die as well."

"That's awful!"

She could feel Cody shrug, "If your soulmate dies, what's the point of living?"

"What if they have children?"

"I'm not sure. My pack didn't have very many Triads either but the three pack members who are part of Triads are all in whole Triads and don't have children yet."

Claire thought about that. A Triad seemed very constricting. Every group member had to be reliant on each other and always get along. From the little she interacted with the rest of the coven she knew that most partnerships weren't happy ones. And those were with only two people! Claire couldn't imagine trying to make three other people happy. It would take a strong and powerful woman to handle three men. Luckily Claire wouldn't have to worry about that.

CHAPTER 5

The sun hit Claire's face as they exited the class building.

"There's Holly. I think the two of you have lunch now while I have to go to Combat Class on an empty stomach." Cody complained.

"Oh don't you dare feel bad for him," Holly's voice came from a distance, like she was still five paces away, "he packed away a more than full breakfast. He'll survive."

Claire laughed with the friends as Holly reached them and took her arm. "Goodbye, Cody, thank you for taking me to class. Don't waste away at Combat Class."

"I'll try not to," Cody's sigh was dramatic, "Goodbye, fair maiden, and the only one who cares about my stomach."

Holly and Claire giggled as they headed towards the dining hall. As they entered, the coolness that radiated from the stone was a welcome contrast from the warm late summer sun.

"Can I lead us?" Claire asked as they entered.

"Lead the way!"

Claire turned as they entered and walked thirteen paces

before making a quarter turn to her right. Counting off the paces rather than the windows, she counted off thirty-seven paces before coming to a stop. While she could see the shadowy figure of a table, she didn't want to let Holly know she saw it. "How did I do?"

"You did great." Bethany's voice sounded from her seat at the table. "The table is another half-pace from your knees."

Claire let go of Holly's arm and felt her way forward with a half shuffle of her feet. With her hand outstretched, she grabbed the edge of the table and lowered herself into the bench seat. "How were your morning classes?" She asked Bethany and Holly.

"Not too terrible." Holly answered. "Mainly first day stuff where they go over the basics or outline the syllabus."

"Same for me," Bethany said. "How were yours? Did Cody behave?"

"He was a great guide." Claire assured her. "And mine were very interesting. Mother Kemp basically filled the role of teacher at the orphanage so I can tell these classes will be much more in-depth but you were right, Holly, Professor Andy is really great."

"Isn't she? And a strong witch. You should see her in battle practice." Holly paused as if realizing what she said. "Oh I'm sorry, Claire, I wasn't thinking."

Claire smiled. "It's no worries, really. I don't expect you to change your wording just for me."

"I don't want to be rude," Holly protested.

Claire shook her head, "I don't know any different. I vaguely remember flashes of color before I joined the orphanage but I was so young that the memories are only in flashes so I must have been losing my sight at that young age. I've grown up not seeing so I don't know what I'm missing out on."

But she did. She did know. From the teasing of the children

at the coven to her own wishes and dreams of being something more. Not that she would ever share those thoughts with anyone. Especially not Holly who had been more than nice to her. "Don't feel bad, please."

"Fine," Holly squeezed her hand, "let's order lunch."

The girls ordered lunch and chatted a bit more about their classes. As they were eating, a shadow approached their table. Claire turned her head towards it.

"Damn, Claire, Cody wasn't kidding when he said your hearing was good," Zack's voice was awed as he sat down with them.

Claire smiled, "I didn't know you had lunch with us."

"My lunch period starts about halfway through yours. They do it to stagger the students out a bit."

Claire nodded, "That makes sense."

As she took another bite of sandwich, another shadow approached the table from behind Zack. She nudged Holly with her foot and slightly inclined her head. Holly cleared her throat and must have motioned to Zack who Claire heard shift in his seat and give an almost inaudible groan.

"Zack, why do you still insist on sullying my father's coven's name and sitting with outsiders?"

While she couldn't see the witch who approached the table, Claire imagined he approached it with as much swagger as was in his voice.

Zack shifted slightly and completely ignored the witch's opening comment, "Brent, good to see you, how were your morning classes?"

"Come on, Zack, answer my question. Why do you insist on sitting with the misfits? You know you have a seat at Ashcraft Coven's table."

"Like we talked about last year, these people are my friends."

"I know my father talked to you about this over the summer, you're never going to find a good job unless you make the right connections. And those connections aren't here at this table. Especially not after you've added a blind, orphan freak from a nothing coven to the group."

While the rest of the words Zack had let roll off his back from a pattern of hearing them before, the rude witch's comments about Claire seemed to strike a different tone. "Hey, watch your mouth." Zack rose from the table.

Claire placed a hand on Zack's forearm, squeezing gently and smiling softly. "It's okay, Zack."

"Oh you're taking orders from her now?" Brent just wouldn't stop.

"What seems to be the problem here?" A new, familiar voice entered the mix, bringing the scent of forest and spice with it. Everett had arrived at the table.

"Just having a conversation with my coven member, Captain Everett," Brent's tone was a lot more respectful now but still held a hint of anger.

"It was a conversation until your last statement and now it's dangerously close to bordering on bullying which you know Headmaster Dorian has a zero-tolerance policy for."

"Just stating the facts," Brent had the confidence of someone who's parents always bailed them out, "didn't realize the Academy was taking just anyone these days."

"Every student here deserves to be here." Everett growled, "But remember, the Headmaster decides if a student should leave. Consider this your second warning and head back to your own table."

Claire felt like Brent wanted to say more but she heard his receding footsteps.

"Thank you, Captain," Zack said, "but you shouldn't have. I can handle Brent."

"He's an asshole," Everett growled, "and we have a zero tolerance for that." Claire felt his eyes on her like Desmond's had been this morning. Did they do this with every new student?

Claire sensed that Everett wanted to say more. She didn't know how she knew that but something about these two men connected her more than she ever had. "Have a good rest of your lunch." Everett's tone was crisp as he retreated.

"I'm sorry about that." Zack apologized, drawing her thoughts away from Everett.

Claire squeezed his arm, "It's okay, It's nothing I haven't heard before."

"It's not okay," Bethany spoke, "but you shouldn't hear it again. Captain Everett was correct, the Headmaster has a zero-bullying tolerance."

"Doesn't slow the spread of rumors though, true or not. Like I said this morning, the walls in this place seem to have ears." Holly said.

"He's part of your coven?" Claire asked.

Zack groaned, "Unfortunately. His father is Coven Leader in case you didn't catch his brag. We're a decent-sized coven, nothing like Brandlevine but we hold our own. Brent and his father think our Coven is more or should be more. Brent's father, Isaac Ashcraft, is like, second cousin to the witch's Councilmember. It's not too bad during the school year but this summer was rough. I'm glad I qualified for summer classes this year. My moms will miss me but they'll understand."

"Can you switch covens?" Claire asked.

"It's rare for a witch or sorcerer to do that on their own. Usually they only leave to join a Triad or if they find their soul flames."

"Soul flames?"

"A witch's version of a shifter's mate. Didn't they have soul flames at Windshire?"

Claire shrugged, "If they did, they didn't advertise it. Our coven rarely traveled. We were on a merchant train's route so everything was delivered to us." She didn't add that they were the last stop on the route and often the merchants had run out of many items.

The group finished lunch chatting about the merchants that stopped through the covens and the unique items they often brought.

* * *

AFTER LUNCH, Holly dropped her off at her Spells and Potions class. Where Professor Andy had been warm, Professor Benton's reception was icy. And his class remained so.

"This should be a review for most of you," Professor Benton said, "so most of you should have no problem keeping up."

At the snickers around her, Claire felt her cheeks heat. Clearly word had gotten round about her orphan heritage from Brent's scene at lunch. She shouldn't be surprised that news traveled fast with a student body of less than 300. The rest of the class hadn't been bad but it was a lot of information and the Professor clearly had his favorites. Three students, Vivienne, Brent, and Christopher being among the favorites. Claire clearly wasn't but Professor Benton mainly left her alone. Claire had a feeling that also meant she wasn't going to be getting any additional help from him.

Luckily, Spells and Potions went by quickly. Instead of Holly, Bethany picked her up after class.

"How was it?"

Claire's face must have given her away as she felt her lips twist in a grimace.

Bethany laughed, the throaty laugh sounding like a purr. "That bad, huh?"

"It wasn't terrible, but you all were right at breakfast about the professor."

"Just keep your head down and we can help you with any of

your questions." Bethany advised, "He picks his favorites for sure. Who are they this year?"

"A Vivienne, Brent and Christopher?"

"Figures," Bethany scoffed, "Vivienne's a witch. She's got two proficiencies, water and air. Brent, you heard about at lunch. Christopher is a pack alpha's son and the nephew of a Councilmember. Christopher's not a bad guy, just cocky. Brent's an asshole and Vivienne's a bitch."

Claire laughed uneasily, "Sounds like a fun group."

"Just stick with us and you'll be fine." Bethany squeezed her arm. "Now let's get to Herbology. The greenhouse and gardens are behind Class Building Two."

The girls hurried along the path and as the building's shadow passed them, Claire could smell the freshly tilled soil of the gardens. The creak of a gate's hinges filled her ears as Bethany pushed it open. "Come on, Professor Helene has us work in plots of the garden with partners for part of the class. We can be partners!"

Bethany tugged her along the right fence line about twenty paces. "Here hand me your bag and I'll hang it on the fence with mine."

Claire tugged her bag off her shoulder and handed it to Bethany before kneeling in the soil. She was glad she had chosen pants today but she was going to have to ask Holly about how laundry worked here.

"Have you gardened before?" Bethany asked as she sat next to Claire.

Claire reached her hands out and enjoyed the feel of the soil trickle through her fingertips. "Yes, it was one of my regular chores at the orphanage. I loved it."

"You'll love this class then. Professor Helene is a Dryad and very knowledgeable. For your mental map, there are about fifteen garden plots in three rows of five. We are the row furthest from the greenhouse and in the back left corner if you were facing the garden plots from the greenhouse.

"There is a large maple tree to the right of us about ten paces from the garden plots and the entire area is fenced in."

"Thank you," Claire went to ask a question but a new voice came from Claire's left.

"Welcome, students, to a new semester." The woman's voice was light, like the wind that whistled through the reeds at the pond at Windshire.

"Like your information packets described, in this class we will learn about the different types of plants used for basic potions and medicinal purposes. I am a hands-on professor so not only will you learn to use these plants, you will also grow and tend to them. These are important skills to learn regardless of whether you are a witch or shifter."

"The garden plot in front of you has six rows. We will be planting two rows of three different herbs. When the weather gets colder, we will move inside the greenhouse. Your partner at your plot will be your partner all semester. You will be responsible for your garden plots for the semester and they may require extra tending outside of class time so prepare accordingly."

"We will get started right away preparing the soil for planting the seedlings tomorrow. Next to each plot, is a bag of fertilizer, a watering can, and a rake. Spread your fertilizer evenly on your plot and rake it into the soil. Once you are done, till six rows and water your rows to prepare the soil for tomorrow. I will walk around and introduce myself to you and your partner as you do this."

Claire turned in Bethany's direction. "How large is our plot?"

"It is six paces wide by ten paces long." Bethany answered her.

"Okay, so we'll do the six rows, one pace wide and ten paces long."

"Sounds good to me. How do you want to do this?"

"If you hand me the bag of fertilizer and direct me to the first corner, I can spread the fertilizer and you can come behind me with the rake? Then I can create the rows if you want to fetch the water?"

"Let's do this!"

That was one of the things Claire really liked about Holly and her friends. Like Desmond and Everett, they took into account her blindness but didn't treat her like she was handicapped. Instead they respected her limits and what she could and couldn't do.

"Here you go," Bethany placed the bag of fertilizer in Claire's arms.

Claire estimated that the bag weighed about three to four pounds. She cradled it in the crook of her left arm and reached her right hand into the bag. The fertilizer felt like small pebbles across her fingers.

She rose to her feet. "Okay, where's the left corner." She asked as she took off her shoes and socks. Bare feet were better to feel her way around.

"One step to your left and a half step forward."

Claire slid her foot off to the left and took a step and then brought her right foot forward and felt for the edge of where the grass met the dirt. Her toes sank into the soil and she took a step forward so she stood fully in the dirt.

Grabbing a handful of fertilizer in her right hand, she started sprinkling it on the ground from left to right as she took slow, measured steps forward. Once she went ten paces, her left toes hit the grass. She brought her foot back, took a pace to the right and then made a half turn before starting down the next row.

She repeated the process four more times, falling into a rhythm. Bethany raked the soil behind her, the rake making soft scratching noises in the soil. Once the last row was completed, the fertilizer bag was nearly empty.

Claire carefully rolled it up and set it on the grass next to the plot. She stepped off the dirt so Bethany could finish raking the last few paces. Claire brushed her hands together, feeling the small grains of fertilizer rub against her palms before falling to the ground.

As Bethany finished raking, the tall shadow figure of the professor approached from the right.

"Hello, girls, how are we doing over here?"

"Hi Professor," Bethany greeted, "we just finished with the fertilizer and raking. I'm Bethany and this is Claire."

"It's a pleasure to meet you Bethany and Claire. Claire, you seem to have done this before?"

"Yes, Professor," Claire said, "I tended the garden at home."

"Excellent," Professor Helene said, "I have no doubt you will do wonderfully in this class. Your book should have been in your room. Have the first chapter read for tomorrow both of you."

Professor Helene moved onto the next pair of students and Claire watched her willowy shadow figure fade into the mass of grey three paces away.

"I'll get the water if you want to wait for me and I can help with the rows?" Bethany asked.

"I can do the rows," Claire assured her, "I've done them before. You can let me know if I get too crooked though."

"Okay," Bethany sounded unsure but headed off to get the water.

Claire stepped back into the corner of the soil and faced the back fence. Kneeling down, she used her hands to find the left edge of the plot and spread them about a pace apart. Digging them into the soil a bit, she brought them together to create a raised mound of dirt. Scooting back a few inches, she repeated the action.

She repeated the movements all the way down the row, keeping her left knee on the edge of the plot line to keep her row straight. Moving over a pace, she started down the next row. She had finished three rows by the time Bethany got back with the first round of water.

"Damn, those are some pin-straight rows," Bethany exclaimed.

Claire sat back on her heels and rolled her shoulders back, shaking out her arms. "Thank you. It's easy when the plot is measured out so well. The orphanage garden never had straight edges."

"Well this watering can should be able to do these three rows but it looks like most are making two trips so I'll get started."

Claire ignored the slight burning in her muscles and finished the last three rows. While Bethany got the last can of water, Claire stood and stretched her aching muscles. Doing the work felt good to Claire, although the whispering complaints from their neighbors around them showed not all students enjoyed gardening.

"She must be really good on her knees." A male student whispered from a few plots over.

Claire frowned, unsure of who he was talking about. What an odd thing to say?

"Alright, students, that's great work today. Remember to read the first chapter in your book tonight and we will be planting the seedlings tomorrow."

Claire brushed her hands together to dispel most of the dirt and leaned down to wipe them on the grass. She would usually just wipe them on her pants but didn't want to get her uniform too dirty until she figured out what laundry looked like here.

"Here's your bag," Bethany offered her.

Reaching out for the strap, Claire slung the bag across her shoulder. "That was kind of fun." She admitted shyly, unsure if liking gardening was okay.

"I agree. Usually shifters don't learn Herbology in our packs or prides but Professor Helene is great at relating it to real world issues."

Even if Claire couldn't access her magic, she would still be able to learn some practical skills that it seemed like she could take back to Windshire. Maybe she should focus on Herbology exclusively? That was something to ask Holly about or maybe Professor Helene. But for now, it was on to combat class.

CHAPTER 6

Malcolm was going to kill Desmond. Kill him. No matter that Desmond was a member of his Triad and one of the few people Malcolm considered family. Desmond was going to die. Everett too, now that Malcolm thought about it. Malcolm's dragon called for blood.

Why? Because of the pair of students walking into the combat arena.

Holly Brandlevine, a second year student and Desmond's cousin, walked into the combat arena with a brown-haired female's hand on her arm. The brown-haired female had to be Claire, the blind new student that everyone was whispering about.

But that wasn't the reason Malcolm was going to kill Desmond and Everett. He was going to kill them because they both *knew*.

They knew like his dragon knew. The beast snarling in his chest as the sweet orange smell of *his mate* swept through his nostrils. He locked every muscle in his body as the beast roared inside his mind, desperate to get out and claim the exquisite female. Her cinnamon-colored curly hair softened her angular cheekbones. And while he knew she was blind from the other students' whispers and Headmaster Dorian's warning, he wasn't prepared for the pair of the lightest blue eyes he had ever seen. So light, they sparkled like pale sapphires in the sun, brighter than any of the jewels in his dragon's hoard.

Malcolm took a deep breath as the pair reached the rest of the group. None of the students had seen him yet as he stayed in the shadows. This gave him time to collect himself without anyone seeing the effect this woman had on his dragon. Because if they saw how close he was to losing it, she would become a target.

Closing his eyes, he wrestled the dragon back down into his mind with promises to seek out Desmond and Everett later and deliver a bit of revenge at keeping the dragon from his mate. He also reasoned with the beast that losing control would not endear him to his mate and could scare her as well as planting a possible target on her from the other students and the Council. The beast settled at that but snarled in impatience.

Feeling more in control, Malcolm strode from the shadows of the wall towards the group. The students snapped to attention and fell silent at his approach. His reputation for being a grueling and demanding instructor was well known. Malcolm almost softened his approach due to his mate but dismissed the thought instantly. She wouldn't be able to see his gruff exterior which hopefully meant he wouldn't scare her. His dragon whined anxiously at the thought of his mate not being able to see him and Malcolm internally rolled his eyes at the vain beast.

"Class." He barked a greeting.

* * *

CLAIRE COULD FEEL Holly stiffen slightly next to her as Instructor Malcolm barked his greeting. Claire wondered what was so intimidating about this man's appearance. Holly had told her a little bit about him on the way over to class. Malcolm was the third member of Desmond's Triad and the youngest combat instructor the Academy had ever employed. Just because he was young though did not mean he wasn't a fearsome fighter according to Holly. He ran his classes with precision and demanded excellence from his group.

Combat was a required class at the Academy apparently although Claire was unsure how she was going to participate. She had no prior training and while the shadows helped her make out vague images, they weren't going to help her when a sword came barreling down towards her.

"Today and for the rest of this week you will learn Warm-up Form A, B, and C. You will be expected to run through these forms automatically at the start of every class after three weeks."

Instructor Malcolm definitely had a commanding aura about him. His tone of voice made it clear that he expected the students' full attention. Claire felt herself giving that to him but not necessarily out of fear. There was something about this man that drew her focus, similar to the feeling she had when she was around Desmond and Everett.

Before Claire could examine the feeling further, Instructor Malcolm had them spread out and Holly tugged her backwards and to the right to give them plenty of room from the group.

"Warm-up Form A is designed to stretch out your major muscles. Like it's name suggests, it should be done first and before anything else. Proper flexibility is important to prevent injury."

As he spoke, he wove in and out of the students making sure they were spaced accordingly. As he neared Holly and Claire, the scent of cinnamon and smoke danced in Claire's nostrils. Claire could have sworn he inhaled as he passed by her. What was it about Triads and sniffing people?

"To start Warmup Form A, stretch your arms out overhead and reach up for the sky. Bend at your hips and reach forward until your torso is parallel with the ground. Repeat this five times in sequence with your breath."

Claire performed the movements with the rest of the students as Instructor Malcolm walked around and made small adjustments.

"Now, reach up to the sky and fold at your waist to try and touch the ground next to your feet. If you cannot touch the ground, this should be your homework assignment. Repeat this action five times."

Claire's fingertips grazed the ground as she felt the stretch in her hamstrings. She was going to have to work on this stretch for sure.

"Take your arms and hold them out on either side of your body. Twist your torso to the right until your right arm is behind you and your left arm is in front of you. Repeat this action to the left and repeat the sequence five times. Make sure the movements coincide with your breath."

Claire could feel her muscles start to warm up as she twisted. This wasn't too bad.

"Now take your left hand and grab your right elbow. Hold your arm straight across your body and turn your head to the right over your right shoulder. Hold on my count of ten.

As Instructor Malcolm led them through the rest of Warm-up Form A, Claire could feel her muscles start to stretch and ache as they went through lunges and calf stretches. Heavier breathing on either side of her showed she wasn't the only student who found the warm-up form difficult.

Instructor Malcolm led them through Warm-up Form A two more times, ensuring it was in the students' muscle memory. At the end of the class, Claire was sweating slightly and while she couldn't see them, she didn't think she was the only student in the same boat,

Instructor Malcolm dismissed the class. Holly and Claire

grabbed their bags from the arena wall and hurried out the gates, letting themselves get swept up in the wave of students.

"Want to grab a quick shower before dinner?" Holly asked.

"I'd love that." Claire admitted. "Oh I was going to ask you, where are the laundry facilities?"

"Ooo, this is where I get to introduce you to the perks of a sentient Academy. There should have been a basket in your bathroom. Place your clothes in there and they will appear magically cleaned and in your drawers."

"Really?"

"Yep!"

That was not the answer Claire was expecting but she filed it away to process later.

"Oh and it didn't occur to me until my last class," Holly said as they approached their dormitory, "but as a first year all of your pants and skirts are black and your tops will be either green or white so you shouldn't worry about not matching."

"I hadn't thought about that," Claire admitted, "but I'm glad I was matching today." At the orphanage, Claire only had two worn dresses that she alternated with. A dress meant she didn't need to worry about matching two items. She hadn't even known what color the dresses were.

"I would have said something this morning if you hadn't been matching," Holly assured her as they climbed the stairs to Claire's floor. "Are you good from here?"

"I'll be fine," Claire said.

"Great! I'll meet you in thirty and we can head to the dining hall. Bring your books and we'll go to the library afterwards for homework."

"Okay sounds good."

Claire turned and walked down her hall, mentally counting off the doors in her head until she got to door eight. She was fishing in her bag for her key when a voice called out to her.

"Hey, Claire, right?"

The girl's voice was familiar but Claire couldn't place her. "Yes?" She said politely.

"I'm Vivienne, we have Spells and Potions and Combat together."

"Oh yes." Claire smiled, this was the girl that was one of Professor Benton's favorites. And Bethany had referred to her as a bitch.

Vivienne was direct. "How do you know Desmond and Everett?"

"I'm sorry?" Claire was confused.

"Desmond was at your table this morning for breakfast and Everett was there for lunch. I was just wondering if you knew them."

"Oh well, Desmond is Holly's cousin and Everett and Desmond were part of the guard who escorted me to the Academy yesterday."

"I see, they were just doing their job." Vivienne's tone was dismissive and not unlike some of the mean girls at Windshire. "Well they are very good at their job. I ask because I'm their potential Fourth and it seemed like you knew them so I wanted to meet you."

"Thank you, everyone has been very welcoming here." Claire knew that was not Vivienne's intention at all. Vivienne meant for her words to be a warning but Claire intentionally misunderstood them. "I'm sorry I don't mean to be rude but I have to meet Holly soon for dinner. Have a lovely evening."

Claire slipped inside her door before Vivienne could respond more than a, "You too."

Claire made a mental note to stay away from Desmond and Everett. Malcolm too now that she thought about it. Girls like Vivienne could be single minded in their pursuit of their targets and Claire did not want to become Vivienne's target. Something in her stomach protested at the thought of not seeing the men but she shoved it down. From everything she had learned about

Triads so far, they only took strong, powerful Fourths. Vivienne had two proficiencies while Claire struggled to use magic. It was an easy choice or not even a choice at all. Claire was not in the running.

Claire showered quickly, finding the basket in the bathroom that Holly described. Feeling a bit awkward at dropping her dirty clothes in a basket for a magical building to clean, she whispered a quick thank you as she did.

Selecting some comfortable pants and a long sleeve shirt as the evening got chillier. She dressed quickly and slipped her room key in her bag along with the books and her guidance orb over her head.

Dinner with the group was a fun affair and afterwards they headed to the library. Claire felt a bit awkward about using the reading spell when the others were trying to study but they insisted they didn't mind and Cody and Bethany even read the chapters from History and Herbology out loud as they said it helped them understand the material better.

As the evening drew to a close, the boys walked the girls back to the dormitory and Claire slipped into bed with a smile on her face. As long as she stuck with her friends and stayed away from one specific Triad, her Academy experience seemed to be off to a good start.

CHAPTER 7

The week continued like her first day had. History class with Professor Storm launched into the beginning of the realms, covering the five main races and their geographic regions. Cody kept her entertained throughout the class and during their study time. Spells and Potions with Professor Benton was almost boring. Professor Benton took policies and procedures very seriously and was going through the extensive background of potions masters before students were allowed to touch the ingredients. Claire spent most of her nights cramming her head full of the various potion masters and significant dates.

Herbology was probably one of her favorite classes. Professor Helene had them planting three different types of seedlings in their garden plots as well as tending to some more mature plants in the greenhouse. Claire spent some of her homework time in the greenhouse, running her hands over the different plants and familiarizing herself with what the adult versions of her seedlings were supposed to look like.

After four days of Combat Class, the students had been

deemed decent enough in Warm-up Form A and were learning the first half of Warm-up Form B which was a series of footwork steps and arm movements designed for hand to hand contact. It felt a bit weird to be punching at air but Claire reasoned it was no less weird than trying to learn hand to hand combat as a blind person.

Runes was where Claire was making the most waves across the student body. Professor Andy kept Runes interesting. The class was working through the four basic runes, one for each element. Student's who had mastery in a specific element usually did the best at that element's rune. Most witches could do one to three elements although they tended to specialize in just one or two elements. Two element masteries indicated a powerful student, like Vivienne. Thankfully Vivienne wasn't in her Runes class.

Claire was a bit of an anomaly in Runes. She had memorized the runes for each of the elements that first night. On the second day, when it came time to push some magic through the fire runes, Claire called into her small well of magic and drew the fire rune above the candle she was supposed to light.

Students who had fire proficiency were able to easily light their candle and create a small fireball in their hand. Claire struggled to call her magic up. It felt like she was pulling it through sludge but the warmth beneath her hand indicated she had lit the candle. Professor Andy praised her efforts and Claire was ecstatic at dinner that night. She had never had a proficiency before and even though Windshire coven members typically had air proficiencies, Claire reasoned that her orphan status was what caused her to be different.

Until the next day, when manipulating water, Claire formed a small ball of water in her palm. It was no bigger than a marble and Claire still struggled to pull her magic up but she had still done it. Again, it was nothing like the water proficiency students who could manipulate large bodies of water but it was still more than most.

Her friends were excited for her at dinner that night when she told them. A bit confused as water and fire proficiencies were not common co-dependent proficiencies but excited for her nevertheless.

Claire almost didn't tell them about the third day of Runes when she moved a piece of paper across her desk. Professor Andy was shocked but very excited. Proficiency of three elements wasn't unheard of but it was rare. Claire almost didn't have to tell her friends. When she sat down at dinner that night the conversation stilled at the table.

"Is it true?" Cody asked, "Were you able to manipulate air today?"

The sound of flesh being smacked was a familiar one at this point in the week as Bethany smacked Cody. At this point, Claire was sure that Cody could see Bethany coming but for some reason let her smack him each time.

Claire smiled in Cody's direction, "I don't know why everyone's so excited. It's not anything like the other students can do. I barely moved the piece of paper from one side of the desk to the other."

"Even if it's just a little bit, it's rare for a student to even be proficient in three elements. Even seasoned witches take a few years to develop the third proficiency and almost none of them develop the element into the mastery level." Zack said.

"I guess. I mean it's not easy though, it feels like my magic almost fights me on every rune."

"That might get easier with practice." Holly was reassuring.

"Maybe," Claire wasn't sure.

"Well either way you should feel proud of it," Holly said, "you've been working so hard at all of your classes that you deserve this win."

"I feel like we are winning at Herbology." Claire protests. "Our seedlings are taking well."

"That's right, partner," Bethany agreed, "ours are doing really well. Hey, maybe you'll have an earth proficiency too."

"Maybe," Claire laughed but it was a nervous laugh. Professor Andy had told her after class today that she shouldn't worry about tomorrow or put additional pressure on herself to feel like she has an earth proficiency. She had explained the same thing that Zack had.

That didn't prevent Claire from feeling like there were eyes on her all the time. Even now as she sipped her water, she heard whispers from across the dining hall and felt the weight of the students' gazes on her.

The weight wasn't comfortable like it was when Malcolm, Everett, or Desmond watched her. Malcolm, she could identify the most because he was her instructor. She kept hearing Desmond and Everett around the Academy but always accompanied by Vivienne's voice. Claire steered well away from those areas. She had enough to worry about.

"Hey, what happened to Brent's face?" Cody broke through her thoughts and changed the topic of conversation.

"Zack," Holly whisper-shouted, "was that you?"

Zack scoffed, "I wish. But no it wasn't me. I actually heard Malcolm partnered up with him in Combat Class and laid him out."

"That's odd," Bethany mused, "I mean Instructor Malcolm is strict but he usually doesn't bruise up a student's face like that. I wonder what Brent did to piss off Malcolm or his dragon?"

"I wonder," Claire felt Holly's gaze rest on Claire as she spoke the words but when Claire lifted her head from her plate, Holly had averted her gaze.

Claire had no time to think about the interaction as Cody launches into a story about him and his brothers roughhousing and giving each other black eyes and how their mother had reacted when they showed up for a pack dinner with matching black eyes.

* * *

As Claire finished her dinner, she was unaware of a table at the direct opposite corner from her. All three occupants of the table kept eyes on Claire in rotating shifts.

"We are definitely bordering on creepy stalkers," Everett grumbled.

Desmond hummed while Malcolm let out a low growl. The dragon had been doing a lot more of that since Monday.

"Is that how you're communicating now?" Desmond arched an eyebrow at the growly dragon.

Malcolm huffed.

"You should feel better," Desmond smirked, "after all, you got to work out some frustrations on Brent Ashcraft's face."

Malcolm's stormy face broke into a smile for a few seconds and Everett rolled his eyes. He should be grateful to Brent he guessed. After Malcolm had learned they met Claire first, his dragon had been out for blood. Everett happened to mention the confrontation between Brent and one of his coven member's Zack and the names Claire had been called and all of a sudden Malcolm's dragon found a new target.

It had helped that Desmond had stepped in and smoothed things over with his silver tongue. Everett wasn't good at that. In fact out of the two of them, Malcolm was usually the smooth talker up there next to Desmond. Everett stayed quiet and in the shadows, just where he liked it. It had allowed him to stalk, he meant, watch, their little mate.

Their little mate who was causing a stir about having three element proficiencies.

"So are we taking bets that earth will be next?" Desmond leaned forward and pressed his fingers together in a steeple in front of his chin. Desmond loved puzzles. He got almost obsessive over them. And Everett recognized the gleam in his eyes as Desmond watched their little mate.

Desmond hid his obsessiveness behind his silver tongue and debonair clothing. But Everett had seen him out on the battlefield and the man was deadly in his own right.

Malcolm, on the other hand, made no movement to hide his obsessiveness. Or his protectiveness. He usually pushed his classes through all three warm-up forms in one day. Here they were, four days into the new semester and he had just moved Claire's class onto Warm-up Form B. In fact Everett was surprised the dragon hadn't snapped yet and claimed Claire. That spoke to the ironclad control Malcolm exhibited in almost every area of his life.

Claire caught the three men's attention again as she laughed at something Cody, an alpha's son said. Everett held in a growl. The only reason Cody was alive right now was Everett knew Cody and the feline shifter, Bethany, were mates although the two hadn't admitted it to anyone, even themselves. Everett recognized the signs. He felt them in his own beast as clearly as he watched them in Cody.

And Zack, the other male sitting next to her mates, didn't bat for Claire's team. Everett had caught him last year behind one of the dormitories with a shifter. Not that the pair saw Everett from the shadows. Everett had stayed long enough to know that Zack was very clearly gay and thus he was still alive after touching their mate so casually all week.

"She's already demonstrated ability at three elements," Malcolm rumbled out.

It took a second for Everett to catch up from Desmond's previous statement. "She's aceing Herbology. Professor Helene appreciates her work."

The Dryad was a fair teacher but she had a softer touch to

her smile when she interacted with Claire. Claire seemed to love being in the gardens.

When he relayed that information to the others, Desmond chuckled, "I'm starting to think you might be the creepy stalker here."

Everett growled and shoved at Desmond. "Like you and Malcolm are any better."

"What can I say, I love puzzles and our little soul flame is definitely a puzzle. An orphan witch from a no-name coven on the outskirts of the witch's territory with proficiency at three of the four elements? Have you ever heard of such a thing?" Desmond's tone was almost gleeful.

"You know we haven't. No one has. If she does have an earth proficiency tomorrow, she'll become a bigger target." Malcolm grumbled.

"Guess you'll have to move on from Warm-up Form B then," Desmond teased, "I've been hearing whisperings that the fearsome Instructor Malcolm is losing his touch."

"Lay off." Malcolm growled, "All my dragon wants to do is sweep her up and carry her off to his hoard in the mountains. That would really cause a stir with the Council."

Everett understood where Malcolm was coming from. More than once he had to restrain his gryphon from the urge to pick her up and flee. "Think of it as protecting her. She's got to be able to defend herself." Everett said.

"She shouldn't have to. That's our job," Malcolm growled.

"We can't publicly claim her, we've talked about this." Desmond said in his annoying, matter-of-fact tone. "To claim her publicly would be to put her into more danger than she is right now. Plus, our little mate is skittish and we all know a Fourth has to be accepting of her Triad. Our added little bonus is she's also each of our mates or soul flames but she doesn't know that."

"So what do we do?" Malcolm groused.

"We spend some time with her, courting her, but discreetly. The less obvious the better but if we need to make it obvious we can. She's going to be the most confused one in the Academy if we come out and claim her publicly. We have to get her to accept us and our bond."

So patience. Everett could do patience. He was a pro at watching and waiting.

CHAPTER 8

If Claire thought last night was bad, the eyes on her today were even worse. It felt like the whole rune class was watching her as Professor Andy talked about the earth element and the magic it can be used for. Although the class was a good mix of proficiencies and masteries, Professor Andy had told them it was important to learn and understand about each element as it would help them defend against them as well.

In front of each student as they came in today was a small pot with a budded plant inside. The rune that they would draw shortly was supposed to encourage the plant to grow. Claire's hands were shaking from all of the pressure so she kept them folded in her lap.

The stares of the students kept on and the whispers increased as Professor Andy dismissed them to practice. To avoid trying the rune a little bit longer, Claire brought out her book and traced the earth magic rune one more time.

When the whispers didn't die down, Claire took a deep breath and closed her hands around the pot, feeling its shape and tracing a gentle finger over the small plant. She focused inward on her magic and tried to call it up. Usually calling her magic felt like she was pulling it through sludge. Today, it felt like she hit a brick wall as she fell into her center where her magic danced. Any attempts she made to call it up were met with firm resistance. Her magic did not seem to want to cooperate with her, almost feeling defensive.

Claire took a deep breath and tried again, coaxing her magic into cooperating. Met with resistance again, her magic seemed to cover its center in a protective fashion and refused to break its protective stance.

Claire dropped her hands, not bothering to draw the rune above the plant. If her magic didn't want to cooperate she guessed that earth was simply not one of her elements.

"How goes it?" Professor Andy announced her presence before laying a gentle hand on Claire's shoulder.

Claire shook her head, "Not well. My magic doesn't have an interest in participating."

Professor Andy squeezed her shoulder softly, "That's okay, no one expected all four."

Except people had. At Claire's head shake, she could hear the other students whisper, *of course she wouldn't get all four* and *I bet the other three were flukes, there's no way she will get proficient at all three.*

Claire ducked her head a bit as the professor moved onto another student. Thankfully the pressure of the eyes on her eased when the students realized she wasn't going to put on a show. Claire spent the rest of the class tracing the fire, water, air and earth elemental runes in her book.

When Professor Andy dismissed the class, Claire waited for Cody at the door. When he reached her, she could almost feel the question from his entire aura. She shook her head as she took his arm and he squeezed her hand quickly before launching into an elaborate story about a prank he pulled last year in his Runes class. Claire was grateful for the distraction and squeezed his arm before taking her seat in History.

History class passed quickly with Claire knowing she was going to have to use a reading spell on her notes. She drifted in and out of focus, the feeling of disappointment swirling in her gut. Earth was the element she felt the most sure about before Runes class had started because she loved being out in the garden so much.

After class, Cody must have shaken his head when Holly approached because Holly didn't ask about Runes. Instead they chatted about idle things like what they wanted for lunch.

"How did it go?" Bethany asked after they had sat down.

Claire shook her head, "It didn't."

"I'm sorry, girlie," Bethany sympathized, "I was sure you were going to get it. You are brilliant at Herbology."

"I was too. I've always loved working in the garden and definitely expected to be able to do the earth elemental rune over the fire or water ones."

"That's okay, you still did the other three," Holly said, "and that in itself is rare. Just focus on those three."

"Oh, being able to do those three is more than I expected. I'm just a bit disappointed in myself. I was so confident until I sat in class and felt everyone watching me. My magic just froze then and didn't want to cooperate at all!"

"Hey, it happens." Holly soothed.

Claire knew Holly was right but she couldn't help but feel she was supposed to be able to do the earth element. Just wishful thinking she guessed.

Zack joined them halfway through lunch and must have heard the whisperings in the dining hall as he didn't ask how it went. The group kept the rest of lunch light.

Sitting in Spells and Potions, Claire did her best to not be as distracted as she was in History. Today, they were going to do their first potion. A simple cough syrup.

"Your ingredients will be in the bags passed out to each of you. Mix the ingredients in the order I describe in the bowl on your desk. This is a simple potion that none of you should have any problem with."

Claire was sure this was just how Professor Benton taught but every time he made a comment like that Claire felt like he was staring directly at her. She was just still upset from Runes, she reasoned.

The student right in front of her was Christopher, one of the professor's favorites. She waited for him to pass a bag back to her. As the bags got back to their section, Christopher fumbled with them. "Oops, sorry Claire, this one is yours."

He placed a bag in her palm and she cupped her fingers around the canvas. Dipping her fingers into the bag, she pulled out three leaves of the same shape, a waxy substance in the shape of a marble, some berries and a vial.

Listening to the professor, she crushed the berries with the provided mortar and pestle and scraped it into the bowl. She crumbled up the dry leaves and mashed the waxy ball into the mixture.

"Finally, pour the contents of your vial into your mixture."

Claire felt for the vial on her desk. Picking up the slender glass bottle, she popped out the cork stopper and poured it into the mixture. With her enhanced hearing she heard the mixture begin to sizzle and shoved her chair back as the mixture exploded upwards.

Students shrieked and dove away as the Professor clomped towards her desk. "What in the Realm happened? How did you manage to screw up such a simple potion?"

"I don't know," Claire stammered, "I followed your directions exactly."

"Well you must have done something wrong because my directions were perfect. That truly is a talent, Ms. Windshire, to fail at cough syrup so badly. I surely hope you weren't planning on becoming a healer back at your coven. You'd likely kill everyone there."

Claire's mood sunk lower and lower with each word the professor spewed at her. She wanted to curl up into a ball under the desk and disappear. Finally he seemed to be done. "Class dismissed as this mess will have to be cleaned up. I'll inform the Headmaster about this."

Claire's cheeks flamed as some of the students snickered. She grabbed her bag, hurrying out the door. She didn't wait for Bethany, instead tracing the familiar route with her feet. She exited Class Building Two out the side door and circled the path around to the back of the building.

Pushing open the gate to the garden, Claire hung her bag on the fence next to their plot. She brushed off the front of her shirt, picking at the dried bits of potion that had stuck to it.

She sighed. How had she managed to screw that potion up? She had followed the professor's instructions exactly. Maybe she had zoned out because of what had happened in Runes. Maybe she got distracted and missed a step. She hoped the Headmaster wasn't going to be too harsh in her punishment.

"Hey, are you okay?"

In her self-deprecating thoughts, she had missed Bethany coming up next to her. Claire jumped slightly, "Yes, sorry I didn't mean to worry you by not being in class."

"Don't worry about that, I'm fine, I'm worried about you. Someone said there was an explosion in class. Are you hurt?"

"No I'm fine, just my pride. The explosion was my fault."

"I'm sure it wasn't." Bethany said.

"No, it was my bowl that exploded. I don't know how though, I thought I followed the professor's instructions exactly."

Before Bethany could ask any more questions, Professor Helene called the class to order.

Claire let herself get lost in the lesson, desperate to feel like she had accomplished something today after two dismal failures. The lesson went by fairly quickly as they examined their seedlings and learned about the proper conditions required for plant growth.

As the half-past bell rang, Professor Helene dismissed the class fifteen minutes early. "Claire, would you mind staying back for a minute?"

"Are you going to be okay?" Bethany asked.

Claire forced a smile and nod, "I don't think I've screwed anything up in this class so far."

"Okay, Holly will be here soon to take you to combat class."

As Bethany exited the garden gate, a different shadow figure came through. "Hi, there, Claire." Professor Andy's warm voice called out as Professor Helene approached from the other side of the garden.

"Sorry to catch you off guard like this, Claire," Professor Helene said. "Professor Andy was telling me about your Runes class this morning. You have a startling affinity for plants and the garden and I was telling her you were one of my star students."

"It's hard for me to watch every student in class," Professor Andy admitted, "I was wondering if we could sit and you can walk me through what you were feeling as you cast the rune."

"Sure," Even though her words were agreeable, Claire forced her feet to stay still. All she wanted to do now was to run back to her room and maybe to Windshire.

Claire lowered herself to the ground next to her garden plot as her professors took seats as well, "I don't know what you are looking for. My magic did not want to participate in this rune."

"Did you try to draw the rune?" Professor Andy asked.

"No, 'cause I couldn't get my magic to work." Claire said.

"How were you feeling?" Professor Helene asked. "In general." She clarified.

"Nervous, I guess." Claire admitted, "There seemed to be a lot of eyes on me."

"Partially my fault," Professor Andy sounded guilty, "I'm

afraid I got a little excited after our class yesterday. You are a very hardworking student, Claire, and I was excited to see you manipulate air as well as fire and water. I'm afraid I did you a disservice, Claire, and created pressure where there shouldn't have been any."

Claire felt awkward having a professor apologize to her after Professor Benton had chewed her out so thoroughly the class before. "It's okay. I think I placed a lot of pressure on myself as well."

"That's why I asked Professor Andy to come this afternoon," Professor Helene said. "I thought a lower-key environment might convince your magic to cooperate. If I had to guess, your magic was feeling a bit defensive in class this morning."

Claire nodded slowly, "It was feeling a bit protective. It had created a dome around my center and it didn't want to leave it."

"I hadn't thought about it until Helene mentioned it but if you haven't been used to using your magic regularly and placed a lot of pressure on yourself, your magic would have been very instinctive and in this case reactive to the pressure."

"So you think I can use earth elemental magic?" Claire questioned, "I thought that was rare. Being able to use all four elemental magics."

"It is, but I think you are a rare student." Professor Andy said.

"But I can't use it to the level that the others can." Claire argued. There wasn't anything special about her. She couldn't even get a simple cough syrup right!

"I'm confident that with practice and your desire to learn, that will change very quickly." Professor Andy sounded confident.

"You think so?" Claire couldn't seem to find the same confidence that Professor Andy had.

"I do."

"And so do I." Professor Helene said. "It's been a while since

I've had a student to whom the plants respond to so well. Not since we had Elven and Fae students at the Academy."

"Are you willing to try again?" Professor Andy asked.

If these two professors believed in her, that had to count for something right? Claire took a deep breath, "Let's do this."

"Here's your pot from class earlier. Like I mentioned this morning, it has a small budded flower. Your goal is to use the rune to encourage the flower to bloom if possible."

"Think about how you feel out here in the garden," Professor Helene advised, "We often can communicate best with an element when we are able to feel it around us."

Claire took the pot from Professor Andy and placed it on the ground in front of her. She took a deep breath and went inwards to her magic. It seemed more relaxed now, but still wary.

Feeling a bit silly, she mentally apologized to it for the pressure she placed on herself earlier. She coaxed it forward, reassuring in her ask. She didn't try pulling it but kept the gentle coaxing until she could feel her fingertips tingling with the stored magic.

Carefully, she drew the rune with her finger, letting the magic fall from her finger into the rune as she traced it. The magic left her finger in a warm rush, not fighting her like it usually did.

"Would you look at that," Professor Andy breathed as the warmth from the magic faded.

Claire carefully let her fingers wrap around the pot, trailing them through the soil at the rim until they ran into the stem of the plant. She traced them up the length of the stem until the soft caress of a petal brushed her knuckles. "I did it," she said excitedly.

"You did," Professor Andy sounded just as excited. "How did your magic feel that time?"

"Much smoother. It didn't fight me as hard. Thinking back

on it, I was probably placing it under a lot of unneeded pressure for the other elements as well."

"Sometimes when we force magic instead of allowing it, we can actually stifle it." Professor Helene said. "The best approach is to build a relationship with your magic so it is always ready to answer your call."

"And as you practice, it should come more easily to you." Professor Andy said. "Now I think we've kept you long enough. Holly is probably looking for you."

"Thank you, Professor, both of you." Claire extended the pot in Professor Helene's direction.

"You are very welcome, Claire," Professor Helene took the pot from her. "Don't forget to read the next chapter over the weekend."

As Claire pushed out of the gate from the garden, her steps felt much lighter than they had been when she had entered.

"There you are," Holly called out. "Is everything okay?"

"Everything's great!" Claire felt a wide smile break across her face.

"Oh?" Holly's tone was cautious.

Claire tugged Holly a bit closer once her hand was on Holly's elbow. "Professor Andy came back to the garden after Herbology and had me try again. I did it. I grew the flower." She kept her voice hushed.

"No way!" Holly barely matched her whispered tone.

"Yes! So even if I almost blew up the Spells and Potions classroom, I still was able to accomplish one thing today."

"Almost blew up the Spells and Potions classroom?" Desmond's voice came from three paces to Claire and Holly's right.

"Desmond," Holly greeted, "what are you doing here?"

"Just checking on Claire to see how her first week at the Academy has been. Sounds like an explosive one."

Claire let out a small laugh. “I don’t know what happened,” Claire admitted, “No one else’s potion exploded like that.”

“Yours was the only one that exploded?” Desmond’s voice had a hint of anger in it.

Claire nodded.

“It sounds like someone mixed up the ingredients you were given.” Desmond said. His tone was cheery but Claire could feel the hint of darkness in it.

Claire shook her head, “Professor Benton distributed the bags so that couldn't have been it. I must have screwed it up somehow.”

“That’s okay,” Holly squeezed her arm, “Mistakes happen.”

“Holly’s right,” Desmond said, “I’m sure it won’t happen again.” His words were spoken with the confidence of someone who seemed to be sure it wouldn’t.

“I don’t know,” Claire said, “maybe Spells and Potions just isn’t my thing.”

“Are you kidding?” Holly asked, “After activating all four elemental runes, I would say your other classes should be a breeze.”

“You activated your earth rune?” Desmond’s voice sounded proud.

“Not in class but afterwards,” Claire said.

“That’s fantastic. You’ll have to tell us the story at dinner tonight.”

“Us?” Holly asked.

“Of course,” Desmond said smoothly, “I figured I would join you for dinner. A quick check-in is never my style, you know that. I always need time for a good story.”

Holly’s body tensed slightly and she seemed like she wanted to protest more but Desmond continued, “Now you two should probably hurry. I can practically feel Malcolm’s glare from here. I suppose you two could always sacrifice my pretty face and tell him I was the one that made you late.”

"We'll make it plenty of time." Holly said.

"See you at dinner later," Claire said shyly, allowing Holly to tug her away.

"See you at dinner, little witch."

Holly and Claire hurried into the arena just as the bell rang four times. Dropping their bags at the wall, they hurried into place to finish learning the rest of Warm-up Form B. Claire found herself distracted yet again during class but this time for a different reason. Her thoughts drifted from the footwork of the warm-up form to a certain playful wizard who smelled of spearmint and seemed oddly proud of her Rune work.

CHAPTER 9

Claire hurried through her shower that evening, not wanting to keep Holly or Desmond waiting longer than necessary. Drying her hair with the smaller towel, she decided on a skirt and soft, long sleeve shirt. She didn't get a chance to wear the skirts often as she always had Combat Class at the end of her day. It made more sense to wear pants throughout the day. Claire wondered if some students changed at lunchtime or during a free period. She would have to ask Holly.

She met Holly outside the dormitory and the two girls walked towards the dining hall. "So you and Desmond are cousins?" Claire asked, "Did the two of you grow up together?"

"Sort of. He's about four years older than I am so he was always closer to my older brother. That is until he met his Triad at age sixteen. Then he, Malcolm, and Everett were joined at the hip. They used to spend the spring months at the coven and then most of their time at Malcolm's family's territory. Malcolm is like dragon royalty so they had the best training grounds the Realm could offer before the Academy."

"Sharing gossip, dearest Cousin?" Desmond's voice surprised Claire and her cheeks heated.

"Just common knowledge," Holly parried back. "You aren't interesting enough to be gossiped about."

"I'm wounded, Cousin." Desmond's shadow figure staggered away from them dramatically.

"You'll recover." Claire couldn't see to confirm but if she had money, she would have bet that Holly rolled her eyes.

"We'll see." Desmond said, "Now ladies, let's get to dinner." Desmond opened the door for them as they entered the dining hall.

"I'm surprised you tore yourself away from Malcolm and Everett tonight," Holly remarked.

"Well Malcolm was called home to his family for the weekend and Everett is on guard duty tonight. So you get me all to yourself."

"Joyful." Holly said dryly. "Oh, Claire, Bethany forgot to tell you earlier but during your Sophomore year you get to use the portal to go home for the weekend and both Bethany and Cody went home this afternoon."

"Is everything okay?" Claire asked.

"Oh yes. Bethany's pride has a ceremony tomorrow and Cody went home to visit."

"That's good. I'm glad it was a trip for pleasure rather than something being wrong."

As they sat down, Claire could have sworn she heard Desmond whisper something like "just the sweetest" but even Claire's advanced hearing couldn't make it out distinctly.

"Claire, have you tried the sweet potatoes and turkey with gravy yet?" Desmond asked.

"No, I haven't."

"It's one of my favorites. You'll have to try it."

"You can order it for me. So I don't screw it up."

Desmond placed their orders and then Holly placed hers. As

she was finishing, Zack approached the table. "Holly, Claire," he greeted, "Assistant Desmond." His tone was respectful.

"We are outside of class," Desmond said, "You can just call me Desmond."

"Assistant?" Claire questioned.

"Assis-, Desmond is an assistant teacher in my advanced spell work class."

"Oh that's right, Holly mentioned that you did that while you were getting your mastery."

"I do, that's why I'm curious to hear the story about your Spells and Potions class."

"Wait," Zack said, "It was your class that had the explosion. I heard about that. Are you okay?"

Claire blushed, "I'm fine. I screwed up the potion somehow."

"I was an assistant teacher for that class last year," Desmond said. "If Professor Benton used the same first potion, a cough syrup, that he did last year, that should have been impossible."

"I guess I'm an anomaly. Or the first to make that mistake." Claire shrugged. "I think I was distracted by Runes. Besides, it's got to be difficult for Professor Benton to teach a blind student."

"How did you mix it?" Desmond was persistent. He seemed to be wanting to prove it wasn't her fault but Claire knew she was bad at potions. The professor had said so. And she didn't blame him. A blind student trying to mix potions had to be a walking disaster.

"Well, I crushed the berries with the provided mortar and pestle and then scraped it into the bowl. Then we crumbled up the dry leaves and mashed that waxy material into the mixture. Finally, I poured the contents of the vial into the mixture. That's when it began to sizzle and then exploded everywhere."

"So it didn't begin to sizzle until you poured the mixture in?" Desmond asked.

"Yes."

"The cough syrup potion?" Zack asked.

"Yes, it was our first one."

It felt like Zack and Desmond were exchanging a look. "I think I agree with Desmond on this one," Zack said. "That's nearly impossible."

"I guess I'm just that talented." Claire tried to joke.

"I have no doubt you are quite talented, little witch. However, in this case I am leaning towards someone switching out your vials. All that was supposed to be in that vial was a syrup. The medicinal properties came from the berries and leaves that you crushed earlier in the potion-making process. If the contents of the vial are what caused the reaction then someone must have switched out the vials."

"Who would do that?" Holly asked.

"It probably wasn't intentional," Zack argued. "Professor Benton is a difficult person but he's a fair professor."

"It probably was an honest mix-up." Desmond agreed, "Maybe when he was preparing vials for another class they got mixed up. I'm sure it was an honest mistake."

Now why did Desmond's words ring false? Claire was broken out of her musings by the soft pop of their food arriving. To break the tension at the table, Desmond launched into a story of how he screwed up a potion in his lab one time causing his eyebrows to be singed off.

While the storytelling was dramatic, Claire felt herself hanging on to every word Desmond said, almost forgetting to eat. She found herself wanting to know every detail about this man, even though he was clearly out of her league and matched to Vivienne anyways.

"Oh, Claire!" Holly said as Desmond finished his story, "Share your good news from earlier today with Zack."

"I love some good news." Zack said from his new position across the table. Desmond had sat in Zack's usual spot and his closeness made Claire feel oddly safe.

"Professor Andy stopped by after Herbology and had me try the rune for the earth element again and I did it!"

"What! That's great!" Zack exclaimed. "Great job, Claire!"

Claire smiled, "Thanks! Professor Helene said that sometimes when we put too much pressure on our magic to perform, it can actually cause it to get defensive."

"That makes sense," Holly said.

For the rest of dinner, the four of them chatted comfortably. Zack, Holly, and Desmond traded stories about the Academy and Claire soaked it all in. It had been a rough start to the day but now, sitting at this table with her new friends, she started to believe that she might have a chance at success.

After dinner, Desmond offered to walk Holly and Claire back to their dormitory. Zack said he was going to hit the library with a classmate to finish up a project.

The summer evening's breeze carried a touch of chill in its flow, warning of colder days ahead.

"Hey, Holly!" A voice called out.

"Oh, that's Bernice from one of my classes. One second, I won't be long."

"I'll take good care of her." Desmond promised.

"Yeah, that's what I'm afraid of." Holly teased, "Feel free to tell him to shove off if he bothers you." Holly hurried towards her friend leaving Claire's side cold.

"Claire," Desmond's warm voice nearly made her stumble as she turned in his direction.

"Yes?" She felt out of breath for some reason.

"Earlier at dinner, you made a comment that you thought Professor Benton found it difficult to teach you. What did you mean by that?"

Desmond was close. Claire could feel his body heat radiate in the cool, late summer evening. She was distracted by the warmth and almost forgot he asked a question.

"Oh, I just meant it is probably difficult for a professor to teach a blind student. I don't blame him for getting a bit frustrated with me."

"Frustrated with you?" Desmond's voice was still warm but there was a slight edge to it.

"He got frustrated when I made the potion explode and vented a bit. It's fine, it was a stressful situation." Claire tried to dismiss it. She didn't want to complain about the professor of an Academy she felt lucky to be in.

"Do you think any of your other professors feel the same way?"

"Oh no, they've all been very kind and helpful. I know Instructor Malcolm probably talks out the warm-up forms we are learning more than usual because I can't see him do it. And Professor Andy is fantastic."

"I'm glad," Desmond's voice was back to being warm. Maybe she had just imagined the edge earlier. "I'll pass along your praise to Malcolm."

Claire's cheeks burned. "I mean, you can but I can't imagine he would care too much. He's very... disciplined."

"I think you would be surprised, little witch, at the things the three of us would care about."

Claire could feel Holly saying goodbye to her classmate and stayed quiet, basking in Desmond's presence for a few precious seconds longer.

Long after Claire snuggled under her covers, that feeling of warmth and security from Desmond's presence stayed with her.

CHAPTER 10

Her first full weekend at the Academy was peaceful and quiet. Holly and Claire grabbed breakfast in the dining hall and then headed out into the courtyard to get some reading done at one of the stone tables that littered the courtyard. Claire preferred studying outside, because she didn't feel like she was disturbing as many people with her reading spell. The air was tinged with a chill that the morning sun struggled to push away.

The girls huddled under blankets from their rooms as they read through their textbooks. Most of their professors had assigned two to three chapters to be read over the weekend and Professor Storm had assigned their first short paper to be completed on one of the five races for the following weekend.

Cody planned to do his paper on shifters and the chatter from the other students indicated they were going to do the same, stay within their own races, witches or dragons. Claire was torn though. She didn't really know what it meant to be a witch. Maybe she would do her paper on one of the lost races, the Fae or Elves.

Sunday, Claire spent most of the day in the garden, tending

to their garden plot. She enjoyed the summer sun on her face and the feeling of the dirt in between her finger tips. The garden seemed more… alive than usual. Claire had always been able to detect a person's energy but she thought it was just to make up for being blind. Now she wondered if there was more to it than that. She made a mental note to ask Professor Helene sometime this week as her fingers caught on another weed trying to take over the seedlings.

The first few classes on Monday morning seemed to drag on. It seemed as though the students and some of the professors were missing the peacefulness of the weekend and had trouble getting back into the school routine.

After lunch, Holly was dropping her off at the door to Spells and Potions when she stopped in the doorway. "What is it?" Claire asked.

"I forgot that after the first week, Professor Benton changes up the layout of the room to make workstations. Essentially, the desks have all been taken out and in their place are long tables with the short sides facing the professor. A wall splits the tables into two skinny sections and there are two students to a workstation. Here, I'll walk you to where you usually sit."

As they walked in, Claire could see the shadow figures of what Holly described. Most of the students were already seated leaving Claire to wonder who her partner would be.

Holly squeezed Claire's hand. "Here's yours. It's in the same back corner as it usually is. It doesn't look like you have a partner yet."

"Thank you," Claire said as she took her seat. Holly lingered instead of heading to her next class, "What is it?"

"Are you going to be okay?" Holly asked softly.

Claire smiled, even though she wasn't sure of the answer, "I'll be fine. You better hurry to class."

Holly squeezed Claire's arm before leaving the classroom. Claire ignored the eyes on her as she used her hands to feel for the new layout of the workstation. The layout was fairly simple. Different size jars lined the top shelf. Some seemed sturdy like clay pottery and others tinkled under her fingertips unveiling their glass composition. Underneath the shelf, several smaller jars and vials were heavier and rattled or sifted as she picked them up.

She wondered how she was going to tell which was which without a partner. Since no one had sat at the other seat yet, she had determined she was going to have to go through this class alone. And possibly with more mishaps like last week.

Professor Benton started to gather the class's attention with a morning greeting. He was halfway through role call when there was a shuffling at the doorway followed by students' whispering.

"Sorry, Professor Benton," Desmond's cheery voice called out. Claire wanted to sink in her seat. Surely, he wasn't here for her.

"Ah, Assistant Desmond," Professor Benton's voice was cool yet polite. "What can I do for you?"

"The Headmaster thought it would be beneficial for the students to have a second pair of eyes as they go through potions and I need another teaching credit. I was wondering if we could kill two birds with one stone and you would have me as your assistant this semester?"

Desmond phrased it like a question but Claire had a feeling he wasn't giving the professor much of a choice as he continued into the classroom towards the back of the room.

"The students would be honored to have a second pair of eyes from a mastery student such as yourself." Professor Benton's voice was tight even as his words were friendly.

"Fantastic! I'll situate myself in the back here and then we can have pairs of eyes from both sides of the room. As a former student of this class, I remember the temptation to play with the ingredients at your stations and as Professor Benton can tell you, I was the worst of them when it came to experimenting."

Professor Benton let out a chuckle that seemed out of practice. "I can definitely attest to that. You certainly made your mark."

Professor Benton continued to call roll as Desmond made his way to the back of the room. He paused at the last two aisles, as if looking for a seat. Claire sank lower in her seat. It's not that she didn't want to spend more time with the wizard that captured her attention, but Vivienne was in this class. And Vivienne had made it clear that Desmond and the rest of his Triad belonged to her.

Desmond was unaware of Claire' inner turmoil though. "Ah, Claire, I see you don't have a partner. Would you mind if I claimed your extra seat as mine to store my things?"

While she knew she didn't technically have a choice, Claire appreciated Desmond asking anyways. "That would be fine," Claire murmured softly to avoid disturbing the roll call.

Desmond's spearmint scent filled her nostrils as he brushed by her back to store his bag underneath the shared desk. He settled in the stool as Professor Benton began teaching today's lesson. Today's lesson was on the different categories of medicinal potions and the main ones in each category.

Claire took handwritten notes in this class, using her free hand to make sure she was staying on straight lines in her writing and keeping track of where the page ended. The Headmaster said she could use a writing spell in every class but Professor Benton had scoffed when she asked and said he wouldn't let her cheat. She didn't really understand how it could be cheating, but she had enough experience writing without the spell that her notes were still very legible for the reading spell she used for homework.

As she wrote, she could feel Desmond's eyes on her periodically as he sat against the corner. Professor Benton had a dry voice and it droned on for the whole period. Once Claire's brain was sufficiently stuffed with information on the differences between cough and fever potions, the bell rang. She shook out her aching hand and carefully blew on the paper to dry the rest of the ink before carefully shutting her book.

After she packed her things, she heard Bethany call her name from the door. Desmond hadn't moved yet, seemingly content to wait for her to fumble everything into her bag. She half-turned and gave a small smile, "See you tomorrow." She said softly.

She made her way down the aisle noting another person was making their way up it. "Desmond," Vivienne's voice called out as the scent of orchids filled Claire's nostrils.

Vivienne brushed by her, hitting her bag and ignoring her. Claire hurried down the aisle, not wanting to hear the two of them together. While she knew she would never measure up to Vivienne, that period of sitting next to Desmond and soaking in his scent of spearmint and safety made her wish for things that would never be hers. And that was dangerous. Maybe Vivienne would convince Desmond to sit next to her so Claire could stop all the wishful thoughts she seemed to have when he was around.

"Are you okay?" Bethany asked.

Claire smiled, "I'm fine. Tell me about your pride's event this weekend."

As Bethany chattered on about the pride ceremony and the latest gossip at home, the wishful thoughts of a different time and place faded from Claire's mind. By the time they got to Herbology, Claire was totally engrossed in the story. Or at least that's what she told herself.

* * *

On Wednesday, when the students got to combat class there was a notice on the arena doors saying combat class had been cancelled. No reason was given and Claire couldn't help but worry that Malcolm was sick. The gruff combat instructor never seemed one to show any type of weakness but Claire knew that didn't make anyone infallible.

"Let's study out in the courtyard before dinner," Holly suggested.

Claire nodded and followed alongside Holly back towards the courtyard. They found an unoccupied spot under a large maple tree and settled in. Claire spread out her light sweater on the soft grass and settled her bag next to her.

Holly sat out in the sun, close enough for Claire to call out but far enough away that she wouldn't be disturbed by Claire's reading spell. Holly also often called herself a sunflower, chasing the sun whenever they sat outside.

Claire leaned back into the tree. While she didn't have a preference over the sun or shade, Claire did like being close to the tree. It was silly, but it almost felt like the tree was embracing her in a rough hug as the bark prickled her skin through her shirt. She dug out her Herbology book, making a mental note to ask Professor Helene about the energy fields she thought about over the weekend. Activating the reading spell, Claire lowered the volume of the spell until it was a soft drone. Opening her notebook, she poised her pen above the page.

While the chapter played, Claire took notes, trying to make connections among the different pieces of information and how it would relate to their garden plot. Halfway through the chapter, a shadowy figure approached from Claire's left, from the main path through the courtyard. As he got closer, the rich, earthy smell of the forest after a fresh rain reached her nostrils. *Everett.*

"May I sit?" His quiet, deep voice asked.

Claire nodded mutely, wondering why he was here. As he

settled beside her, his back to the tree as well, the spicy smell of cinnamon peeked through his forest scent.

Claire's Herbology chapter filled the silence and Claire forced herself to focus on her notes. Everett was silent, seemingly content to just sit and as the silence continued Claire felt herself relaxing into it. His presence was like his scent, the quiet stillness you find deep in the forest.

Claire could feel Holly's eyes on her from her spot. Claire looked up from her notes and sent a small smile Holly's way, letting her know she was fine. As the chapter came to a close, Claire called a bit of magic up to her fingertips and pressed them to the book "*Finito*," she said quietly.

Feeling Everett's eyes on her, she finished making a few notes on the chapter and then closed her notebook.

"Is Malcolm alright?" Claire asked quietly.

"What?" Everett said, seemingly caught off guard.

Claire smiled, "Is Malcolm alright? Combat class was cancelled and I was worried he was sick."

Everett's gaze felt searching but warm, "He's fine," he said, "he and Desmond were called for a patrol in the woods."

"Do they not usually patrol?"

Everett paused for a breath "Not usually but they will occasionally to keep their skills up."

"That's good." Claire murmured, feeling a breath of relief that Malcolm wasn't sick but a spark of worry that they were in danger.

"They'll be fine," Everett said, "both are excellent warriors, despite Desmond's terrible sense of humor."

Claire smiled. "He really is quite persistent, isn't he?"

Everett let out a low chuckle and Claire's insides warmed. "He is. How are you finding the Academy?"

"It's... big," Claire said, finding herself wanting to be honest with him, more honest than she was with even Holly, "and a bit overwhelming sometimes. It's hard to feel like I belong here."

Instead of dismissing her, Everett hummed an agreement. "It takes time to adjust."

"That sounds like you speak from personal experience?" Claire couldn't fathom how this quiet, confident man could feel out of place.

"I am." Everett was silent for a few moments. "I was also an orphan. I actually grew up with Malcolm, I was fortunate enough to be adopted by his aunt and uncle. They didn't know who my parents were and when I hit sixteen and my gryphon came out, I felt even more alone."

"What do you mean?" Claire's heart ached for him.

"Gryphons are rare shifters to begin with but also can be used in several spells and potions. Before the war, gryphons without a colony were often hunted."

"Oh, Everett," Claire reached a hand out and placed it on his knee, squeezing gently. She understood what he wasn't saying, his birth family was likely dead.

Everett placed a hand over hers and squeezed gently. In the distance, the bell rang six times for dinner. An approaching shadow figure clued her into Holly's approach. "Would you like to sit with us for dinner?" Claire asked impulsively. Holly paused and Claire turned to her, "That is if you think it'll be okay with everyone?"

"He can't possibly be more annoying than my cousin so it's fine with me." Holly said.

Claire turned back to Everett, aware her hand was still under his. "Would you like to sit with us?" She repeated her question.

He squeezed her hand again, "That would be nice actually. Malcolm and Desmond will be on patrol the rest of the evening. And you're right," he added to Holly, "I don't know if anyone can be more annoying than your cousin."

Holly laughed with Everett as Claire placed her notebook in her bag. Everett released her hand almost reluctantly, trailing big fingers down the back of hers. Claire stood to distract herself from the butterflies that fluttered in her stomach at that movement.

"Don't forget your sweater," Everett's tone was a little gruff as he pressed the material into her free hand.

"Thanks," Claire smiled up at him.

Dinner was a quieter affair than when Desmond had joined them. Unlike Desmond, Everett let the others lead the conversations, providing short answers to the questions asked of him. Claire had a feeling he wasn't trying to be rude but was just naturally a man of few words.

After dinner, Everett walked with them back to the dorms. Bethany, Holly, and Claire split off from the group at their dorm, calling goodnight to the others.

"I thought you were going to stay away from them?" Vivienne's voice was like a blade, slicing through the hallway.

Claire paused, a few paces from her door, "I'm sorry?"

"Are you really as blind as you seem?" Vivienne asked, "My Triad. Desmond, Everett and Malcolm."

Claire was still confused. "Malcolm is my Combat instructor and Desmond is an Assistant Teacher in my class."

"So that's why Everett spent the whole afternoon with you and your friends?"

"He was just being friendly," Claire murmured.

"Everett isn't friendly with outsiders." Vivienne said. "Look, I'm going to spell it out for you because clearly you are blind in all aspects. I am their Fourth. Which means I am their everything. Their Fourth. Their Lover. Their Friend. And I don't need them distracted by some poor blind girl act. They've got bigger things to worry about then helping you get through the Academy. Maybe you just aren't cut out for this."

Claire was stunned at the force of Vivienne's attack. They had barely exchanged more than a few words over the last week. Certainly nothing that Claire felt deserved this level of animosity.

"Claire," Holly's voice called from the middle of the hallway, by the foyer to the stairs.

"Over here," Claire called, still feeling the weight of Vivienne's anger. It lingered in the hallway like a thick hot blanket, the woolen scratchy kind.

"Vivienne." Holly's voice was cooler than normal.

"Holly." Vivienne's voice was equally cool.

"Excuse me, I have to borrow Claire for a question on an assignment. Claire, could we use your room?"

"That's fine." Claire said softly. "Have a good night, Vivienne."

She turned and walked the remaining few paces to her door. Holly stayed close behind like a shield.

"What did she say to you?" Holly questioned once the door was closed.

"She was just enlightening me about a few things," Claire was polite. Vivienne was going to be like family to Holly, it wouldn't do for Claire to complain about Vivienne.

"Mmm," Holly didn't sound quite convinced.

"You said you had an assignment question?" Claire quickly changed the subject.

"Nothing that can't wait." Holly said. "We can talk about it in the morning."

"Okay," Claire smiled even though her insides were still a bit shaky, "In the morning then."

Holly paused at the door, "Whatever she said to you, Claire, know that Vivienne comes from a family of power-grabbing witches. She'll say anything to get ahead. If she's threatening you, it's because she views you as a threat."

Her? A threat? The thought made Claire grin a little wider at the ridiculousness of it. "It was nothing of the kind. She was just filling me in on a few things. Good night."

Holly repeated the farewell before slipping out. Claire walked the two paces to the door and leaned her forehead against the smooth wooden surface. She would leave the Triad alone. She wouldn't jeopardize their relationship with Vivienne by being a distraction. She could make it through the Academy without any additional help from them. The idea of belonging with a Triad is a fanciful dream for a low-level witch like herself. She would keep her feet firmly on earth and her head clear of daydreams.

CHAPTER 11

Thursday, Claire was decently successful at staying away from the Triad. Professor Benton was still lecturing on different properties of the various ingredients they would be using so she had no reason to engage with Desmond. After class, she packed up quickly and hurried off, forgoing her usual goodbye.

Malcolm had returned from his patrol and seemed to be in a gruffer mood than normal. He quickly pushed them through Warm-up Form C and told them they would start running laps next week. Claire made a mental note to go running this weekend.

Everett was easiest to avoid because she didn't have any direct classes with him. Still, she seemed to get hints of his scent as she moved around campus, the soothing scent of the forest seemingly around every corner.

Thankfully for Claire, she is able to repeat the same pattern on Friday. Sitting in Spells and Potions, her knee bounced anxiously as her internal clock counted down the minutes until class was over. Desmond had greeted her warmly at the beginning of class, but she was saved from answering by Professor

Benton starting the class before she could sit down. That was intentional on her part. She had lingered in the hallway with Holly carrying on a conversation from lunch before hurrying into her seat.

As Professor Benton finished up, she could feel Desmond's gaze on her. While she usually felt it on her throughout class, it had remained steadier today as if she was his favorite puzzle to figure out. His spicy spearmint scent filled her nostrils as he leaned in close, "Are you okay, little witch?" His voice was soft in her ear as his warm breath skittered down her neck.

Claire just nodded, her voice seeming to disappear at his proximity. Desmond lingered for just a bit before retreating back to his space, letting Claire breathe again.

Professor Benton dismissed class and Claire shoved her books into her bags and hurried down the aisle. She felt fingers on her elbow briefly from behind her as Desmond tried to get her attention but she let herself be caught up in the shuffle of students towards the door.

A shadowy figure passed her in the next aisle and Vivienne's lily scent filled her nostrils, "Des," Vivienne's voice bubbled, "I missed you at lunch today."

Claire was gone before she heard Desmond's answer. If she had stayed, she would have seen Desmond disentangle himself from Vivienne as quickly as possible and hurry into the hallway to look for his little witch but she was gone.

* * *

"DESMOND!" Holly's voice stopped Desmond's trek across the courtyard. He had been up late into the night, working on a boundary spell for the forest and the early morning sky had started to brighten by the time he let his eyes close in his desk chair. After only a few hours of sleep, Everett had shaken him awake so he could get to Spells and Potions on time. His stomach grumbled at his missed lunch while his mind stayed on his little witch.

Claire had seemed anxious today, her knee bouncing under the desk and her gaze staying locked on Professor Benton. He wondered if Benton had said anything to her again. After learning from Claire that Benton expressed frustration at her, he had asked around discreetly. Several students including Vivienne, confirmed that the Professor had blown up at his little witch and that simply wouldn't do.

"Cousin," he forced cheeriness into his voice. Malcolm had once told him that a grumpy Desmond was a scary bastard and Desmond had a reputation to uphold here. "What can I do for you this fine morning?"

"It's after lunchtime," Holly corrected him and Desmond glanced up at the clock tower.

"Sorry my head must still be lost in a spell. Anyways, what can I do for you?"

"Vivienne cornered Claire in their hallway a few nights ago." Holly's voice was matter of fact but her eyes were questioning. "I didn't hear what was said but the weight of the anger was still strong when I found them."

In addition to her earth witch talents, Holly was an empath. She was just coming into her power. She could pick up on most emotions if she was standing right next to a person so for the anger to be so strong that Holly could feel it from a floor away was something.

"You felt it from your floor?" Desmond confirmed his thoughts.

"Yes. The closer the relationship I have to the person right now the easier it is to feel them. I felt Claire's shock and then a bolt of panic and came up to the two of them." Desmond's mind swirled with anger at the thought of Claire's panic.

Holly paused and looked him over. "Now from what I can gather on campus, Vivienne is your potential Fourth."

"Our what?" Desmond was lost in his thoughts of rage and protectiveness that he almost didn't hear Holly.

"Your Fourth." Holly said. "Can I guess by the waves of shock coming from you that that rage and protectiveness is over Claire and not Vivienne?"

Desmond nodded mutely. "Who the hell is telling people that Vivienne is our potential Fourth?"

Holly broke eye contact for the first time. "It's just a rumor going around campus."

Desmond could understand Holly's hesitation. Vivienne's family was powerful and had a past history of cruelness. Vivienne had always seemed sweet enough but clearly inherited some of her father's temperament if she was out threatening Claire. *Desmond's soul flame.*

"Holly, who's been telling people that?"

Holly glared at him, one of the few people on campus brave enough to do that. "If she finds out it was me I will totally throw you under the carriage and say you forced it out of me under duress."

Desmond rolled his eyes, "Noted."

"It was Vivienne. Vivienne's been spreading the rumors, mainly among the girls dormitory, that she's your potential Fourth."

"And no one finds it odd that we barely spend any time with Vivienne?" Most Triads when they find their Fourth are inseparable. If it's a potential Fourth, the males spend a lot of time with the potential Fourth in order to court them and see if they are a potential match.

"The key word there was barely. Individually, you three spend enough time with her that the rumors never die. In addition, Vivienne's added the rumor that the three of you are waiting until she finishes the Academy to begin courting. Something about you wanting a strong warrior witch."

Desmond thought back to earlier this week when Vivienne

stopped him after Spells and Potions to chat about the lesson. Recalling the memory was easy and he let it replay in his mind. The student she had brushed by was Claire and now that Desmond watched it a second time, he saw how Vivienne hit Claire's bag lightly.

He blinked away the memory to see Holly staring at him expectantly. "So from the way I see it, and the way that campus sees it," she began slowly, "Vivienne is your potential Fourth member of a very powerful and very beloved Triad and instead of spending time with her, you all are showing interest in what the campus perceives as a low-level blind orphan witch."

"Perceives as?" Desmond raised an eyebrow.

Holly rolled her eyes, knowing full well he was avoiding the rest of her statement. "Both you and I know that Claire has more potential in her than meets the eye. But stop deflecting. Claire is my friend. She's sweet and kind and sees the good in people and she is also blind. And not just physically but with her magic as well. I have a feeling that her upbringing suppressed more than just her self-esteem. So if the three of you are just playing some game or have some hero's complex, you're not only going to hurt her, but you will encourage others to hurt her too. Remember, interfering with a Triad's Fourth is looked down upon and right now the campus thinks Vivienne is your Fourth."

"We'll kill anyone that touches her." Desmond snarled.

Holly took a step back at his ferocity, "Who? Vivienne?"

Desmond ran a hand over his face and shoved his anger down into his dark place deep inside of him. "No."

He stepped closer to Holly, looking around the courtyard. With a flick of his wrist, he threw up a privacy spell that he probably should have thrown up at the start of their conversation. "What I say to you next can not be repeated."

Holly rolled her eyes, "Give me a little credit, Cousin, I'm not a blabbermouth and I'm always firmly in your corner."

"I'm serious, Holly." Desmond's use of her name had the intended effect. Her mouth clamped close and she nodded.

"Claire is my soul flame. She is Malcolm's mate. And she is Everett's mate."

Holly's eyes widened. Triads were often alliance-based matches. Sure some Fourths found their mates as part of a Triad and joined them but it was unheard of for all three Triad members to have the same woman be their everything.

"She means more to us than anyone could ever know. I don't know where Vivienne got these ideas..." Desmond paused, "Actually, yes I know where she could have gotten them but I will handle them. I guess I will tell the others that we need to step up our courting of Claire. We hadn't wanted to draw a target on her back but I guess it's already been drawn."

"She's not going to understand if you all overwhelm her at once." Holly said, "So maybe tone it down and get to know her first before throwing words like soul flame, intended, and mate at her.

Desmond nodded. "Keep an eye on her for us?"

Holly nodded, reading between the lines of keeping an eye on her emotions. If Holly felt she was being overwhelmed, she would step in.

Stepping back, Desmond dropped the barrier. "Thank you, Cousin. I'm going to charm the cooks into a late lunch.

Holly rolled her eyes. "Good luck with that."

* * *

After Herbology, Claire lingered telling Bethany she would catch up with Holly at the arena. "Professor," she called as she gingerly picked her way through the garden plots towards the front of the garden.

"Claire," Professor Helene's voice sounded like the wind that whistled through the leaves of the trees in the deep stillness of the forest. "What can I do for you?"

"I had a question, it might be silly." Claire paused. She hadn't thought about how the question would sound to a professor.

"No question is ever silly," Professor Helene said, "What is it?"

"Is it possible to, I don't know, sense another person or being's energy?"

Professor Helene was silent for a few seconds and Claire fought hard not to fidget. "It is possible," Professor Helene conceded, "but it is rare. Let me amend that statement, it is rare in people with sight. Have you been experiencing this?"

"Yes, for a while now, even before I came to the Academy. I had wondered if it was just because I was blind but I was working in the garden last week and I could almost feel the energy of the plants beneath the soil's surface."

"Every being, plant, animal, or person has a living energy inside of them. That energy also exists in the air, water, fire, and earth elements as well. Think of it as an energy circle that encompasses the being, it starts in the being's center and expands outwards depending on how much energy it has and how it is being used. For you, people are probably easier to sense than plants?"

Claire nodded and Professor Helene continued. "I would think that your sensitivity to energies is probably your magic's way of helping you navigate through life."

"My magic's way?" Claire was confused.

"Your magic is your own energy. It is an instinctive part of you. Whether you knowingly tell it to or not, it guides and protects you. The most powerful witches and wizards know that to be at your best you have to develop a relationship with your magic. Think back to when you were trying to call the earth rune in class. You felt defensive and your magic responded to that by protecting your center. Later, when you tried it with Andrea and I, your magic was more relaxed and more inclined to work with you."

"How does one develop their relationship with their magic?"

"The easy yet complicated answer is to spend time with it. You have to develop a focus on it. Wait here. I think I have a book that you would find interesting on the fields of energies."

Claire waited while Professor Helene retrieved the book. When she pressed it into her hand, Claire tucked it carefully into her book bag. "I'll take good care of it."

"I know you will. Now hurry along, I see Holly's been wondering where you are."

The sound of the gate opening in the back clued Claire into Holly's entrance. Her heart warmed at the concern of her friend.

"Everything okay?" Holly asked.

"All good," Claire started towards her, "Thank you, Professor."

Claire took Holly's arm as they headed towards the combat arena. "I was just talking to her about the energy fields I've been sensing."

Holly's steps slowed, "Energy fields?"

"Yes, Professor Helene thinks it's because of my blindness that I've been able to sense the energies of other plants, animals, and people. She gave me a book on it."

Holly tugged Claire to a stop and stepped closer, "I'm thrilled for you but as your friend I have to warn you to keep that ability on the downlow."

"Why?"

"Because what Professor Helene forgot to mention is that is not a common ability for a witch even in our most powerful witches."

"Then why is there a book on it?"

"Because it was a common ability in the Fae."

CHAPTER 12

In the Fae.

Holly's words echoed in Claire's mind through combat class, dinner and well into the evening. She was distracted in Combat Class, stumbling through a few steps and causing the other students to snicker softly. While Claire's cheeks were red, for the first time she wasn't consumed with thoughts about what the others thought of her when she made a mistake. Instead she stayed on those words. *In the Fae.*

Something about that felt right as odd as it sounded. But heeding Holly's warning, she kept it quiet at dinner, playing off her silence as exhaustion from a long week. Bethany and Cody's familiar bickering kept the conversation light. Claire ate her meal barely tasting the delicious turkey and sweet potatoes that Desmond had introduced to her last week. It had quickly become one of her favorite dishes but her thoughts kept her so distracted she couldn't enjoy it.

"Claire," Holly's hand on her arm clued her into the fact that the table had been trying to get her attention for a while.

"Sorry, lost in my head," Claire gave a sheepish smile.

"Are you feeling sick?" Cody asked.

"No. My brain just feels over packed with information. I think I need to pace myself better with studying."

"It's hard to get into a routine your first year," Zack agreed. "Don't worry about it though, you are only two weeks in so you'll find your rhythm."

"I hope so,"

"You will," Bethany comforted. "We can study together this weekend in the library. I have a big test next week. I want to get started on the material for this weekend."

"That sounds good," Claire smiled.

"Bethany? Studying? In the Library?" Cody teased. "The world must ending!"

"Hey!" The sound of Cody getting smacked was a familiar one at this table, "I study."

"Yeah, now. I remember when we were little, the last place you wanted to be was lessons. Always a tomboy trying to run around with the older kids."

"And I remember kicking your ass even when we were little. Would you like a repeat of that memory?" Bethany said sweetly.

"You two grew up together? I thought that the shifter clans didn't mix?" Claire questioned.

"My pride and Cody's pack share a boundary line and a truce that our grandfathers started before the Great War."

"Wow."

"I know right," Cody teased, "Cats and dogs getting along together was definitely a sign of the end times."

Bethany smacked him again and Cody just laughed. Claire wanted so bad to ask what was going on with the two of them but she held her tongue.

After dinner, Claire begged off going to the library to turn in early. Vivienne's voice was still holding court at one of the center tables and Claire refused to look in that direction as Bethany and Holly walked her back to get their books.

Shutting the door behind her, Claire sighed and leaned back

against it for a few breaths. Suddenly feeling like her bag weighed a thousand pounds, she pushed up from the door and placed it on the desk. Pulling out the books, she carefully stacked her textbooks on her desk.

Her fingers dug in her bag again and brushed against the leather bound book on energy fields. In the Fae.

She pulled the book out and placed it on the bed instead of the dresser. Her mind probably wasn't going to quiet until she got some more information.

She finished her bedtime routine in the bathroom, brushing her teeth and splashing some water on her face and neck. She had already showered before dinner.

Drying her hands on the towel, she changed into her sleeping clothes, dropping her used clothes in the basket by the door before climbing into bed.

Snuggling under the covers, she grabbed the book and brought it up to her chest. Opening the front cover, she traced the front page, calling some magic up from her center. It flowed into her fingers quickly and Claire took a moment to feel it swirling inside her. She whispered a silent thank you to it, thinking of Professor Helene's advice on building a relationship with her magic. "*Legere*," she whispered, letting the magic flow into the reading spell.

With reading spells, the voice of the reader was something the caster could choose. When she first got here, her reading spells always sounded like Mother Kemp's flat voice. Once Holly had let her know about the ability to change it, Claire had used the voice of each professor for their respective class text-book. Tonight, Professor Helene's willowy voice started reading the introduction.

"This book has been written for the Fae and Witches strong enough to read energy fields and for all others who are inter-ested in the practice whether they have the magic strength or not."

Read energy fields? Not just sense them?

Claire listened as the introduction and first chapter went on to discuss in greater detail what Professor Helene had outlined earlier this afternoon. Each being in the Realm had an energy field including the four elements. Like Professor Helene had said, the energy came from the innate magic at each being's center but the first chapter also described the differences in energy fields based on the being. For plants, the energy field was small but steady. It was sluggish to respond because of the growth cycle of plants. A Fae or Witch could pour all the magic into the energy field that they wanted, the book said, but they would never be able to influence most plants to move quickly.

There were a few exceptions to that rule and they were the plants that naturally grew faster than others like most vines. Trees were almost impossible to influence and the larger the tree the bigger and more steadfast the energy field. Smaller trees could be influenced but mainly at their roots and younger branches. Witches with an earth affinity could influence plants more than most but still not as much as the Fae. The first chapter referenced another book on Fae gardening techniques that Claire made a mental note to find in the library. Seedlings were the easiest to influence because small influences led to big changes. That's probably why Professor Andy used the seedling as the earth rune test.

After the brief introduction to the energy fields of plants, the first chapter moved onto its next section: the energy fields for elements. Elemental energy fields felt a lot like the elements did. Fire's energy field was warm and got hotter depending on the size of the fire. It flickered and expanded, reaching out to touch the energy reader almost like it was consuming them. This corresponded to fire's ease of an element overall and why most second elemental proficiencies were fire because of its easiness to work with.

Air, the book described, was the easiest elemental energy to read because it was all around Readers. The slight draft from a cracked window, the gentle summer breeze in the evening that lifted the hairs on the back of one's neck, or the bitter winter wind that whipped through you no matter how many layers one had on. Air's energy felt like air but also had a cooler energy field. Most Readers could easily read air so the book recommended it as a good starting point for beginning Readers.

The elemental energy of water was next. The book described the energy like the water's element, it rushed and flowed towards a reader if the water was moving or reflected a deep still energy if the water was still. Some Energy Readers when traveling were always able to identify the closest body of water making it valuable to travel with one.

The elemental energy of earth was hardest to read despite it being at one's fingertips. The book described the earth's energy as steadfast and unyielding. Readers could eventually tap into that energy but convincing it to work with you was difficult. The book described that the best earth Readers could track troop movements at distances up to a mile. It was hypothesized that with enough power, Readers might be able to even shake the earth by its energy but that was just a hypothesis.

Claire yawned so hard her jaw popped. Her eyes popped open realizing she had dozed off a bit as the reading spell kept going, moving onto the energy fields for people. "*Finito*," she whispered, closing the book and setting it on the windowsill next to her bed. Pulling the covers up to her chin, she snuggled into bed. That night her dreams were filled with trees and vines and voices that called her name that sounded suspiciously like Desmond, Everett, and Malcolm.

CHAPTER 13

Groggy, Claire woke up the next morning. Eyelids heavy, she rolled over in bed wondering what had woken her.

Another knock on her door gave her the answer. "Claire, it's Holly. Everything okay?"

Groaning, Claire resisted the urge to roll back over and snuggle under the covers. "One second," she called, throwing the covers back and stepping carefully to the door. Her room was brighter than usual this morning, the shadows easier to see.

She pulled the door open. "Good morning."

"Good morning," Holly's voice was amused, "Are you okay? I've been knocking for five minutes."

So that was what had woken her. "Sorry, I was up late reading. I must have overslept." She stepped back to let Holly in. "Give me a few and I'll get ready."

"Take your time. I'll take a seat on your bed."

Claire looked at her bed longingly for a few moments and Holly busted out laughing, "You look like I'm stealing your lover from you."

Claire's face heated but she smiled, "And what if you are? I'll have you know that bed is the best thing at night," she wiggled her eyebrows at Holly and both girls giggled.

"Well it will be waiting for you tonight. Maybe tonight you won't cheat on it with a book."

"Oh, on the contrary," Claire's tone was airy, "the bed gladly shared me with the book last night. It doesn't make me choose between two good things."

"Does it make you choose between it and breakfast?"

"No it doesn't," Claire kept up the game and stroked the covers lovingly, "but that doesn't mean I'm not going to miss it when I'm gone."

Holly shoved her shoulder lightly laughing, "Go get dressed. My stomach has only one love affair and it's bacon at the dining hall."

"Only one lover?" Claire teased as she fetched a pair of pants and a long sleeve shirt from the dresser, "How boring." She didn't know where her new boldness was coming from? Maybe it was always there and Claire just needed to find a friend to share it with.

Claire dressed quickly and the pair headed to breakfast. "What are your plans for today?" Holly asked.

"I think I'm going to spend most of the day in the garden. I want to read more of the book Professor Helene gave me last night and I have some other reading to get done."

"Do you want any company?"

"No, I'm okay. I know it's hard for you to focus when my reading spell is going."

"It's not that much of a bother if you want the company."

Claire squeezed Holly's arm, Holly's thoughtfulness warming her heart. "I appreciate you." Claire leaned her head briefly on Holly's shoulder.

"What?" Holly seemed surprised.

"I appreciate you. And I don't tell you this enough. You've made these last two weeks possible." Claire truly meant that.

Without Holly as a guide, there was no way she would have been able to navigate the Academy even if she could see much less when she was blind. Holly's guidance and information was invaluable.

Holly was silent for a few paces, but it wasn't awkward. Claire had a feeling that she may have surprised Holly by her words. Holly placed her hand on top of Claire's and squeezed it back.

Just as they were entering the dining hall, Holly leaned closer, "You are a treasure. Don't ever let anyone tell you otherwise."

It was Claire's turn to be speechless as they walked up the steps to the dining hall doors. She hadn't ever been called a treasure. Come to think of it, she couldn't remember the last compliment she received. Holly's words warmed her in the way Desmond's little witch did.

* * *

AFTER BREAKFAST, Claire walked the familiar path to the garden by herself. At her insistence, she was walking alone as the others were heading to the library which was in the opposite direction from the gardens. Both Zack and Cody insisted it wouldn't be any problem to walk her there. Cody even boasted he could run back without getting winded but Claire held firm. Her friends already did so much for her, she could handle a walk by herself.

Even so, Holly insisted that she use her guidance stone. Even though Claire knew she could get to the gardens unaided, there was something about Holly's tone that wore her down. The orb lay on her chest, under her shirt, bouncing slightly with her steps as she made her way down the path past the Class Buildings. The orb warmed in small increments as she made the turn around Class Building 2 towards the gardens.

Even now she laughed internally at the names of the Class

Buildings. All the prestige of the Academy and they were still Class Building 1 and Class Building 2. Zack had told her one lunch period that there were several council members at the time of the Academy's construction that had wanted the buildings named after them but the original Headmaster insisted that none of the buildings on campus would be named after anyone to preserve the Academy's neutrality as a welcoming place for all students.

Three paces out, the shadowing shape of the garden fence appeared in her field of vision. Her ability to see shadows had developed overtime. When she was younger, most of her vision was darkness. Over the years, the darkness had lightened incrementally until shadows started to form around her 16th birthday. She could only see shadows of people or objects when they were within a three pace distance from her.

Light played a big role as well. On a sunny day the shadows were more pronounced and on a cloudy day they were harder to distinguish. Claire acknowledged that shadows were probably the wrong word to describe them but no one had ever asked her. With very few at the orphanage to talk to and no friends to speak of, Claire had never mentioned the ability or how it became easier to see the shadows.

Unlatching the garden gate, Claire stepped through and shut it behind her. The rough wood was still a bit cool from the chilly night last night. The warm late summer weather was starting to get a tinge of fall chill especially at night. She settled in at the corner of her and Bethany's garden. Pulling her bag over her head, she settled it at her side rubbing her arms slightly. The sun's morning rays were still trying to chase away the night's chill. She would have to ask Holly about getting a jacket.

Claire shifted herself to the left of the first row of plants and started running her hands gently over the row, shuffling forward on her knees as she made her way down the row of seedlings. Their garden plots mainly consisted of common kitchen and medicinal herbs. Some had dual uses as she learned from her Spells and Potions book. Professor Benton seemed more interested in the medicinal effects of the herbs but the kitchen effects were also interesting to Claire. Mainly for their preventative measures. A balanced diet with herbs could go a long way to improving the health of a person.

Maybe that's what she could do after the Academy. Set up a small herb shop and provide a coven with her services. But not Windshire. She had no interest in returning to that coven even after the Academy. Maybe Brandlevine or a neighboring coven would take her. That could be a good goal, she mused as she finished the first row and started down the next. Find a way to make herself useful enough that after the Academy she could settle somewhere other than Windshire.

For the next two rows, she let her thoughts wander on that dream. She would get a little cottage on the outskirts of a coven with enough room for a few garden plots. Maybe she could even have a small orchard at the back of the property if she had enough land. Maybe she could work something out with the coven that she would provide a portion of her produce in exchange for a larger plot. She would have a kitchen herb garden plot and a medicinal herb garden plot for the village's healer. And then she could raise her own food. Maybe even get a few goats?

Her fingers caught on a weed and she worked her hand into the soil to get all the way down to the roots to excavate it completely. She had repeated the action a thousand times before but holding the weed in her hands she stopped herself from adding it to the pile at the end of the row. The words from the energy field book last night made her pause. What did they say about feeling the fields around the plants? Plant's energy fields tended to stay close to the physical plant and felt 'sluggish' if she remembered right.

She added the weed to the pile at the end of the row and started down the next row. This time, as she ran her hands over the seedlings and mounds of dirt, she tried to focus on the energy that surrounded the plants. Nothing. She paused at a struggling seedling. Sitting on her heels, she took a few deep breaths. Professor Andy had taught them that centering themselves before casting was a helpful way to strengthen their cast. Reaching down to her center, where her magic resided, Claire tried mentally telling her magic what she wanted to do, read the energy field of the seedling and see if it was healthy.

While she felt a little silly mentally talking to her magic, it seemed to work. A tendril of magic departed from her center and warmed her palms. She cupped them around the seedling and took another deep breath, clearing her mind. There was a pause and then Claire felt it, a dryness in the back of her throat like she was thirsty. It took a second for her to realize that was the plant's energy and not her own but she smiled when she realized. "Alright little seedling, let's get you some water."

Standing up from the row, she stepped towards the fence. Following it around the garden plots, she came to the rain barrels next to the greenhouse. A few small watering cans sat next to the barrels and Claire reached out for the handle of one. Pulling it over, she carefully positioned the opening under the rain barrel's spigot and turned the handle. Letting the water run for a few seconds in case there were other seedlings that needed some, she twisted the spigot off and hauled the water back to the plot.

She was rounding the corner of the plots when she heard voices.

"Desmond, why did we all have to come with you to get this leaf?" Claire recognized that gruff tone from her Combat Class. Malcolm.

"It's a good team building exercise." Desmond said cheerily

as the clink of the garden gate's latch sounded. "Oh look, it's Claire."

Claire placed the watering can down at the corner of the garden plot as the three shadowy figures made their way towards her. While the third shadow hadn't spoken yet, Claire instinctively knew it was Everett.

This was the first time she had been in close proximity to all three members of the Triad at once. Each man seemed to fill the space before her while simultaneously seeming to pull her into their presence. Claire forced her feet to stay grounded before she did something embarrassing like step towards them.

"Hello," she said shyly, thankful that her voice came out clear.

"Good morning, little witch." Desmond said cheerfully, "Getting some work done in the garden?"

"A little bit. I've got some reading to do as well." Why did she tell them the last part? It wasn't like they were interested.

"Don't you have a leaf to get or something?" Malcolm asked Desmond.

"Oh, yes," Desmond seemed distracted, like he forgot his original purpose.

"We'll keep Claire company." Claire couldn't see Malcolm but if she could she wondered if the satisfied tone in his voice would match an expression on his face.

Desmond's shadow left the Triad and Claire breathed a bit easier now that the three of them had split up. The pull didn't feel as strong now. She leaned down and picked up the watering can again. Counting down the rows, she came to the right one and walked in a bit until she got to the thirsty seedling. Gently tipping the watering can, she focused on the sound of water hitting the soil. She didn't want to overwater the seedling so she stopped after a few moments.

"Why are you watering that seedling?" Everett's voice was quiet.

She settled on a simple answer. "It's thirsty."

"And the others are not?" Malcolm asked.

"Not so far." She shrugged.

"And how can you tell?" Malcolm asked, his gruff tone seeming almost amused.

"They tell me. This seedling was struggling a little bit and since no other seedlings around it are struggling, that rules out bugs so water was a likely option." Claire explained it carefully to avoid talking about the energy fields, remembering Holly's warning to not share the energy field ability with anyone.

"Hmm," Malcolm's hum made it seem like he knew she wasn't telling the full story but he let it go. Both he and Everett's shadows shrunk as the men took seats with their backs to the fence two paces from the edge of her garden plot.

Claire forced herself to ignore them, telling herself that they were just waiting for Desmond. She shuffled on her knees down the rest of the rows, her hands carefully feeling over every seedling. She found two other seedlings that were a bit smaller than the others so she carefully watered them aware of the two pairs of watchful eyes on her.

Finishing the rows, she set the watering can off to the side and dusted off her knees. Thankfully the soil wasn't wet so she shouldn't have mud stains on her knees but it never hurt to check. Desmond's shadow appeared off to her right and she turned her head to look at it.

"How did you know he was coming?" Everett asked, his voice quiet but curious. Desmond's shadow paused at Everett's words and Desmond also settled into a seated position off to Malcolm's left.

Sighing, Claire took a seat as well, not wanting to be awkwardly standing while the Triad was sitting and waiting expectantly for her answer if the weight of their stares was anything to go by.

"It's hard to explain," she twisted her hands in her lap.

"Try us," Desmond said, "or try me at least. I'm clearly the brains of the group."

Desmond's words had their intended affect and Claire's lips tilted upwards. "I've never tried to explain it to anyone before, but it's like I can see shadows?"

"Shadows?" Everett's voice soothing even as it questioned. Claire could listen to his voice all day.

"Well maybe that's not the right word but it's the word I call them. I see these outlines? Of people, buildings, and things but I have to be within three paces of them. On cloudy days it's harder to distinguish them and on brighter days it's easier to see so I think that's why I call them shadows."

"But why do you think shadows is the wrong word?" Malcolm asked.

"Because… it's hard to explain. But it's almost like the objects I see aren't shadows but holes? Like it's an absence of energy rather than a shadow that's cast because of the light? That's not making much sense, is it?"

"It does." Desmond soothed, "The energy signatures make sense."

Claire flinched internally, energy signatures sounded like energy readers. She needed to do better at hiding that. "I guess so. I've always called them shadows because it just seemed easier."

"Shadows work then," Desmond said.

"How clear is the outline for them?" Malcolm asked.

"Okay, I guess," Claire shrugged, "Larger objects like people are easier to see. I have a harder time with smaller objects but I usually rely on feeling for the smaller objects."

Malcolm made a noise of acknowledgement. "Next week we start cardio training for Combat Class but we will move on to swords after that. I will try and figure out a way you can use the shadows to help predict moves."

"Oh you don't have to do that, I don't want to cause any extra trouble or work for you."

"It's no problem, Claire. It would be my pleasure." Malcolm's words cause a different type of heat to fill Claire, not only in her cheeks but in her stomach as well.

"It's the job of all instructors to help their students." Desmond said firmly. "Besides your Combat Instructor being grumpy, how are the rest of your classes going?"

Malcolm's growl at Desmond made Claire giggle. At the sound of her voice, the growl shut off immediately and Claire blushed as she covered her mouth. "I'm sorry," she said.

"Don't apologize," Desmond said gleefully, "we all know he's a grump."

"But he's really not." Claire defended Malcolm, "He's a bit growly and stern but it's only to make the class take it seriously." She knew some of her classmates didn't take Combat Class seriously as they thought they would never need to defend themselves.

"See, Claire likes my growls," Malcolm shot back at Desmond.

Claire opened her mouth, because that was not what she said but Everett leaned over and placed a hand on her knee, "This argument has been going on much longer than these past few minutes." He squeezed her knee once and let it go, the spot where his hand was felt chilled despite the sun's rays. She shivered slightly.

"Where is your coat?" Everett's question stopped the other two men's bickering.

She shrugged, "I don't have one yet. I was going to ask Holly where I could get one."

"We can help with that." Malcolm grumbled.

"Oh I wouldn't want to trouble you. Holly can help me."

Malcolm grumbled but Desmond or Everett must have shot him a look because he quieted.

"So your classes?" Desmond prompted.

"Professor Andy is great and Runes seems to be going well. It's only the second week so we are still practicing the elemental runes. I still can't do anything big with them but Professor Andy says it's going to take time."

"Professor Andrea Brandlevine?" Malcolm asked.

"Yes, I guess you know her?" Claire directed the question at Desmond.

"We are acquainted but I don't know her well. She is spoken of highly around the Academy though."

"I really like her." Claire said, "she gave me a book of etched runes so I can trace them with my fingertips and I think she and the librarian actually made it for me."

"Good. Professor Andy has always been very invested in her students. What about Professor Storm."

Claire paused and Desmond pressed, "Is he giving you trouble?"

"Oh no! He's... nice? No, that's probably not the word. He's very fair and polite but it doesn't seem like..." Claire trailed off, "truthfully, I feel bad for him. The students all whisper about how he lost his Triad and Fourth in the war. He's a fair professor and has allowed me to use the writing spell in his class but I almost get the sense he's just... sad all the time. Which is probably silly because he's a great warrior."

"A great warrior who's suffered a huge loss." Malcolm said, "that's enough to knock any warrior off balance. He's always been friendly, but like you said, a bit distant from the others."

"He helps the patrols sometimes," Everett said, reminding Claire he was one of the captains of the guard.

"But you're not having any trouble in his class?" Desmond questioned.

Claire laughed and rolled her eyes a bit, "No, Holly." she teased. "No trouble from the polite but sad history professor."

Malcolm and Everett laughed. "You can tell him to fuck off," Malcolm said, "he's perpetually nosy."

"Hey, I resent that term. I prefer inquisitive." Desmond's mock snooty tone had the group breaking into laughter.

Once they all caught their breath, Claire smiled at Desmond. "I don't mind it, honestly." She paused, letting her fingers sift through the grass in front of her, "I didn't have many people that cared about my activities growing up so while the questions are unexpected… I don't mind them." She kept her eyes on the ground.

"Tell us about it. Growing up." Malcolm's voice was soft but threaded with a command that warmed Claire's insides.

Claire shrugged, "It's not much of a story."

"We want to hear it." Everett's voice was quiet but firm.

"Well, I was found wandering in the woods at five years old. I don't remember how I got there or a lot about it. A Windshire coven member found me and brought me to the coven. They sent out missives to the surrounding covens but no one stepped forward to claim me so I went to live at the orphanage. Mother Kemp raised me and a few others. Some of them got adopted but no one wanted a blind child of unknown parentage. I helped out around the orphanage as much as I could. I tended the garden and did the laundry and other tasks I could do, well, blind."

"You must miss her, Mother Kemp." Desmond asked.

Claire shrugged, "I mean I guess I should but Mother Kemp was never… motherly." Malcolm let loose a small growl and Claire hurried to explain, "She was never cruel but she was never particularly kind either. She was there to make sure our basic needs were met."

"A lack of kindness can still be cruel. Especially to a child." Everett's voice held a thread of tension.

"I don't know any different." Her use of the present tense instead of the past tense caused tension to thicken the air. She puzzled about it for a second and realized they must feel sorry for her.

"Don't feel sorry for me," she said, quick to reassure, "I had a good childhood. The orphanage had a small library and one of the coven members who volunteered at the orphanage taught me a reading spell so I could listen to the books as I did the chores."

"Do you have a favorite book?" Desmond asked.

"I like fairytales." Claire blushed, "It was nice to escape the world for a bit."

This set off a conversation about the Triad's favorite fairy tales and specifically the heroes in them that they pretended to be when they were boys. Desmond informed her that they used to play king of the mountain in the Dragon Mountains on this small boulder that they thought was huge.

Claire laughed with them for a bit and a comfortable silence fell. "Did you need to get some reading done?" Malcolm asked.

"I have a little bit to do. I was going to do it when I was here though. I have to use the reading spell so it disturbs the library's silence."

"You can start the reading spell if you want." Everett said quietly. Claire smiled but her stomach panged at the thought of them leaving. "We can keep you company." He finished.

"Oh, you don't have to do that. I'm sure you have better things to do than listen to a History of Realms textbook."

"Nonsense," Desmond said, his shadow slouching down, "It's always good to have a refresher. Learn from past mistakes and everything."

"You have to have better things to do though." Claire insisted. Very few students visited the gardens on Saturday preferring to enjoy the first day of the weekend. Claire couldn't imagine what Vivienne would do if she found her Triad sitting with Claire or if one of Vivienne's friends found them.

Everett touched her knee lightly, "Claire, there is nowhere else we would rather be."

Claire didn't understand but brushed it off. All she could do was hope that no one happened upon the four sitting in the garden.

"Okay," she said demurely, reaching for her bag and digging out her History of the Realm textbook.

Opening it to the marked chapter, she called up a little bit of magic and pushed it into the reading spell, *"Legere."*

To her mortification, the voice that started reading the chapter wasn't Professor Storm's but Everett's. *"Finito,"* she whispered desperately.

"Is that Everett's voice reading your book?" Desmond sounded gleeful.

Claire buried her face in her hands, "I'm sorry. The reading spell does whatever voice I am thinking about at the time."

"And you were thinking of my voice?" Everett sounded like he was teasing her. The teasing tone sounded more familiar on Desmond's voice but she liked it on Everett's voice as well.

"You have a nice voice." Claire said, her face burning. "I'm sorry, I'll change it."

"Don't," Everett said, "I like that you like it."

Claire's face was still hot but she started the reading spell again. For the rest of the afternoon she enjoyed the Triad's easy company. They filled in some of her questions about History and gave her more current background on the Realm and its current politics.

When the bell clanged for dinner, Everett helped her pack up her textbooks and notebooks and handed off the bag to Claire. "Thank you all," she said shyly before leaving the garden.

"Bye, little witch." Desmond.

"Bye, Claire." Malcolm.

"Bye, Claire." Everett.

A smile split Claire's face as she left the garden. Spending time with all three men had been wonderful. Now she knew why Vivienne was so possessive over them. That thought cooled her mood a bit. As wonderful as it had been, the Stonemont Triad belonged to Vivienne and Claire was the interloper. Hopefully no one had seen her with Vivienne's Triad.

CHAPTER 14

If only Claire would have been so lucky.

Sunday evening, Vivienne cornered Claire in her hallway again, ripping into her about spending time with her Triad and telling her that if she caught Claire spending time with the Triad again, she would expose her as a whore to the whole Academy and make her an outcast and possibly get her expelled.

Claire firmed her resolve from last night. She would stay away from the Triad. Even though she had a wonderful time with them on Saturday, it wasn't worth losing her place here in the Academy. Not when she was learning so much and starting to feel like she belonged.

She stayed close to Holly and her friends and if they noticed her clingingness the next few days, they didn't mention it. Holly seemed to stick closer than normal and Claire was grateful for it. Desmond tried to speak with her Monday after Spells and Potions but Claire made an excuse that she had to talk to Professor Helene before class and slipped away. He didn't try again on Tuesday or Wednesday but steadily watched her throughout class like she was a puzzle he was trying to figure out.

Everett didn't approach her directly but she caught hints of his scent on the wind as she hurried around campus. Enough that her heart clenched every time. She shouldered herself on though. Classes were starting to pick up and she was often at the library until late studying for the various assignments their professors had loaded on them.

In Combat Class, they had started running on Monday. After running through Warm-up Forms A, B, and C, Malcolm had them run 10 laps around the arena wall before dismissing them. Some students had clearly been running for years and finished quickly. Others, like Claire, were a little bit more out of shape and did a mixture of running and walking. Claire insisted that Holly didn't have to wait for her but Holly was equally as stubborn that she would wait. They compromised by Holly waiting outside the arena for Claire to finish.

Claire felt Malcolm's eyes on her as they made laps around the arena throughout the week but he didn't approach her until Thursday. As one of the last students in the arena, there was nowhere for her to go when she felt his energy approaching her on her last lap. She was up to running three laps around the arena, alternating between running one lap and walking two laps. She was finishing up her last lap when she felt him.

"Claire, can you stay after class?" His voice was calm but firm and Claire found herself nodding before she realized what she was doing.

She finished her lap and waited by her bag while the other students finished. "Is there a problem, Instructor Malcolm?"

She deliberately used his title in front of his name to remind herself of the stakes. She would distance herself from the men to keep her place here.

"Yes." Malcolm's voice was tight and the word was almost a growl.

"Is it my blindness regarding weapons training next week?"

Malcolm informed them that they would begin training with wooden staffs next week in addition to the running he expected them to continue outside of class.

"No. We need to discuss something with you."

We? Claire was so distracted by Malcolm's presence that she missed the other two shadow figures entering the arena. The pull she felt towards them identified them instantly.

"Hello, little witch." Desmond's voice was cheery but tight. Like he was upset but trying to hide it. Claire took a half step backwards.

"Assistant Teacher Desmond." Claire nodded at him, "Captain Everett."

The tension stretched between the men at the use of their titles. "Can I help you with something?" She asked politely, her stomach in knots. Maybe Vivienne had told them about Claire's behavior and that Vivienne was upset. As her Triad, the men would be bound to carry out Vivienne's wishes. Claire braced herself for their next words.

"You've been avoiding us." Everett's voice was quiet... and sad? "Why?"

That was not what Claire was expecting him to say. "I'm sorry?"

"You've been avoiding us." Desmond spoke this time. "Did we do something to offend you?"

"No," Claire was quick to reassure them. "It's just not... proper that I've been taking up your time."

"Not proper?" Malcolm growled the question.

"Yes. You all have important positions in the Academy and the world and it's not proper or efficient for you to be spending your time helping a low-level witch out."

"Efficient?" Malcolm bit out the word, his shadow turning away, was he running his hands through his hair? "Desmond!"

He barked and Claire jumped slightly, unsure of what was happening.

"Little witch," Desmond said, stepping closer. "Who's been filling your head with those words?" While his voice was calm, he couldn't hide the tension in his words.

Oh no, they thought she was going to tattle on Vivienne. "No one," Claire said quickly, "it's just how it is. You have more important things to do than help me and that's perfectly okay. I'm sorry it took me a few weeks to realize it but I don't want to keep you from your duties."

"Duties?" Desmond choked out and Claire nodded.

There was a pause as if Desmond couldn't find the words he wanted to say. Maybe they thought she was going to argue with them and were surprised at her easy acceptance. "If that's all..." She inched towards her bag.

Everett stepped silently to her side, grasping her elbow and halting her movements. "Claire," he breathed softly, "I think there has been a misunderstanding."

"Oh I know," Claire nodded. "Don't worry, I won't make the same mistakes again."

Malcolm growled and Everett tugged Claire closer. She stumbled at the motion and landed against his chest. At this proximity, the pull to him was almost impossible for her to ignore but she found the reserves of her strength and straightened, stepping a half pace away.

"No, Claire. I think there's been a misunderstanding with our intentions towards you." Everett reluctantly let her elbow go but didn't step away, causing her head to spin slightly with his scent.

"Our intentions?" The question was out of Claire's lips before she could stop it.

"Yes. Spending time with you is our choice. We want to get to know you better."

"But why?" Claire said, "There's nothing interesting about me except for the mistake the Academy made in sending me an invitation to come here."

"A mistake?" Malcolm growled again and Claire idly wondered if there was something wrong with the man that he could only speak in one word growls.

"Claire, who's been telling you that we don't want to spend time with you?" Desmond asked, his tone carefully even.

"No one," Claire said quickly, but even she could hear her voice pitch higher, "It's just easy for everyone to see and I didn't know until recently but I won't make the same mistake again."

"Nothing about you is a mistake." Malcolm growled and Claire took a step back stunned at the intensity and sincerity of his words. What?

"Claire," Everett's voice was quiet but cut through her swirling thoughts at Malcolm's declarations, "We want to spend time with you. That is our choice."

"But why?" Claire asked bewildered. They had Vivienne, a very powerful witch with two proficiencies.

Desmond huffed out a laugh, "Never thought we would see the day that we would have to explain to a woman that we wanted to spend time with them. We must be losing our touch, lads."

He didn't sound angry, almost amused? Claire was so confused.

Malcolm stepped closer, boxing her in between Everett on her right and Desmond on her left. Malcolm invaded her space forcing her to lift her head as his shadow grew the closer he got. She wished she could see his face, their faces. She was missing something here and her blindness quite literally left her blind.

"I don't have the silvered wordsmithing that Desmond possesses so I'm going to lay this out plainly for you, Claire."

The growl in his chest should have scared her but that

combined with the pull between them had Claire fighting to not step closer to him. His next words broke the spell though. "We want to spend time with you because you are our Fourth."

There was more there but he cut himself off, possibly seeing the panic spread across her face. "What is it?" he growled.

"I can't be your Fourth." She stepped back away from the three of them. "Vivienne is your Fourth."

"Is that who's been filling your head with those lies?" The animosity in Desmond's voice stunned her.

"She's your Fourth." Claire repeated, "That's a sacred bond. I can't interfere with that. I won't interfere with it. I won't risk my place here even if it was because of a mistake."

"Vivienne is not our Fourth." Everett said firmly.

"She is." Claire insisted, her voice pitching with a bit of hysteria. How dare they toy with her like this. "She is your Fourth and you are just waiting until she graduates. Is that what this is? You pretend to show interest in me to take the pressure off of her? Because no one would care if a low-level witch got kicked out of the Academy and punished by the laws of the Realm for interfering with a Triad's bond." Claire's mind raced, was this all a joke to them?

"What? Claire, no..." Desmond tried to talk but Claire whirled away, grabbing her bag and darting for the entrance. The men shouted behind her but didn't pursue her.

She ran out of the Combat Arena and straight into Holly. "Whoa, what's wrong? Did they do something to you? Desmond slipped by me but I should have known Everett was in there too."

Claire just stared at her blankly. Who all had seen her in the arena with the three men. Were people telling Vivienne or worse, the Headmaster right now?

"Claire, Claire, are you okay?" Claire refocused on Holly who was shaking her slightly.

"I need to get out of here." Claire stared blankly at Holly who nodded at her.

"Okay, let's go to my dorm room." Claire nodded, letting Holly lead her away. Grateful she had offered her room because Claire didn't want to risk running into Vivienne.

Holly turned halfway to look behind her quickly but she didn't falter in her steps. When no steps sounded behind her, Claire realized that Holly must have done something to dissuade anyone from following them.

Claire followed Holly mechanically, her thoughts still swirling at the Combat Arena and the three men there. She barely registered climbing the steps to the dormitory or making her way into Holly's room. Holly guided her to the bed and sat her down, grabbing her hands. "Claire?" Holly said quietly, "Are you okay?"

Claire's eyes filled with tears at Holly's kindness. Would she still treat her the same if she knew Claire came in between a Triad and their Fourth.

"Oh, Claire," Holly stood and gathered her close. Wrapping her arms around her shoulders, Holly hugged her into her chest. Claire let the tears spill out over her cheeks. Once the first tears were spilled, Claire couldn't seem to stop. Sobs wracked her body as she let all of her fear and confusion and the deep ache that seemed to only be filled by the Triad pour out of her.

After fifteen minutes, Claire pulled herself out of her wallowing and sagged against Holly in exhaustion. Holly stroked her hair and Claire wrapped her arms around Holly's waist and squeezed her thanks.

"Do I need to curse anyone for you?" Holly's quiet question made Claire huff out a laugh.

"Maybe me? I screwed up."

"I'm more inclined to believe that the three buffoons you left in the Combat Arena are at fault here."

"No, this time it was definitely me who screwed up. Like always."

"Hey, that's not true." Holly pulled back slightly, her hand moving from Claire's hair to her chin, tilting it up.

"You don't know that. Maybe I'm just... an awful person."

Holly moved both hands to Claire's head, cradling her cheeks, "You, Claire Windshire, are not an awful person. You are so far from an awful person it's not even funny. You are full of kindness and goodness and light, always seeing the best in people but for some reason the worst in yourself. Now tell me, what happened in the arena. Powerful Triad or not, I will kick all of their asses for you."

"I don't deserve you," Claire said through a watery smile.

"Yes you do. You deserve me, Bethany, Cody, Zack, Desmond, Everett, and Malcolm. Now stop avoiding the subject and tell me."

Closing her eyes, Claire spilled the entire story starting back at the beginning. Of how Desmond and Everett picked her up from Windshire and how she thought they were just checking in on her these last few weeks out of some feeling of responsibility. She told Holly about how Vivienne had cornered her the first time and the second time before Holly intervened. She told Holly about the wonderful day she had on Saturday with the Triad and how Vivienne had threatened her place here at the Academy when she found out, telling Claire she could be kicked out of the Academy and punished by the realm for interfering with a Triad and their Fourth.

She confessed how scared she was of that threat that even if she didn't feel like she deserved to be here she wanted to be here and learn. She wanted to learn so she could be of use to a coven eventually, not wanting to go back to Windshire. She rambled about the tiny cottage she wanted with the garden in the back and how no coven would want a witch who was kicked out of the Academy for interfering with a Triad bond.

She spilled the whole story out, all her thoughts and feelings over the last few weeks. Holly kept her warm hands cupping Claire's face the whole time, her thumbs brushing away the tears that spilled and her energy staying so calm and steady throughout Claire's mess. Claire finally quieted, awaiting Holly's words and judgement.

"I'm going to kill them." Holly declared unexpectedly.

"Wait, what?" Claire was confused.

"Don't worry about it," Holly said, "but listen to my words. You did nothing wrong. Even if Vivienne was their Fourth, the fault would lie on the Triad and not you."

"Even if?" Claire was confused. Vivienne was their Fourth.

Before Holly could respond, there was a knock at the door. "Holly?"

"That's Bethany," Holly said, "what do you say about having a girl's night tonight? I think we deserve it."

Claire just nodded mutely. She didn't deserve anything but she wasn't going to argue with Holly.

Holly moved to open the door and spoke to Bethany in a low, hushed voice. After a few minutes, she closed the door and returned to Claire. "Bethany's going to grab us all dinner and some treats from the dining hall."

Claire started to protest against the trouble but Holly placed a finger on her lips and Claire quieted, "While she does that, let's go down to your room so you can shower and change real quick. I'll come with you."

Although a pang of fear about possibly seeing Vivienne went through her, Claire nodded obediently. Holly's energy was as steadfast as the earth element she wielded. There would be no arguing with her on this.

Holly escorted Claire up to her room and thankfully the hallway was empty. Claire grabbed a change of clothes while Holly waited on her bed. Standing under the shower, Claire let a few more tears escape her before she composed herself. She could do this. She could stay away from the Triad. She could be a model student. She could graduate from the Academy and get her cottage. Maybe she could go with Holly to Brandlevine. That is if Holly wasn't sick of her by then.

Holly made Claire grab her pillow and a blanket from her bed and she followed Holly back downstairs. As they reached Holly's hallway, Claire heard the familiar sound of Bethany and Cody's bickering.

"I didn't ask for your help."

"Oh shut it, Bethany, there was no way those measly feline arms were going to carry all of this. You needed the big bad wolf, admit it."

Cody was saved from Bethany's sharp response when Holly cleared her throat.

"Evening ladies," Cody greeted, "having a girl's night?" His tone was light but Claire felt his eyes trace her puffy cheeks and red eyes from crying. "Need anything else from the big bad wolf?"

Bethany didn't pretend to have subtlety, a trait that Claire loved. "Claire, what's wrong?"

Claire smiled at Holly's exasperated sigh. "I'm fine," she said, "I did this to myself."

If Holly could growl, Claire was sure she would. "You did not." Holly said.

"Do I need to kick someone's ass?" Cody said.

Bethany smacked him, "Not everything is solved by beating it up."

Claire wasn't entirely sure they were still talking about her so she kept silent.

"Some things are," Cody shot back, "and besides, it's Claire. She's the sweetest person we know. In this case, someone probably does need to be beaten up."

"Thanks, Cody," Claire broke in, "but no one needs to be beaten up."

"Well, maybe not tonight," Holly disagreed, "Tonight we need to stuff our faces with this delicious food and have a girl's only night."

"So it's a boy I need to beat up?" Cody was persistent.

"Tomorrow." Holly was firm. "Thank you, Cody."

Something must have passed between them and Cody backed off. "Okay, I'm going to go bother Zack at the dining hall. Let us know if you need anything."

Holly directed Claire to sit on the floor and Bethany and Holly started dishing out the contents of the boxes onto plates they pulled out of the bags. Claire must have had a questioning look on her face because Bethany spoke up, "The head chef is a really sweet witch who is mated to a cougar shifter in my pride. She'll sneak me a few extra things occasionally."

Holly handed Claire a plate and they spent the next fifteen minutes stuffing their faces. Claire was starving after her breakdown earlier and she scraped her plate clean. After finishing up, the girls cleaned up by shoving most everything back in the bags the food had come in.

Arranging themselves on Holly's bed, Claire sat sideways with her legs crossed and back against the wall. Holly took the head of the bed and Bethany sprawled on the remaining space.

"So what is off limits for topics tonight." Bethany was as blunt as over. "I'm down to have a distracting girl's night or to talk out whatever is bothering you."

Claire fiddled with her fingers for a few moments, it wasn't that she didn't want to tell Bethany, she was just worried what Bethany would think of her afterwards. Holly covered her fiddling fingers with her warm hand and Claire took a breath.

She briefly recanted the last few weeks' events to Bethany with less waterworks then earlier with Holly. Once she was done, Bethany summed up her thoughts succinctly.

"Holy fucking shit, what a bitch."

Claire reared back slightly, confused as to who Bethany was calling a bitch.

"I could murder Vivienne with my bare hands!" Bethany continued, "She's a bitch in general but lying about being a Fourth takes the cake."

"How are you so sure she's lying?" Claire asked, "She could be telling the truth and I was the one who interfered with the Triad bond."

Bethany shook her head so hard she shook the bed slightly, "No way. Vivienne's always been a manipulative bitch. Honestly, it runs in her family. You… don't take this the wrong way… but you're the sweetest person I've ever met, Claire. Like sickeningly sweet to the point that I feel dirty sometimes when I'm with you, like I'm going to corrupt you or something. There's no way you are at fault here. Like even if Vivienne was their potential Fourth, you wouldn't be at fault here."

Claire looked at Holly as Bethany mirrored almost her exact words earlier. Holly clasped Claire's hand, "See I told you it wasn't your fault."

Claire sagged backwards. "But if Vivienne was lying, that means…" she trailed off as she thought of the Triad's words earlier.

She sat up straight, startling Holly and Bethany, "I can't be their Fourth!"

"Why not?" Bethany demanded.

"Cause… I'm me. I'm a low-level witch from a no-name coven who's blind on top of it."

"Why do you always call yourself a low-level witch?" Holly asked.

"Because…" Claire trailed off. Because that's what everyone's always called her.

"You have a beginning proficiency in all four elements and a gift for Herbology." Holly was quiet but insistent. "That doesn't sound like a low-level witch to me, that sounds like someone coming into her power and is where she belongs, at an Academy that will teach her."

"But..." Claire wanted to protest but didn't have a rebuttal as everything Holly said made sense.

"Claire," Bethany was as direct as ever, "Why do you call yourself a low-level witch."

Claire's cheeks burned as the memories surfaced. "The children at the coven were not particularly kind," she twisted her fingers in her lap. "Neither were the adults for that matter. When my coming of age ceremony was performed, the elders could find no significant magic in me and declared me a 'basically useless witch'."

Bethany growled, "Your coven sounds like a bunch of dicks."

"Bethany!" Holly chastised.

"What? You were thinking the same thing."

Claire giggled, "They kind of are, aren't they?"

For some reason Claire's giggles grew and spread until all three girls were clutching their stomachs with laughter. After they quieted, Claire felt lighter with the recognition that her coven had for some reason put a label on her early on and Claire had let herself carry that label.

"So what are you going to do now?" Bethany asked, breaking the easy quiet.

Claire shrugged, "I don't know. I don't even know what it means to be a Fourth or if I'm even qualified to be one. I have so many questions I don't even know where to start."

"I think you need to talk to the Triad. Not tonight," Holly adds quickly, "maybe not tomorrow, but soon."

Claire nodded but her stomach clenched at the thought of facing them after she had stormed out of the arena. Plus, she still wasn't convinced that Vivienne wasn't their intended Fourth. Vivienne was a powerful witch with a powerful family. She was a much better match for them then Claire would be.

"But we can start answering your questions tonight."

Bethany said, moving into a seated position. The sound of her rubbing her hands together made Claire smile.

"Okay, so Triads 101."

CHAPTER 15

"The concept of Triads was formalized over 2000 years ago after the Realm was formed. The Council was trying to instill unity across the different territories and came up with this idea of an elite fighting unit formed by different members of different powerful bloodlines. The idea was that if you were bonded together in a Triad, your families were less likely to fight each other. However the Council also had a secondary reason for forming the Triads. Basically, for every powerful female, there are three powerful males. Bloodlines were important to the Realm's leaders as they indicated power. To ensure the power was passed from generation to generation, multiple males pairing with one female became common among the powerful."

"To no one's surprise, except apparently the Council's," Bethany rolled her eyes, "placing a bunch of powerful males into the same relationship did not go peacefully. Thus began the triad concept. Powerful males are matched as a trio at age 16 when they come into their power. They grow up together, live together, and enter the Academy together. The theory is that once the males form bonds with their other Triad members, a relationship with the Fourth is easier to start and stay together.

"There are some exceptions to the rule. Your Triad, for example, met when they were 12 and formed their own Triad bond. They've been one of the most powerful Triads to pass through the Academy in generations and the Council has watched their steps closely. Honestly I think that's why they are still here, the Academy and Headmaster Dorian provide them a certain amount of protection from the Council's eyes but I digress."

Holly picked up the explanation here. "Usually, the Council helps Triads find their Fourth or perfect match but not always. My cousin and his Triad didn't want anything to do with the Council or their families' matchmaking and made that clear from the beginning. Now the Council has helped many Triads find their Fourth and those Triads are strong and very much in love."

"In love?" Claire questioned.

"Yes, in love. What did you think a Fourth was?"

"I don't know what I thought," Claire admitted, "Vivienne made it sound like the Fourth boosted the Triad's power."

"I mean the Fourth can but that's not always their primary purpose. Many Fourths help hold their Triads together and give them something to focus on."

"That sounds..." Claire wanted to say clinical but she didn't want to sound like she was being dismissive of Holly's explanation.

Bethany laughed, "You can say it. It sounds weird. It's really not as bad as it sounds. Like Holly said, many Triads are madly in love."

"But not all of them." Claire said.

"That's true," Holly conceded. "But that's to be expected. Nothing is 100% absolute. Anyways, yes, the Council often helps introduce the Triads to their Fourths but it's always done as a potential match. Both the Triads and the females have the ability to say yes or no to the match and usually Triads will court the females that they are interested in. Once both parties have agreed to the match, there will be a bonding ceremony that binds the Fourth to the Triad."

"But not all males are part of Triads and not all females are Fourths. How do mates fit into all of this?"

Holly laughed, "Bethany, do you want to take this one?"

Bethany grumbled but answered Claire's question. "Mates are most common among shifters and witches. I would say Elves and Fae but they were always secretive even before the Great War so I don't know about them. Shifters call them mates and I think witches call them soul flames. Basically, it's like your other half. You have no choice who it is but they are your fated pair so you are both usually compatible. It's not common but not as rare as being in a Triad. And then for everyone else, they fall in love and choose life partners the old fashioned way."

"So you can either have a mate or a Triad or choose your own life partner?"

"Well there have been instances where a Fourth has been the mate of a Triad member. Those Triads sometimes break up if the Triad member has a super possessive animal."

"Break up?"

"Remember the Fourth bond is a choice the Triads and Fourths make. A mate bond would technically supersede that choice. There have been some instances where the Triad was so tightly bound that the member didn't view his other Triad members as threats and instead they all peacefully co-existed but usually the only romantic relationship that developed would be between the Fourth and the mated Triad member."

"What does a mate bond feel like?" Claire asked.

Bethany huffed, "It's supposed to be like an intense pull towards the other person when you are in their presence. They smell really good to you and you feel safe in their presence. The pull only intensifies until the pair accepts and solidifies the mate bond."

"How do you solidify a mate bond?" Claire's question made Holly giggle softly.

"Sex." Bethany said bluntly, "Lots of sex. And a bite if you are a shifter. Witches have their own thing."

"There's a soul flame spell that witches will do before or after the coupling." Holly said.

Bethany snorted when Holly called it coupling and Claire lapsed into giggles with the girls.

"So if there's a mate bond between the Fourth and a Triad, it's with just one Triad member?" Claire asked when she caught her breath. She didn't want to overanalyze Bethany's description of a mate bond but what she was describing sounded like the pull Claire felt towards the Triad. Her cheeks heated as she thought about what that meant and quickly changed her thoughts.

Holly answered this time, seeming careful in her word choice. "There's only ever been a public record of one Triad member having a mate bond with a Fourth but that doesn't mean that more than one Triad member can't feel a mate bond with a potential Fourth."

"It would be extremely rare though," Bethany said, "occasionally, in the shifter clans, twins have been known to share the same mate bond but that's rare as well."

"Got it," Claire said. See, there had to be a different explanation for the pull she felt to the Triad. Maybe it had to do with her energy reading ability and the fact that they were powerful. Maybe the more powerful the person the easier the energy was to read? She would have to read more of that book that Professor Helene gave her.

Her thoughts were broken by a yawn that seemed to come out of nowhere and made her jaw ache with the size of it.

"That shit's contagious," Bethany said through her own yawn.

Claire giggled, the yawn seeming to set off a wave of tiredness through her body that made her slump back into the wall.

"Do you want to stay with me tonight?" Holly asked Claire.

"No, I don't want to disturb your space anymore than I already have."

"Stop that." Holly said, "you are welcome to sleep here anytime."

The girls were silent for a few moments, no one wanting to move just yet. "I'm not sure I'm ready to face them tomorrow." Claire said quietly into her lap.

"Then you won't." Bethany said simply. "Take a sick day or just the afternoon off. A ton of students do it."

Claire wasn't super comfortable with the idea of just not showing up for class.

"How about this," Holly suggested, "Let's go to morning classes and then I'll run to the Headmaster's office and get us slips to go out into the city tomorrow afternoon. We can get you a jacket, Claire, and a few other winter things and explore the city a bit."

"Would the Headmaster be okay with that?"

"Of course. Especially if I explain it like we need to get you some things for classes as well."

"If you're sure." Claire said.

"I'm sure," Holly said confidently, "now Bethany and I will walk you up to your room. We've got a busy day ahead of us tomorrow."

Claire was worried sleep wouldn't come peacefully to her after the chaos of the day but she shouldn't have been. As soon as her head hit the pillow, Claire fell into a deep sleep, dreaming of mates and Triads and three voices calling out her name.

CHAPTER 16

She really did have the best friends, Claire thought while sitting at breakfast the next morning. Not only were Holly and Bethany outside her door that morning, Zack and Cody had met them outside the dormitory and provided a light-hearted escort to the dining hall. As they waited for their breakfast, the table kept Claire distracted with funny stories from their first year at the Academy. Cody must have clued Zack in to last night's events as the sweet wizard leaned over during one of Cody's stories and quietly asked if she was okay.

"Better," Claire whispered back, "better this morning."

They were halfway through breakfast when Claire felt the Triad enter the dining hall. It seemed she was more sensitive to the pull of their energy since last night. She couldn't be sure without seeing their shadows but she knew the second they entered the dining hall. She hoped in equal parts they would stay away and come over but the staying away thoughts prevailed. She felt emotionally drained after last night and needed the day to recover, the promise of going into the city with Bethany and Holly was one of the only things that got her out of bed this morning.

Holly squeezed her arm, "I'm going to go talk to the Headmaster. Zack, could you walk Claire to class this morning?"

"Sure," Zack said before Claire could protest, "why do you need to talk to the Headmaster?"

"Bethany and I are going to take Claire into the city this afternoon to show her around and get her a few winter things."

"Ooooo an outing," Cody said excitedly, "can we come with?"

Claire laughed at his childlike glee. "You want to go shopping?"

"Of course, who is going to carry all of your bags?"

"You just want to get off campus." Bethany laughed.

"Well, duh. If shopping is the reason then I'll survive it."

"I'll ask the Headmaster but no promises. We'll leave after lunch. Zack, you want to come too?"

"I'd love to but I have an exam in Runes this afternoon." Zack said, "make Cody carry extra bags for me?"

Holly laughed as Cody protested, "Will do. Okay, I'm off. See you at lunch."

* * *

DESMOND CAUGHT Holly's eye as she left the table where his little soul flame sat, their Fourth. By the Realm, his Triad had fucked up last night. They had no idea their little witch was struggling with so much insecurity and his Triad had forgotten she was not used to their world and had muddled their intentions towards her. And Vivienne... growling was Malcolm's domain but Desmond might just challenge him on this subject. That manipulative witch has apparently been filling the campus with her lies and filling Claire's head with them and threats to her place here.

He inclined his head towards the door Holly was exiting from and Everett and Malcolm rose to follow him. Their gazes shifted back to the back corner table where their Fourth sat and

Desmond would have laughed at the look of despondency and longing on their faces if he wasn't sure that his face wasn't mirroring the same look.

The Triad descended the steps and found Holly standing under a tree in front of the administrative building.

"You all screwed up epically, Cousin." Holly's voice was quiet but full of censorship.

Malcolm let out a little growl at the accusation and the look Holly shot him could have melted the dragon where he stood.

"I would highly suggest not growling at me at this moment. After last night, I could bury you in the ground where you stand and grow daisies out of you. What the hell were you thinking? I told you Vivienne was spreading those lies around campus and had cornered Claire once already. When the hell were you going to do something about that?" Holly laid into them, ignoring their winces.

"Holly," Desmond began.

"No, I don't want to hear your excuses. You fucked up. All of you. You should have come clean with Claire at the beginning and I should have made you after our first conversation and as a result of all of our inactions, Claire has spun herself a story she firmly believes in, that she's not worthy of being a Fourth, your Fourth."

"That's absurd," Malcolm growled.

"Is it? Her entire life she's been told she's a low-level witch from a coven that most of us have to look up on a map to find. She's told the Academy made a mistake placing her here which only emphasizes the point in her mind. Then she gets attention paid to her by the most powerful Triad the realm has ever seen and gets told by a powerful manipulative witch that the Triad is hers and that the Triad only sees her as a duty, a fact that the Triad perpetuates by not coming clean with Claire and not cutting off Vivienne's machinations months ago."

"Her father..." Desmond begins.

"I don't care who Vivienne's father is. Are you or are you not the most powerful Triad this Realm has ever seen? You've been playing politics too long if that's your excuse."

Everett spoke, "We fucked up. I won't make excuses for that. Help us fix it?"

Holly paused in her rant and looked Everett over, "I always knew I liked you best."

"Cousin, I'm wounded," Desmond exclaimed, placing his hand over his heart.

Despite her stern countenance, Desmond could see the corner of Holly's lip quirk up. Even though he wasn't enjoying the tongue lashing, he was glad their little witch had someone as fierce as Holly in her corner.

"Not today." Holly raised her hand to cut off Malcolm's growl. "Not today," she repeated, "today we are going to take her into the city to get her a few winter things and take her mind off things."

"Are you taking her to Pinscer Street?" Malcolm asked.

"I was going to. I think she will enjoy the Market Square as well but once you pull your heads out of your asses I figure that would be a nice place for you to take her."

"I knew you loved me," Desmond said, inwardly grateful.

"I love Claire and seeing her like that last night..." Holly trailed off, eyes in the distance, "If I ever see her like that again, I will bury you where I find you."

"And we will let you." Everett agreed. "Not today, but let me send a guard with you into the city."

Holly shook her head, "If you send a guard she'll know who sent them. Cody offered to go with us and I was going to ask the Headmaster if he could come as a guard."

"Cody Clawmoon, Alpha Bryce Clawmoon's son?" Malcolm asked.

"Yes."

"He's a good student," Malcolm grumbled, "it should be one of us but he will do."

Holly laughed softly, "I'm glad you agree because it wasn't your choice."

Malcolm growled, "That's my mate."

"Who doesn't know it," Holly shot back, "because you conveniently forgot to mention it. All she knows is you told her she was your Fourth after Vivienne told her that Vivienne was your Fourth but you were keeping it quiet till Vivienne graduated."

Holly took a breath to compose herself, "She asked about it last night. What being a Fourth means. What being a mate feels like. We explained it but I don't think she believes it. She thought that a Fourth boosted the Triad's powers and therefore had to be powerful which she doesn't believe she is."

"She has beginning proficiencies at four elements." Desmond said.

"And she has no idea how rare that is. Sure people have told her but she doesn't believe it. I think... I think her coven was a bit cruel."

Malcolm grumbled, "She told us a bit about them last weekend. Neglectful at best but I agree."

"So then you know that's how she grew up. You are going to need to have lots of patience with her. Bethany and I got her to agree that she needs to have a conversation with all three of you but it's not going to happen today. I'll see when she wants to have it but it will be on her terms. And even after you have the conversation, that's not going to fix everything. She'll need time to process probably, and you'll have to be steady and reassuring. No outbursts."

She eyed Malcolm who folded his arms with a grunt.

"And I know you didn't want to," Holly continued, "but you'll have to show publicly that she's your Fourth."

"It paints a target on her back," Desmond rubbed a hand over his eyes.

"You know Headmaster Dorian and the Academy will provide protection. Either way, she has three years of protection here. By then, she will be able to defend herself from potential threats."

"That's our job," Everett stated.

"Yes it is, but you will do her a disservice if she feels helpless," Holly looked at them pointedly and Desmond nodded.

"Now I'm going to go talk to Headmaster Dorian."

"I'll go with you," Desmond said, "if he gives you any trouble I'll let him know it was our fault."

"Oh, I planned on telling him that anyway," Holly teased.

"When you go to Pinscer Street, bill your purchases to my account. I'll call ahead to let them know you have permissions." Malcolm said gruffly.

Holly shook her head, "She'll never go for that."

"Tell her it's part of the Academy stipend that students can bill to. That part is true." Everett said.

"Fine, but if it blows back it's on you."

Malcolm went to make the calls and Everett melted into the shadows like the gryphon often did, probably to go spy on their little witch, Desmond mused ruefully. He fell into step beside Holly, "Can we fix this?" He asked her quietly.

Holly looked over at him, "Yes, this time. You'll need to be patient with her and lay out your intentions clearly. Believe in her as she learns to believe in herself and it'll be fine."

* * *

PINSCER STREET WAS LOUD, Claire thought as she was sandwiched between Holly and Bethany as Cody brought up the rear. They had portaled from the administration building into the start of the busy street. All of the noise made it impossible to tell who was where or what was happening and Claire felt a little vulnerable.

With so many people, the shadows blended together and the girls were jostled until Cody let out a vicious growl that was so unlike him, Claire tripped over her feet slightly. Holly righted her and they briskly made their way from the portal.

"There are ten stores on either side of the street," Holly painted a picture for her, "it's really crowded as you can probably already hear. The stores are a mixture of clothing and magical item stores and range in prices. The Academy has accounts set up at all the stores and they know to bill it against the stipend you receive so don't worry about paying."

Bethany broke in, "You might also like the bookstore at the end of the street. There's a small cafe attached to it where we can grab a bite to eat before we head back."

"That sounds good." Claire said. While Pinscer Street was overwhelming, the chaos was proving to be a good distraction. She had muddled through classes this morning, knowing she was going to have to read over her notes tomorrow to remember anything. Her mind was still whirling from the conversation last night. She couldn't be Desmond, Everett and Malcolm's Fourth, could she?

Somehow in the light of the next day (and a more logical brain), the notion wasn't as absurd as she had originally thought. She had more questions now then ever though. As Holly and Bethany guided her into the first store, she shoved the questions down until later. She would enjoy this time here with friends.

And enjoy it they did. Holly was a great shopper with an eye for styles and for Claire's clothes, for textures. She didn't think she ever felt a material as soft as the coat she ended up getting. Holly and Bethany told her it was a deep brown that brought out the blue in her eyes. The colors meant nothing to her but the girls assured Claire that it looked great. Bethany, the ever practical shopper, said it would hide the dirt stains when she wore it in the garden and Holly assured her that the

Academy would take care of any stains she happened to accumulate on it.

Claire also selected a few pairs of fleece lined pants for the colder days ahead and a warm sweater Holly said that matched the pale blue of her eyes. Holly and Bethany picked up a few things as well and by the time they made it to the small bookstore, Cody was loaded down with bags. Claire felt bad and offered to carry her items but Cody assured her he was a big bad wolf and had the muscles to do it. Claire had giggled at that and she was sure Bethany had rolled her eyes. She would have to ask Bethany soon about what was going on between her and Cody.

Since they were running out of daylight, they decided to come back to the bookstore another day and instead ordered some things to eat at the attached cafe.

After they finished eating, Bethany cleared her throat.

"Got a hairball stuck in there?" Cody teased, safe from retaliation on the other side of Claire.

"No." Bethany growled, "Cody, why don't you head back to the Academy with all of our bags."

"What? No, I'm supposed to be your guard for the day."

Guard? Claire thought but was interrupted by the feeling of Bethany's leg brushing by hers to deliver a swift kick to Cody's shin.

"Ouch, woman, why do you always resort to violence?" Cody yelped.

"So you know I am perfectly capable of taking care of myself." Bethany said sweetly. "Now, why don't you head back to the Academy with our bags. I think a pride leader's daughter, a Brandlevine witch, and a witch with four proficiencies can handle walking back down the street and to the portal."

"Please, Cody," Holly must have intervened, "I promise you won't get in trouble for leaving us."

"Fine," Cody grumbled, "but if you aren't back at the

Academy in an hour I will be coming back to find you. Probably with reinforcements." The last part was muttered under his breath.

"Thank you," Bethany said sweetly as Cody walked off grumbling about feline shifters and their violent tendencies.

The lighthearted mood at the table dimmed slightly after Cody left and Claire knew it was time to have the conversation she had been avoiding.

At her frown, Holly placed a hand over Claire's and squeezed. "We don't have to talk about it if you need more time."

"No, it's fine," Claire said, "I don't know if it's a conversation I'm really ever going to be ready for. It just doesn't seem real."

"But it is," Bethany, blunt as ever, "It is real. You are their chosen Fourth. You are a witch with four beginning proficiencies which is super rare. You just need the Academy's help to grow into your powers and then you'll be out there kicking ass. Preferably Vivienne's ass."

"Bethany," Holly chided.

Claire let out a small laugh, "No, you're right. It's just… so different from what I've ever known."

"And that's why you have us," Bethany said, "to remind you that while it is different that doesn't mean it's bad."

"I'm worried I'm going to let you down. Let them down," Claire admitted softly. "What if I can't do it, what if I can't believe in it." What if you and they realize I don't belong here, Claire added silently.

"You will," Holly's quiet firmness was more soothing than her words. "You will. You have us, Cody and Zack but more importantly you have Desmond, Everett, and Malcolm. And if my Cousin's expression was anything to go by this morning, those three will move mountains for you. The question isn't whether or not you believe in it right now, the question is whether or not you are willing to try."

Bethany and Holly stayed silent, letting Claire think. As terrifying as it seemed she did want to try. She just wasn't sure if she could trust herself. Trust her magic. Trust her power. But trusting them didn't seem as far of a stretch. Nor did trusting her friends.

"I want to try," she said.

Holly squeezed her hand. "That's great. We'll be right here with you but I think you know the first step."

"I have to talk to them," Claire was both excited and nervous about that.

"Don't think that you have to make a decision about being their Fourth during the conversation," Bethany said, "just think of it as a conversation to get answers to the questions you have."

"But won't they expect an answer?" Claire bit her bottom lip.

"No," Holly said firmly, "they won't. They aren't that type. Sure Malcolm might growl a bit but he's a dragon and for as long as I've known him, growling seems to be his preferred method of communication."

Claire giggled at that, imagining Malcolm growling to respond to anything wasn't a far stretch from what she knew about the grumpy Combat Instructor.

"There you go," Bethany chuckled, "anyone who can laugh at Malcolm's growling is more than suited to be their Fourth."

Claire didn't let her mind go there just yet. The thought of having a conversation to get her questions answered seemed easier for her brain to digest. "Okay. So just a conversation."

"Just a conversation," Holly confirmed, "I can set it up if you want, on neutral ground and away from prying eyes. I shouldn't be in the conversation but Bethany and I can be close by if needed."

"Do you think we could do it in the garden? Would Professor Helene mind?" Claire felt most at peace out there.

"For her favorite student, I think she would let you do just about anything there." Bethany teased.

"Oh, I can't be her favorite." Claire protested.

"Yes you can be and you are." Bethany volleyed back. "You clearly love the garden and her class and I overheard her talking to Professor Andy about how much potential you have in Herbology."

"Oh," was all Claire could say even as a warm feeling spread through her.

"To answer your question then," Holly said, "yes, we can do it in the garden. I'll ask Professor Helene and Desmond to throw up a privacy shield to prevent people from listening in. Bethany and I can stay close by. When would you like to do it?"

Claire thought about it. While she wanted to put it off till later, she knew she wouldn't be able to focus on anything else till she had it. But would she be able to focus afterwards? When she voiced her thoughts to the girls, Bethany saw her point.

"What if you did it tomorrow afternoon. After lunch? That way you can come with us to the library after breakfast and get some work done, maybe the assignments that are due the soonest, and then after lunch we can walk you over to the garden."

"Do you think they'll be able to do that?" Claire asked Holly.

"I think they would drop everything else to make it work."

"I don't want them to do that if they are busy." Claire felt bad.

"Claire, I don't think you understand," Holly said, "a Triad's Fourth is their top priority. They will always be there for you."

Now that was a concept that made Claire sit back in her chair. Someone, or multiple someone's, that were always there for her. The very thought seemed foreign to Claire.

"Okay. If you think so," Claire took a deep breath.

They took their time getting back to the portal. Bethany wanted to time it as close to the hour as possible and Claire and Holly just regarded their friend with quiet amusement. The noise on the street had died down as the sunset, clearing the air for what the next day would bring.

CHAPTER 17

By the time lunchtime rolled around the next day, Claire's stomach was a pit of nerves banging at her insides and telling her to flee. She barely picked at her lunch and eventually gave up eating all together, pushing her plate away. She could feel the eyes of all her friends landing on her at different times as they kept up a light conversation through lunch but Claire didn't know what to tell them.

Yesterday it had seemed like a good idea to talk to the Triad and get answers to her questions but as they got closer to the arranged meeting time after lunch, the more Claire was beginning to think this was a bad idea. If she opened her mouth to reassure her friends she was okay, she was just as likely to blurt out a reason why she shouldn't go to the garden.

The only saving grace of the day is that Vivienne was absent this weekend. Something about a last minute family affair had pulled her away. Even though she felt bad, Claire was secretly thrilled. She most definitely would have backed out by now if Vivienne was still on campus, regardless of the number of times Holly assured her that the privacy spell would give them privacy.

"I know you are probably doing a great job of talking yourself out of this already," Bethany's voice cut through Claire's thoughts, "but since you are looking a little pale, I feel obligated to let you know that you don't have to have this conversation."

Claire let out a nervous giggle, "That obvious?"

"You look like you're going to your execution." Cody said, "Remember, my offer still stands to beat them up for you."

"As if you could." Bethany scoffed, "those are three of the most powerful warriors the realm has seen since the Great War."

"And I'm sure if I told them Claire wants me to beat them up for her, then they would let me get at least a few hits in."

"Focus." Zack chided, "We are trying to help Claire not moderate another one of your arguments."

"No, it's okay," Claire said. "I appreciate the concern and the offer, Cody, but I need to do this. It'll be better for my brain if I have answers rather than letting it keep swirl with the what-ifs. Besides, I promised to try yesterday."

"Exactly," Holly reassured, "you're just getting answers to your questions. No decisions need to be made, just a conversation."

"Just a conversation," Claire repeated.

"Okay then!" Bethany clapped her hands together, "Let's get to the garden then. You can play with the plants to relax until they get there."

"Bethany," Zack warned.

"What? It's fine. If you had Herbology with her you would understand, it's like watching a forest dance when she interacts with them. Honestly, I feel bad because Claire definitely does most of the work because the plants love her best. I just fetch the watering can when she needs it."

Claire laughed as she stood up from the table, "You help too," she protested weakly.

"Mhmmm, thank you for the attempt to make me feel better

but that was a weak protest if I ever heard one." Bethany said as she also rose from her seat.

Holly linked arms with Claire and Bethany took up the other side of her. As they entered into the chilly afternoon air, Claire was glad she wore her coat today. Fall had definitely set in, almost overnight. The rustle of the leaves on the trees was sharper now as the leaves turned and dried up.

As they approached the garden's gate, Bethany sighed, "Looks like playtime with plants will have to wait because of eager Triads."

As she spoke, Claire could feel the energies of the three men on the other side of the gate. They were early. As their energy pulled her in, she got simultaneously more nervous and more relaxed.

"Oh look, they brought blankets so you all don't have to sit on the ground." Bethany's observation and the almost sarcastic way she said it made Claire smile and she squeezed Bethany's arm in gratitude.

Bethany held the gate open for them but didn't follow them into the garden. Holly guided her over to the blankets, the pull intensifying

"Cousin," Holly greeted.

"Holly, lit- Claire." Desmond responded.

"Bethany and I are going to wait outside the garden and the privacy spell. Professor Helene has closed the garden for the rest of the afternoon but the conversation is over when Claire wants it to be." Holly's words were meant to comfort Claire as much as they served as a warning to the Triad.

With one last squeeze of Claire's hand, Holly let go and the sound of the gate latching had Claire flinch.

Desmond began whispering the words of the privacy spell. One of the men, Everett, approached her cautiously coming to stand right next to her. "Hi, Claire." He whispered in that lovely deep voice of his.

"Hi, Everett," Claire whispered back shyly.

"Can I lead you to the blanket?" Everett asked, keeping his voice low and soothing.

Claire noded lightly and held out her hand. When he grasped it with his much larger one, she sucked in a breath as the pull intensified between them, radiating from their joined hands. As his breath stuttered as well, Claire knew she was not the only one feeling it. In a way that made her feel better instantly, that the men, or at least Everett, felt the same way she did.

Everett gently led her over to the blanket. Malcolm stood tall, like the mountains his clan called home, on the other side. Hitting the edge of the blanket, Claire toed off her shoes and stepped onto the soft material. Everett settled into a seat on the blanket, hand still wrapped in hers, he gave it a soft tug and she followed him down. He was so close, his knee touching hers but Claire can't find it in herself to shift away. To shift away felt like she was making a decision she didn't want to make.

Malcolm was still standing looking down at her. "Sit down, Malcolm." Desmond said, finishing the spell and coming to settle on Claire's left, opposite of Everett, "You'll scare Claire, standing there like a growly warden."

Malcolm dropped into a seated position so fast Claire jumped a bit. She offered him a small smile before pulling her hand out of Everett's and folding them in her lap.

"Claire," Desmond began, "we owe you a massive apology."

"Oh, no I should be..." Claire was cut off by Desmond's hand covering hers.

"Us first, and if you still feel the need to apologize, even though none of us think you need to, we will let you."

Claire nodded and Desmond continued, "We owe you a massive apology and an explanation for why we acted like we did. I think it's safe to say, none of us expected to find you. Triad's are usually matched within two years of their coming-of-age ceremony. When the Council and our families came to us with potential matches, all those girls wanted was the status they felt that came from being matched with us. Not a single one was looking to actually match with us. Moreover, all of these girls came from powerful families that were looking to strategically align themselves with ours.

"After a massive temper tantrum by our favorite grumpy dragon," Malcolm grumbled at him, "they backed off and we escaped to the Academy where Headmaster Dorian promised to help develop us into the warriors we are now as well as fend off our families and the Council as the Academy sits on neutral ground."

Claire twisted her hands, feeling sad for them. She would give anything to know who her family was but it seemed that knowing wasn't all it could crack up to be.

"Don't feel bad," Everett nudged her lightly, "our families aren't as bad as Desmond is making them out to be but they have been playing the political game for so long that it is second nature to them."

"It's still not an excuse," Claire said quietly, "they should have listened to you."

"They did, and that's why we are here." Desmond said. "And we've been here for six years now, two years past the required time, learning all that we can and searching for a Fourth that we choose and who chooses us. That's not confidential unfortunately and has led to several females here trying to insert themselves into our lives or stake claims. Unfortunately, Vivienne is one of them as her family is very powerful. Believe me when I say this though, little witch, we want nothing to do with Vivienne as our Fourth."

"You always talked to her after class though," Claire didn't mean it to sound like an accusation but the slight thread of accusation was there and to her embarrassment, a little hurt colored her voice as well.

"She was smart and always asked questions about the class or the lesson so I couldn't brush her off completely. If you stayed," Desmond took one of her hands with his, "you would have heard me brush her off as quickly as possible."

"I can hit him for you if you would feel better," Malcolm offered.

The words did their intended job and brought a small smile to Claire's face, easing the hurt inside her. "No, that's okay. I think he's safe for right now." She teased lightly.

Malcolm chuckled as Desmond let out a dramatic gasp. "Little witch!"

Claire giggled and Everett let out a soft laugh, "She's got you down," he teased his Triad brother.

"Well then," Desmond brushed it off but the smile in his voice told Claire he wasn't actually mad, more like pleased. "I have to admit I wasn't expecting to get picked on by the quiet, captivating witch we found in Windshire that day."

Everett picked up the story here. "We never expected to find you there, true, but we were so glad we did. Although we were admittedly a little stunned and probably fumbled your first impression of us."

"What? No." Claire protested, "I thought you were really nice. More than I expected. I think I was still in shock from getting the Academy's invitation."

"And that surprised us too." Desmond said, "not that we don't think you deserve to be here because you do, especially as a witch with four proficiencies." He was quick to reassure her. "But we've been searching the surrounding territories for the last six years for our Fourth. We had never been to Windshire before and we weren't supposed to be on that trip actually. Two guardsmen got food poisoning right before and the Headmaster asked us to step in. Now I'm wondering if that wasn't fate."

Claire blushed that they thought meeting her was fate.

"So when we rode up to the town square, we were directed

to the coven's small orphanage. And sitting on the steps was the most beautiful creature we had ever seen."

Claire wanted to protest but it was Everett who squeezed her knee this time, "The most beautiful creature that we've been searching the Realm for."

"How could you know though?" Claire questioned, "That I was your Fourth right away. I thought that was a choice you made."

Malcolm' deep gravelly voice explained, "They knew like I knew the first day in Combat Class."

Claire's brow furrowed, "What?"

"We knew because my magic recognized you as my soul flame."

Desmond's words had Claire sucking in a quick breath. Soul flame? She knew what that was, there were a few lucky couples at Windshire who were each other's soul flames. Similar to mates for shifters and dragons, a soul flame was a powerful connection.

"And I knew because my gryphon recognized you as my mate." Everett's words quite literally stopped her thoughts. Desmond's soul flame and Everett's mate? That should be impossible. But what about Malcolm?

Even though she couldn't see him, she looked across to the grumbly dragon. "My dragon recognized you as my mate that first day of class."

"But..." her brain struggled to make sense of it all, "That's impossible. I can't be your soul flame and both of your mates at the same time."

"Not impossible," Desmond corrected her gently as if aware her brain was frying, "just very rare that's all."

"So rare, everyone thinks it's impossible," Claire shot back, she would not be soothed when they clearly didn't get it. "It's impossible, you must be mistaken."

Malcolm let out a loud growl that made Claire jump, "No

mistake." he ground out, sounding more dragon than man, "You are ours."

"But..."

"No but's," Everett picked her hand up gently, playing with her fingers, "you can feel the pull to us like I feel it to you."

"But one can't have multiple mates," Claire knew she sounded like a broken record but that's all her brain was focusing on.

"While it's not common in shifters and witches, it does happen. It was more common when the Fae and Elves attended the Academy as both cultures had multiple matings." Desmond was a fountain of knowledge as he tried to give her brain something else to focus on.

"We aren't lying to you." Malcolm sounded like he had gotten more control over his dragon, "You feel the pull to us?"

Claire couldn't lie to them either, "I do, but..."

"No but's," Everett repeated. "This doesn't mean you need to jump into our Triad immediately but know, there is no other for us."

Malcolm growled and Everett ignored him. He wouldn't sugarcoat it but instead spoke to her with the steadfastness she had come to expect from him, "This is a lot, I can imagine, but I'm sure, Malcolm's sure, and Desmond's sure. Our beasts and magic call for you and you alone. There will never be another. Not Vivienne, not anyone else. Only you."

His certainty helped calm Claire's brain a bit.

"I just need time to think," she said, "I'm not saying no, I'm just... I need time. I... I never expected this when I came here and I just need time," she finished lamely, frustrated with herself for not being able to find the words.

"It's all right, little witch." Desmond cut off the rumbly growl coming from Malcolm. "We can give you time. We won't rush you. But we do want to start getting to know you better so please don't ignore us. We can give you time and take things slow but we still want to see you."

Claire nodded, "That sounds good. I... Bethany and Holly explained some things to me the other night and I know what they said makes sense like what you are saying here. My heart wants to be all in but my brain is having a hard time..."

"Believing." Everett finished for her and Claire nodded, eyes downward. He placed a finger under her chin and coaxed her gaze up, "We'll help you believe, you have my word."

Claire reluctantly climbed to her feet, Desmond's hand steadying her elbow as she stepped back and slipped on her shoes. They stood in an awkward silence and Claire psyched herself up, stepping closer and slipping her arms around Desmond's shadow.

The spicy scent of spearmint filled her nostrils as she let her nose burrow into the soft silk of his shift. Desmond froze for a split second and then wrapped his arms around her, brushing his cheek against her hair. "I'll see you later, little witch," his voice, a steady promise that warmed Claire's insides.

Giving her one last squeeze, he released her and stepped back. Everett didn't wait for her to initiate the hug, but instead stepped into her space and gently turned her around, tugging her into him. Claire was more confident this time as she stepped in close and let his arms close around her.

Stepping back from Everett, she shyly turned towards Malcolm. Of the Triad members, she had the least interaction with him, despite seeing him in Combat Class every day. That almost made it harder because he was formally her instructor. The large dragon remained deadly still, waiting for her to come to him. Finding her courage and shoving down her embarrassment, she stepped closer, lifting her hands to rest on his chest.

His hands came up to her hips, neither tugging her closer nor pushing her away. "Is this okay," she whispered, unsure if he even wanted her to invade his space.

At her words, Malcolm tugged her closer and she rested her cheek on his chest, inhaling his familiar scent of cinnamon and smoke. "This is better," he whispered in her ear. Claire was glad her face was hidden because she was sure her cheeks were red.

Relishing the feeling of his arms around her, and the presence of the two others at her back, for the first time, she felt like this wasn't out of reach.

CHAPTER 18

They tried. They really did.

Actually, that's a lie. They really didn't.

It turns out that Triads are terrible about giving space. She had made it all Sunday without seeing them though she swore she kept smelling Everett in between the bookshelves of the library as she studied. Each whiff made her smile at the sneaky gryphon.

Yesterday, Holly and Bethany had taken her back to her dorm room. Although the girls expressed shock that all three were her mates (Holly less so than Bethany which led Claire to think Holly had already gotten Desmond to spill the beans), they agreed with the men.

"If your animal knows, you know." Bethany had said.

Claire had gone to bed early that night and Sunday night, tossing and turning before she fell into a restless sleep. It was true what she had told the men, her heart wanted to be all in but her brain kept telling stories of how it was a mistake and she wasn't worthy of being a mate. Sunday night she had finally struck a deal with her brain, she would believe in herself for one month. After one month, if she didn't think she could do it, she would tell them.

Her heart whispered that they were mates and they wouldn't let her walk away but the deal seemed to make her brain feel better. Her magic seemed to watch the inner debate with a quiet amusement. It was on her heart's side, or maybe her magic and heart were the same. Either way, her magic was drawn to the men.

But back to her Triad. They had made an effort but Claire wasn't surprised when Holly and her got to their table Monday morning and Desmond was sitting there.

She could feel his slight nervousness so she let out a small smile to let him know she wasn't upset, "Good morning, Desmond."

"Good morning, little witch,"

Claire took her usual seat which was conveniently next to him, the length of his leg pressed into hers and the hum of the pull quieted at the contact.

"Pay up," Zack said.

"What?" Claire was confused.

Bethany groaned, "Claire, I love you and all of your sweetness but you just cost me 10 marks."

The teenagers at the Windshire coven used to play pranks and place bets on her screwing up but Claire brushed off the tension she was feeling. "And what was the bet?"

"Bethany thought you were going to be angry at Desmond for sitting with us at breakfast."

"Not angry," Bethany corrected, "I don't think it's possible for Claire to be angry, but I did think she would say something about Desmond being here when just two days ago they agreed to give her space."

The protectiveness in Bethany's voice chased away any remaining tension Claire was feeling about the bet, her feline shifter friend was more aggravated at Desmond than she was. "I appreciate it, Bethany, but it's fine."

"Does everyone know about the garden time?" Desmond asked lightly but Claire could sense a little annoyance.

"Yes," she spoke firmly, her tone brooking no argument, "they are my friends."

Desmond squeezed her hand in apology as their food appeared at the table. Claire squeezed it lightly back to show him the apology was accepted.

"Yes, we do, Cousin." Holly said after everyone dug in, "Someone has to keep the three of you in line around Claire."

"I don't know," Cody said, "I think Claire can handle all three of them just fine."

Claire smiled at Cody. She knew her friends meant well but Cody was right, Claire could and should stand on her own two feet.

"Besides," Claire started lightly, "I can't be mad at Desmond when Everett was stalking me through the bookshelves in the library yesterday and Malcolm made sure I got back to the dormitory last night after the library."

Desmond choked on a bite of food and Claire bit her lip so her smile wouldn't get too big. Cody had no such problems and his deep belly laugh caused everyone to lapse into laughter, drawing the attention of students from the other tables.

To be honest, Claire wasn't entirely sure if she was correct before she said the words. She just knew she had smelled the two men and took an 'educated guess' as Professor Andy would say.

"How could you tell?" Desmond croaked as he recovered, the laughter in his voice impossible to hide as he took a sip of his juice to wash down the bite of food he choked on.

Claire shrugged, "I could smell them."

"Damn, your senses really are as good as a shifter's," Cody said.

"What do you mean?" Zack asked

"The first day of classes when I went to the Runes Classroom to walk her to History, she could hear me running."

Claire had forgotten about that, "I think it's just due to not being able to see. I rely on my other senses more."

"Impressive," Desmond said and warmth filled Claire. Her brain rolled her eyes at her reaction but her heart and magic were thrilled with his praise.

The bell rang in the distance, signaling that first class was only a half hour away. Claire quickly finished her breakfast and took a few sips of her juice.

"I have to run," Desmond said almost sadly, "Mastery classes wait for no one. I'll see you later, little witch."

Claire smiled at him, "See you later, Desmond."

As they walked to class, Holly asked her, "Are you truly okay with him sitting with us for breakfast? If you need more space, I can tell him to back off."

Claire squeezed her arm, "I'm okay with it. I made a deal with my brain last night that I would believe in all of this for one month and then take it from there?"

"Made a deal with your brain?" Holly was amused.

"Yes, you know the part that's always telling me I don't belong here and I don't deserve this. That part has to be silent for one month."

"And after one month?"

"I'm hoping it will be up for a renegotiation," Claire shrugged and both girls laughed.

"Let me know if you need help with the negotiations." Holly said as she dropped Claire off at the door to Runes.

"I will. Have a good morning."

Claire made her way up to her desk at the front of the room, returning the morning greetings a few of the students made as she passed them. She settled into her desk and pulled out her Rune book. The last few weeks, the students had been studying the four elemental runes. Practicing their proficiencies each class period, most students had grouped themselves into their proficiency groups.

Claire had continued to remain alone as she practiced all four. She still couldn't do them as well as the other students, her efforts seeming to yield a response that was 50% as effective as a student with a single proficiency. While she still had to coax her magic forward, it responded to her easier now though. She could still only coax a little bit forward at a time but Professor Andy was happy at her progress, insisting that practice would make it easier over time.

Today, she was going to practice the air rune. Professor Andy had given all air proficiency students a feather to practice with and Claire drew it carefully out of an inner pocket in her bag before hanging the bag on the hook next to her desk.

Placing the feather on the desk, she flipped the Rune book open to the air elemental rune. She traced it unnecessarily a few times with her fingers. At this point in the class, like most students, she had memorized the four elemental runes. Taking a deep breath, like Professor Andy taught them to, she called a bit of her magic forward, coaxing it until she could feel her fingers tingling.

Releasing the magic as she traced the runes, she felt it flow from her into the air under the feather, focusing like Professor Andy said, she focused on directing the air under the feather and lifting it into the air. At first the air seemed confused but Claire remained firm and insistent. Sluggishly, the air moved under the feather and Claire could feel the slight updraft lifting the feather up. After ten seconds, she lost her grip on the element and the air dispersed, causing the feather to land lightly in her outstretched hand.

"Very good, Claire," Professor Andy praised as she came up to her desk. "That seems like it's getting easier."

"It is," Claire agreed, "Air seems to be the hardest, almost like it's too playful to obey."

"I've heard some students describe it like that," Professor Andy said, "But remember air can be purposeful too. The winds in a storm can fell trees with their might. Air, like all elements, is diverse."

Claire nodded, "I'll keep that in mind, Professor."

Professor Andy moved onto the next student and Claire returned to coaxing her magic into the air rune. As she practiced, she also tried to read the air's energy signature a bit more.

Air was supposed to be one of the easiest elements to read, it's energy signature feeling like the actual element with a slight coolness. Thinking about the energy signature, Claire tried something. Instead of starting the feather on the desk, she started it in her left hand.

Calling her magic up, she pushed it through the rune and focused on reading the energy signature telling it what she wanted. When the feather lifted from her hand, she felt the cool ribbon of energy weave around the feather as she directed it's path to rest in her other hand. Claire grinned big, she had done it! Maybe that was the key, combining the rune with the element's energy signature.

Not too long after her discovery, class ended. She made a mental note to talk to Professor Andy about her theory this week. If she was right, then maybe that was the key to getting better at Runes, the elemental ones at least.

Cody was waiting for her after Runes and they walked together up to History. "Do you have your paper?" Cody asked.

Claire nodded, digging it out of her bag and placing it in his hand. This was the paper Professor Storm had assigned them to learn more about a species. She had decided to do it on the Elves, unlike most of her classmates, Cody included, who had done it on their own species.

Luckily the librarian was able to help Claire out and had

shown her the meager collection of books on the Elves. When Claire had asked why the books took up less than a half of a shelf, the librarian had told her that most of the books had disappeared after the Great War. No one had removed them which led the librarian to tell her that the working theory was the Academy had removed them at the Elves and Fae's bidding in order to hide the species secrets.

Cody plopping into his seat caused Claire to jump. "You okay?" He asked her.

"Yes, just lost in my thoughts. Hoping I did a decent job on the paper."

"I'm sure you did," Cody assured her.

Professor Storm called class to order before Claire could respond and she activated the writing spell for her notes.

After class, Cody guided Claire out of the building, with the rush of students heading to lunch. "For the Realm's sake," he groaned.

"What is it?"

"We have an angry Vivienne headed our way, straight ahead. Her face is so red, I bet you could feel steam coming out of her ears," he whispered in her ear, "don't worry, I won't let her do anything."

Once Vivienne was three paces away and had entered Claire's field of shadow vision, she understood what Cody meant. The waves of anger pouring off the witch choked the air around them.

"You just don't get it, do you?" Vivienne raised her voice, drawing the eyes of students around them, "I tried to be nice and tell you privately but your thick brain doesn't seem to understand."

"Back all the way off," Cody growled, the tone of his voice was the most serious that Claire had ever heard. Every inch of his Alpha Heritage seemed to make an appearance, as he bulked up under Claire's arm.

"Oh, shove off, shifter." Vivienne was cutting, "Or is she spreading them for you too?"

Claire's cheeks burned at the insinuation as the students around them gasped and whispered.

"You're looking a little green there, Vivienne." Cody was relentless in his defense, "Jealous that Claire is getting the attention you so desperately crave by simply being her when you have to resort to nasty rumors and blackmail to get your way?"

Claire squeezed Cody's arm then released it, cutting off his rant, "Vivienne, I'm sorry if you feel I am taking something from you but I'm not taking anything that's yours."

Claire worded her response carefully, she had just decided last night to give this a chance and she didn't want the entire Academy to know while she tried to process.

Vivienne didn't share her same concerns. "That's rich. You're talking like you took my desk. No, you took my Triad."

Gasps from the students echoed around them and they turned their censured glares at Claire.

"What is going on here?" A sharp voice cut through the gasps. Everett.

Claire's knees sagged a bit before she caught herself. Maybe he was here for Vivienne and not her. She held her breath.

"Everett," Vivienne's voice turned sultry, "just having a discussion with our newest student, helping her understand her place here."

Vivienne was in a delicate position, Claire realized. If what Holly was saying was true, Vivienne had been spreading rumors about how she was Everett's Triad's Fourth to everyone but the Triad.

Everett spoke as he continued walking into the circle of students, "And what place is that?" He asked Vivienne, his voice icy. Everett halted next to Claire, the pull between them easing at his closeness.

"Are you okay," he leaned over to Claire, the warmth in his

tone in direct contrast to how he addressed Vivienne. It also held a hint of apology in it, as if he knew Claire had wanted to keep this quiet and Everett wasn't going to be able to honor that.

"I'm fine," she said quietly, "she just doesn't understand." Without saying the words, she asked him to be lenient with Vivienne.

Vivienne scoffed at Claire's insinuation that Vivienne was the one blind in this situation. "Everett," she whined, "let's go to lunch. The blind student has her own help."

"No." Everett's voice was flat and firm. His attention stayed focused on Claire, letting the students around them know which side he was picking. Cody took a step away letting them have their moment and wisely not challenging Everett's gryphon. For the first time in her life, Claire chose bravery. She chose to belong somewhere.

"Everett, would you like to join us for lunch?" Claire asked, intentionally ignoring everyone else, especially Vivienne's gasp of indignation.

His knuckles brushed her cheek, "I would love to, little mate."

Students around them gasped but Claire smiled at him and placed her hand on his arm.

Cody chuckled, "That lasted all of a day." A bit louder he said and waved his arms, "Nothing to see here, people, keep moving."

The students eventually dispersed as Everett placed her hand more firmly in the crook of his elbow, sliding her bag off her shoulder and onto his. Claire opened her mouth to protest, but his finger under her chin gently pressed it closed and Claire decided to pick her battles.

Cody flanked them as they made their way up the dining hall steps. Not all students had witnessed the courtyard scene so a hush fell over them as they watched one of the most powerful warriors the Realm had seen in this century escort a slight blind witch to the table.

"So much for the down low," Bethany's voice was amused as they took their seats.

"Yeah, Vivienne kind of ruined those plans," Cody said.

"What happened?" Holly's concerned eyes fell on Claire.

"I can give you a play by play," Zack said as he took his new seat on Cody and Bethany's side of the table. Claire wondered what would happen if the entire Triad ever joined them. They would need more chairs for sure.

"You were there?" Bethany asked.

"Had a back row seat." Zack said.

"Well, I had a front row seat so let's tell them a story," Cody said, rubbing his hands together.

Together, Cody and Zack launched into a dramatic retelling of the events of the courtyard which included Vivienne having actual steam coming out of her ears and dramatic proclamations of love.

Claire laughed and rolled her eyes at them as she dug into her sandwich. Everett stayed quiet through the story although his hand landed on Claire's leg as Cody recounted the nasty words Vivienne had sent her way. Almost like he needed to ground himself to prevent him from seeking out Vivienne.

Claire dropped her hand under the table and patted his quickly before returning to eat his sandwich. Everett let his hand rest there for the rest of lunch, the warmth of it pressed against her leg a pleasant feeling.

After lunch, Everett walked her to Spells and Potions where Desmond is waiting at the door. "I hear the cat's out of the bag?" He asked lightly.

Claire shrugged, unsure of how she felt about it. She had been with Everett since and now she was going to spend a class period with Desmond and then Malcolm. Since no one would say anything with one of the Triad around, it remained to be seen how it would affect the other students or professors' behaviors toward her.

"Well, let's get to class, little witch."

Claire took Desmond's arm and Everett handed him her bag. "I can carry that, you know," she said with a small smile on her face.

"I know, but we want to do it for you." Desmond said, "so let us act like big, strong men and feel good about ourselves."

Claire laughed which seemed to be Desmond's intended response. "Okay then, thank you."

Turning to Everett, she repeated her words with inflection, "Thank you."

Everett bowed slightly, "It was my pleasure, little mate."

* * *

IT SEEMED that news did indeed travel fast at the Academy.

"Claire, can you stay back?" Malcolm's question was sudden but not unexpected.

Claire nodded while lifting the edge of her shirt to wipe away the sweat that had beaded her brow after their running laps, ignoring Malcolm's growl as she did so. He was always growling at one student or another for slacking off in class. Some of the wealthier students seemed to think they would either always have bodyguards or that their magic would always be enough to protect them.

She waited by her bag for the others to be finished.

"Are you going to be okay?" Holly asked, clearly thinking about the last Combat Class Claire had attended where she had run out in tears.

Claire nodded, "Can't be worse than last time," she joked.

A rumbly growl from across the arena told her that Malcolm didn't find her joke funny which only made Holly and Claire giggle more.

"Okay," Holly said when she caught her breath. "I'll be waiting outside for you."

The students cleared out and Claire was left alone with the magnetic pull towards Malcolm. The pull lessened as he strode across the arena towards her. "Why did you stay on that side during the lesson today?" She asked, the thought occurring to her.

Malcolm paused briefly before stopping before her, "Because if I didn't, I would be right here the whole lesson."

He tentatively brought his hand up, cupping her cheek. "I'm sweaty," Claire protested weakly.

"And I don't care." Malcolm returned as Claire nestled her cheek into his hand, despite her words. "I heard you had an eventful day."

Claire smiled, despite her entire body feeling lazy at his touch, "I don't think I'll ever get used to word traveling this fast here."

Malcolm shrugged, his palm caressing her cheek at the movement, "Small Academy. Nosy students and staff." Claire tentatively lifted her hands and placed them on his chest. Out of all of them, she had the fewest opportunities to spend time with Malcolm outside of class and a part of her relished this time now. Specifically, her heart and magic part of her relished it.

A small rumble that sounded more like a purr than a growl exuded from his chest and he took a half step forward towards her. "Are you okay?"

His question took a little bit to register as Claire was distracted by his closeness, "I'm okay. Cody defended me until Everett got there. It was all over rather quickly."

"It shouldn't have happened at all." Malcolm grumbled, "I'll have a word with Vivienne."

"No!" The word tore from her lips before she could catch it, the feeling of possession was odd but felt right, "I mean, don't worry about it please, I think Everett made it clear to her. She just needs time to understand."

"You're too sweet." Malcolm said softly, "but if that's what you want, I will honor your wishes this time. If she continues to be a problem, however..."

Claire nodded, changing the subject "What did you need to talk to me about?"

Malcolm hesitated, "There is a large Market in the city. I was wondering if you would like to go with me this weekend?"

"I'd like that," Claire said shyly.

"You would?"

Claire didn't like the disbelief in his tone. Apparently it was okay for her brain to have doubts but it didn't like it when one of her men had doubts. Her men?

Ignoring her brain, Claire said firmly, "I would. I don't get to see you much during the week outside of class so doing something on the weekend sounds nice," she finished shyly.

"Then it's a date, little treasure."

While the nickname warmed her insides, she had a question, "Why do all three of you keep calling me little? Desmond calls me little witch, Everett called me little mate, and you just called me little treasure."

Malcolm laughed, a rich throaty sound that Claire instantly fell in love with, ignoring her brain's warning signals. "That's because you are little. Little and so precious."

"I'm not little, you three are just gigantic." Claire grumbled although she really wasn't actually upset. Maybe she should be but she liked being little next to them. It was a feeling of safety she wasn't used to experiencing.

"And that makes you little," Malcolm teased.

Claire rolled her eyes but smiled so he would know she wasn't really mad. "I should get going," she said reluctantly, "Holly is waiting on me."

Even though she said the words, her body made no movement to step back from him and he made no movement to release her until her stomach let out an embarrassing growl that had her blushing.

Malcolm chuckled and Claire decided then and there that his laugh was more dangerous than his growls. "Go, little treasure, before the dragon hoards you away."

Claire reluctantly stepped back and grabbed her bag. "See you tomorrow, Malcolm."

"Until tomorrow, little treasure."

CHAPTER 19

Claire thought she might actually be able to do this. The Triad was still terrible at giving her space but their attention wasn't overwhelming her.

Desmond joined her table for breakfast practically every morning and Everett joined them for lunch. She spent a few minutes with Malcolm after every Combat Class and she was looking forward to their outing tomorrow to spend more time with the growly dragon.

After Everett's declaration on Monday, the other students had given her a wide berth, seeming unsure of how to treat her. She still felt Vivienne and her friend's glares across that courtyard or dining hall but Claire ignored them. While she didn't understand Vivienne's motivations, she could see why she wanted the Triad's attention for her own.

The men were very attentive to Claire. Desmond and Everett insisted on carrying her bag for her. Claire didn't mind the attention but she had asked Desmond on the way to Herbology one day, why they hadn't said something to her when she first joined the Academy.

Desmond had told her they didn't want to overwhelm her,

moreover they didn't want to attract the wrong kind of attention to her. Even though the Headmaster and Academy provided a layer of protection, they had thought that by keeping distance from her they would protect her further.

Desmond had tugged her to a step and cupped her face in his hands as he insisted that if they knew how Vivienne was treating her or what Claire's brain was telling her, they would have never given her space. As it was, he worried they were going to be too overbearing for her. Claire had stepped forward and hugged him in the middle of the path. She reminded him that there would be an adjustment period as she and her brain weren't used to the attention but she didn't mind it.

And now it was Saturday. After class yesterday, Malcolm had informed her he had patrol in the morning and to be ready after lunchtime for their outing to the Market Square.

"Are you excited to see the Market Square?" Cody asked her as they finished up lunch.

Bethany smacked him, "Idiot."

"What?" Cody asked indignantly, "Oh. Sorry, Claire, I wasn't thinking."

"It's okay, Cody," Claire said, "I knew what you meant. I am. Even if I can't see it, the new sounds and smells will still be entertaining."

"And there's lots of things to touch," Holly said, "all sorts of vendors bring their wares to the Market. It's a massive courtyard."

"What are you going to wear?" Bethany asked.

"What's wrong with what she's wearing?" Cody asked. "I think she looks fine."

Claire knew what Bethany was talking about though. Since they were just studying this morning, she had opted for comfort over fashion. "I was hoping you or Holly would be able to help me pick something out."

"Of course," Holly said. "Are you ready to do that now?"

Claire nodded as she stacked her silverware and cup carefully on her plate. She knew the Academy automatically cleaned the tables but she felt bad just leaving it there. She gave the table a discreet pat, thanking it as she usually did.

Bethany joined them as they made their way back to the dorms. In Claire's hallway, Bethany let out a dramatic sigh, "Head's up," she whispered to Claire, "bitch witch alert."

Claire smiled at the nickname Bethany had adopted for Vivienne. Vivienne stood in the hallway with two of their friends. They had spread out loosely, blocking the hallway down to Claire's room.

"Excuse us," Holly's voice was polite but firm.

No one moved.

"Do you really want to do this?" Bethany scoffed. "Move the fuck out of the way."

"Such vulgarity," Vivienne mocked, "I know why your mate wants nothing to do with you."

The vicious growl that ripped out of Bethany didn't seem to phase Vivienne but her two friends shuffled backwards.

"Shut up, Vivienne," Holly's voice was stronger than Claire had ever heard it. "And get out of here before I let Bethany rip you to shreds for that comment. And she would be well in her rights to do so. I thought you were classier than to mock a mate bond."

Vivienne scoffed but she didn't reply. She didn't move either.

"Move." Holly said, "Because after I let Bethany have her fun, I'll call my Cousin to deal with you. My Cousin and his Triad, who I might add, has left you alone at Claire's request, despite *you* being the one who has interfered with a Triad relationship."

"Whatever," Vivienne scoffed, "she's clearly tricking them somehow."

"Oh, come on." Bethany said, "Make up your mind. She's either a low-level witch or she's powerful enough to trick the most powerful Triad in this century."

Without waiting for Vivienne to reply, Bethany strode down the hallway, shoulder checking Vivienne and letting out a terrifying growl at her friends who squeaked and jumped back. Holly and Claire followed in her wake, slipping inside Claire's room.

"Are you okay?" Claire asked Bethany who still seemed to vibrate with anger.

"Am I okay? I should be asking you that." Bethany said.

"I'm fine, she's just confused." Claire brushed Vivienne off. "I'm more worried about you."

"I'm fine." Bethany sighed heavily. "It's nothing I want to get into right now."

"Okay." Claire accepted. "Let's pick out an outfit then."

Bethany squeezed her hand gratefully before plopping on the bed. "I'll let Holly take the lead on this one. She's got the best eye for colors."

"You're no slouch yourself," Holly returned, "But let's start with the base. Pants or skirt?"

"Skirt," Bethany said before Claire could, "but give her leggings underneath it so she's not cold."

Holly pulled a skirt out of the dresser followed by a pair of leggings they had gotten during their shopping trick last week.

"Oh, you have to wear that new sweater you got," Bethany said, "it'll make your eyes really pop."

"And you said you weren't good with colors," Holly teased, "but yes, that'll look great on you. Even though it's a little chilly, if you wear an undershirt under your sweater, you shouldn't need your coat."

"And if you get too cold, I'm sure you'll have a rumbly warm dragon to warm you up." Bethany teased.

Claire blushed and covered her cheeks with her hands, "Bethany," she protested weakly.

"Mhmmm, you know what I mean. Get it, girl," Bethany broke down in laughter and Holly and Claire joined her.

"Okay, go change." Holly handed her the clothes. "We're cutting it close."

Claire jumped up and hurried into the bathroom. Quickly stripping out of her comfy long-sleeve shirt and pants, she tugged the leggings and undershirt on before layering it with the sweater and skirt. She felt a little warm in the bathroom but figured that meant outside would feel perfect.

"Damn," Bethany whistled, as Claire exited the bathroom.

"What? Does it match?"

"It looks fantastic," Holly assured her, "You look great."

"Good enough to eat," Bethany agreed, "like a little dragon snack."

"Bethany," Holly scolded as Claire blushed.

"I'm sorry, Claire,"

"It's okay," Claire said, "one day I won't blush so much."

"Oh no, don't change that. If you do, I'll just have to get more ridiculous."

"Yeah, let's avoid that," Holly laughed, "you're ridiculous enough as is."

"Please, you love me and my ridiculousness."

"Of course we do," Claire assured her as they exited her room, slipping her room key in her skirt pocket.

Thankfully, the hallway was clear and the girls hustled down the stairs and into the warm fall sunshine.

"Perfect timing," Holly said, "Malcolm's heading over from their dormitory building now."

Claire turned in that direction, the pull between them activating a few moments before he entered her three-pace field of shadow vision.

"Ladies." he greeted politely, "Little treasure, you look beautiful."

Claire blushed, swearing she would figure out how to cool down her overheated cheeks one day. "Thank you, Malcolm, I'm sure you look great as well." She said with a smile.

Malcolm let out that dangerous laugh, "Thank you, little treasure. Are you ready?"

Claire held out her hand and waited for him to take it. He secured it in the crook of his elbow. "See you later," she told Holly and Bethany.

"See you later, Claire." Holly said.

"Take good care of her," Bethany instructed.

Malcolm raised his opposite hand in acknowledgement and led her towards the front of the Academy, in front of the administrative building. "I figured we could take a carriage to the Market rather than a portal to give us more time together."

"I like that idea," Claire said shyly.

During the short thirty minute ride, Malcolm asked questions about her classes and Claire answered with some of things she had learned this week. The conversation was light and easy and Claire found herself relaxing back into the seat. Malcolm had his arm up on the seat back and Claire leaned her head back into it even as they kept a respectable distance in between their bodies.

All too soon, the trip was over as the noise in the distance became louder and louder until the carriage rolled to the stop. People talking and shouting greetings and prices filled the air. Music twined itself through the conversations as various street musicians performed for the bypassers. Smells of baked goods, sweet fruit, and the tart smell of iron filled her nostrils as Malcolm helped her down from the carriage.

"It's a bit overwhelming at first," Malcolm read her face.

"Just a bit, but that's okay. Can you paint me a mental map of the area? That'll help me sort through the noises, smells and shadows."

"Of course, little treasure. The market is a large rectangle and we are at one of the short ends. It's made up of two squares of tents, each square with a fountain in the middle. The musicians tend to stay in the front half of the market. Around the fountains are tables and chairs that people can sit at and enjoy the food they bought or listen to the musicians."

"Are the vendors split into sections at all?"

"Not really, although the back square tends to me more material goods like leatherwork or metalwork and more regular food. The front square tends to be more baked goods or exotic food and material goods like clothing or other handmade crafts like baskets."

"That all sounds wonderful," Claire said, wishing she could see what he was describing.

"Come, little treasure," he said, reading her face again, "you can touch all the wares and let me know if something catches your fancy. I will make sure you don't touch anything sharp or an enchanted spindle."

Claire smiled at a reference to a popular fairytale in which a young witch touches an enchanted spindle and has to be rescued by her Elven lover.

Claire took his offered elbow and they walked through the entrance, framed by two tall trees. Malcolm guided her to the left, whispering to her ear what each tent held as they approached it. Claire felt too nervous to touch anything, afraid she was going to ruin something or knock something over. About the third vendor in, Malcolm must have caught on to her nerves.

At the next tent with two tables on either side of it, he took her hand from his elbow and gently laced their hands so his palm was at the back of her hand, like a reverse hand hold. He guided her hand over the cloth materials on the table, letting her fingertips trail over the soft, woven fabric.

"They've got quite the selection of scarves here," he spoke low as he moved her hand over to a pile of soft, but silkier fabric.

Claire could tell from the feel of it that this fabric was more expensive than what they were previously touching, the weave of the material so tight it was hard to distinguish. "It's so soft," she observed.

"Have we found something we like?" The shopkeeper came over from the back of the tent.

Claire went to tell her they were just looking when Malcolm spoke, "Yes, we have. We'll take this scarf."

He gently tugged the scarf from under Claire's fingertips and held it up for the shopkeeper.

"Excellent, would you like me to wrap it for you?"

"No, thank you," Malcolm said as the jingle of coins passed hands.

"Malcolm..." Claire started but trailed off when Malcolm brushed a thumb across her chin.

"You started to look a little cold," he gave a weak excuse and Claire smiled and shook her head.

"You didn't have to buy me anything though," she finished her protest as they moved away from the tent. She didn't want the shopkeeper to think there was anything wrong with his wares.

Malcolm stopped and placed the scarf around her neck, gently tucking the soft material around her shoulders. "There. Warmer already." His voice was gruff but warm and Claire decided not to argue further.

That decision was quickly rescinded as Malcolm attempted to buy her something at every tent they went to after that. A leather bound journal, a new writing set, gloves for the garden.

Claire gently tugged on Malcolm's arm, forcing them to stop by the fountain's rushing water. She stepped in front of him and reached up to cup his jaw with her left hand. For not the first time since meeting her men she wished she could see.

"Malcolm," the stubble of his jaw scratched her palm as he leaned into her touch. "I appreciate that you want to buy me everything I look at" she smiled wryly, "Or touch. But that's not why I accepted your invitation to come to the Market today."

"And why did you accept?" His voice was growly, like his dragon was close to the surface.

"I wanted to spend time with you." Claire said. Her cheeks heated a bit at the simple answer but she didn't back down. "I came because I wanted to spend time with you, not have you buy me things."

Malcolm's arm came around her lower back, pulling her closer so she was plastered against the front of his body. His very hard body. His chest was rumbling but she didn't get the sense he was angry. More that, he was pleased?

"What if I want to buy you everything you touch?" His warm breath tickled her face and her cheeks heated further.

"If you truly want to," she began, "then you may. But don't do it because you're trying to buy my affection." She took a breath, this acceptance of being a Fourth still feeling very new. "You already have my affection."

"I do?" His voice sounded amused but his arms pulled her impossibly tighter. As if he was afraid she would take it back.

"You do." Claire let go of his arm with her right hand and brought it up to his chest. Smoothing it over his shirt as his chest rumbled.

"If we weren't in a crowded place," Malcolm mumbled so softly she didn't think she was supposed to hear it.

He leaned down and placed a gentle kiss on her forehead, the heat emanating from that spot long after he pulled away. He tucked her back into his side again, closer this time. "Then let's go enjoy each other's company. I still reserve the right to buy you another pretty scarf or two."

Claire laughed and leaned in closer to him. "Okay, my dragon."

For the rest of their time at the Market, Malcolm held her close and described each tent's wares to her. They enjoyed hot sweet buns next to the street musicians and Malcolm had her in stitches at his colorful descriptions of the people around them.

He seemed to treasure her laughs and his descriptions got even more and more elaborate. They had made it halfway through the large Market when she noticed that the air had taken a chill despite her sweater and new scarf and the sun's rays were starting to set.

"Time to go," Malcolms hand was warm on her lower back.

Claire looked back over her shoulder towards the section of the market that seemed to pull her. Malcolm followed her gaze, "We'll come back." He promised. "I have more scarves to buy you." He teased.

Claire laughed and squeezed his arm. "Thank you for a lovely afternoon."

Malcolm leaned down and brushed a kiss on her cheek, "You are absolutely welcome, little treasure."

CHAPTER 20

If this was what it was like to have a Triad, Claire thought that just maybe she could do it. The men were attentive yet respectful as they continued a similar pattern over the next few weeks. While they didn't make it back to the Market, the men made sure to spend parts of the weekends with her either all together or individually. During the week, Desmond ate with them at breakfast, Everett at lunch, and the three of them usually joined the table at dinner.

That first night, her friends had been quieter, unsure if their usual banter would offend the Triad or make them feel uncomfortable but the table soon fell into an easy rhythm. Like Claire's earlier assumption, the Triad had to add some chairs around the table to make them all fit but Claire liked the coziness and her friends didn't seem to mind.

Classes had buckled down, the professors providing them with a steady stream of work as they headed into the winter. There were many an evening spent in the warm library studying and a pair of gloves and a knitted hat had appeared in Claire's bag mysteriously after one breakfast smelling a bit like cinnamon and smoke.

Nevertheless, Claire wore them gratefully as the winter chill has well and truly set in. Between her coat, scarf, hat and gloves, Claire had never been warmer in a winter, ever, and she enjoyed the fresh breeze across her cheeks as she hurried across the courtyard towards the Combat Arena. Combat Class had started with the staff a few weeks ago, first just walking through Warm-up Form C with the staffs, making small adjustments so the staffs swung in a wide arc around their bodies.

This week, they started sparring with partners. Claire had partnered with Holly for a few days before realizing that Holly was going to need a more challenging partner than Claire. Holly had been good-natured as she always was but Claire had insisted she partner with different people to actually learn. Claire had separated from the group, working through the actions that Malcolm barked out on one of the practice dummies. Claire got the sense that the rumbly dragon actually preferred this set-up but he told Claire he would train her separately on the weekends.

So here she was on a chilly Saturday morning, meeting Malcolm at the Combat Arena before breakfast. Predictably, when she entered the Arena, the strong pull of at least one of her other mates was there as well.

"Morning, little mate," Everett greeted from his position next to Malcolm.

"Morning, Everett. Morning, Malcolm," she hugged each man in turn. Affection was starting to get easier for her to give and accept.

"Morning, little treasure. Ready for training?"

At Claire's nod he continued, "First, I want to get an idea of your shadows and how we can use them. Everett's going to be our practice dummy."

Claire took a half step back, "I don't want to hit him," she protested.

Everett chuckled, "Don't worry, little mate, I'll have my own staff. You'll have to get really good before you could land a hit on me."

Malcolm grumbled, "Cocky gryphons."

Everett stretched out the long shadow that was a staff. "Here's your staff."

Claire took it, wrapping her fingers around the worn wood in the middle. She took a few steps away from the men and twirled it around her body. Like always, there was something about the staff that was familiar but as familiar as it seemed to be, there was a part of Claire that also felt like it wasn't the right weapon for her.

Her thoughts must be splayed across her face as Malcolm asked, "What is it?"

"I don't know," Claire said, "there's just something about the staff that seems familiar, like I used it in another lifetime, but it doesn't feel... right at the same time."

Malcolm just hummed an acknowledgment and Claire finished Warm-up Form C.

"Okay, what's next?" She asked.

"How easy is it for you to make out the shadow of the staff?" Everett asked.

Claire held the staff out in front of her and focused on the shadow. "It's a very thin shadow. If it moves too fast, I lose it completely."

Everett moved two paces in front of her as Malcolm moved to her back. "I want you to watch Everett as he uses the staff. He'll start off slow and go faster. Tell me when you lose the shadow of the staff."

Claire nodded, determined not to be distracted by the heat of Malcolm at her back and focused her attention on Everett. He began to move the staff in a figure-eight pattern. Claire nodded, while it was very thin, she could still see the staff as he moved it.

Everett gradually began to move it faster and after only twenty beats, Claire shook her head. "I've lost it."

Everett slowed it down again until Claire saw the thin shadow cutting through the space again.

"Let's try something different," Malcolm said, "instead of focusing on the shadow of the staff, try focusing on Everett's shadow. See if by the motion of his arms you can then estimate where the staff is."

Claire nodded and Everett began moving faster again. Like before, she lost the shadow at twenty beats but she could keep track of Everett's arms for a little bit longer.

She shook her head when she lost it. "I've lost it."

"That was better though," Everett encouraged, "it took you longer to lose my arms."

"I'm worried though, it won't be as easy when we move to weapons that don't require such large movements away from the torso." Malcolm was in full instructor mode.

"Let's cross that bridge when we come to it." Everett suggested.

For the rest of the time, Malcolm had Everett move closer and Claire practiced blocking and attacking. They started slowly, Malcolm was hyper focused on her form and making sure she got it correct. It felt kind of awkward to slow everything down like that but after thirty minutes when Claire's muscles felt shaky, she was grateful for the slow speed.

Everett and Malcolm must have noticed that too because Malcolm called a halt to the practice. "It gets easier with practice," Everett read the frustration on her face.

"Hopefully," Claire grumbled, "I know I'm blind but I don't want to fall behind the rest of the class."

"Keep practicing that form and you'll be ahead of the class," Malcolm said, "half of those students don't listen to a damn word I say thinking their magic will always be there to save them."

"Won't it?" Claire asked.

"Not always." Everett answered, "In the Great War, there were Elven sorcerers who were able to cast spells to freeze magic users. Witches and Wizards who had always relied on magical use were slaughtered unless they were powerful enough to break the spells."

"That's awful."

"That's war," Malcolm said bluntly.

Abruptly changing topics, he strode to the far side of the arena, "Follow me."

Everett took Claire's staff as they both followed the dragon. He stopped before a long table that leant against the far wall of the Arena.

"You said the staff didn't feel right," he started, "I'm wondering if a different weapon would be better. This is a collection of the wooden practice weapons we will train with later."

Claire moved closer to the table, hand stretched out, till she contacted the edge. The first few weapons she touched and lifted were different variations of the staff. Some were shorter and thicker, others had points on the end or had a curved end, none of them felt right in her hand.

She moved down to the swords section. She could barely pick up the first sword. She picked up a few more, not liking the weight in her hands. Some of these swords were as long as she was tall. There was no way she was going to be able to effectively wield them.

At the end of the table, she picked up a sword that was much lighter than the others. Running her hand down the blade, she realized that the sword was half as long as the others. It was the length of her forearm, and her palm wrapped around the grip comfortably. This was the one.

"That's a rondel dagger" Malcolm's voice sounded behind her. "It's meant to be wielded as a pair."

He stepped up next to her and picked up another short sword from the table. He pressed it into her palm.

She wrapped her fingers around the pommels. Even though the swords were wooden, something about them felt right in her hands. She took a few steps away from the table and Malcolm and gave them a few practice swings. The lightness of the swords allowed her steps to be nimble as she started working through the footwork of warm-up form.

Finishing, she gripped the short swords, "I can't explain it, but these are the ones."

Everett stepped up beside her and ran a finger around the blades, "I don't love it from a defensive perspective. Short blades mean you have to get closer to your opponent to strike a blow."

"But if trained correctly, her size and speed could provide her a larger advantage as a longer weapon means more momentum to stop and start."

Claire placed the daggers back on the table, ignoring the feeling of loss even though they were just practice weapons. "I'll learn."

Malcolm nodded. "I won't go easy on you. I can't, even though you are my mate."

Claire stepped into his arms, "I wouldn't want you to. I want to learn."

"We'll meet every morning before breakfast," Malcolm warned.

"Okay," Claire nodded. It wasn't that she was very excited to get up early and train but something inside her told her she needed to do this. She had to be prepared even if she wasn't sure what she was preparing for.

"Okay then," Malcolm said, "let's go get breakfast."

CHAPTER 21

Malcolm wasn't joking when he said he wouldn't go easy on her. Every morning for the next two months, Claire met him at the Combat Arena an hour before breakfast started. Most times Everett joined them but sometimes he was on patrol. Desmond rarely joined them as he claimed he wasn't a morning person. The few times he did join them, he was as grumpy as Malcolm could be.

Claire trained with the staff until her arms no longer shook at the movements. Malcolm had started to spar with her, keeping his strokes light and Claire had to focus on predicting where his strikes would land. As she heaved herself up from the sand for the fifth time that morning, she didn't think it was going well.

"You have to focus," Malcolm said and Claire wanted to hit him. She couldn't see to focus!

"I'm trying," she said shortly.

"Try harder. Let's do it again."

A few minutes later, Claire was staggering sideways from a hit to her stomach. "This isn't working," she said hotly, "I can't see where it's coming from when you go that fast."

Everett came to her side as she leaned over, hands on her knees and staff on the ground in front of her. He placed a gentle hand on her back and kneaded the tight muscles there.

"What if it's not about seeing it?" He asked.

"What do you mean?" Malcolm questioned.

"We've been placing such an emphasis on her seeing a shadow she can't see but what if it's not about seeing?"

"What are you proposing?" Malcolm asked.

"I don't know. I just think we are placing the emphasis on the wrong thing. Claire?"

Claire was silent as she thought through it. As much as she had been practicing Combat, she also had been doing her other class work. In Runes they had moved to more intentional action with the four elements and her precision had improved. There might be something there with manipulating air but that would help her on the offense and could help her soften a blow but how would she know the blow was coming?

But what about...

She reached down and grabbed her staff. Class work wasn't the only thing she had been practicing. She had also been working on her Energy Reading skills quite a bit. She had reread the book Professor Helene had given her before returning it and Professor Helene was searching for another book on it for her. She had a feeling Professor Helene was keeping her secret quiet as well.

In the book though, it talked about feeling the disturbance in the air as a way to help sense air's energy. Holding her staff in one hand, she ran the other hand up and down the smooth wood. What if she combined the disturbance in the air with the solidness of the wood. Wood like this was hard because it wasn't connected to a living plant but traces of that tree's energy was still around it, enough that if Claire focused she might be able to sense it coming.

"I think I have an idea," she said finally, "let's go again."

She gripped her staff as Everett moved away. Taking a deep breath to center herself, she internally explained the plan to her magic, asking for help. Then, she closed her eyes.

Her world was plunged into complete darkness but Claire didn't let it deter her, instead she sent her magic out to sense the airfield around Malcolm. His body was a disturbance in the air field and Claire smiled softly. He twirled his staff a few times and then began slowly.

It was hard to keep the focus on the air's energy while moving her body but Claire relaxed into the sensation, feeling the air brush her own skin and going back and forth between her and Malcolm.

His first strike was a slow, sweeping move from the side. Claire lifted her staff to block it. The reverberation of wood hitting wood traveled down her arms and she almost lost the focus but caught herself, letting the energy from the contact flow off her skin and back into the air. She was going off instinct alone here.

Unbeknownst to Claire, no book would ever teach her this.

Malcolm's next strike was low and aimed for her knees. Claire dropped her staff point to the ground to block the strike and leapt over his staff once it made contact. Then she decided to go on the offense and lifted her staff quickly to tap him in the stomach.

"So it's like that?" Malcolm teased.

Claire smiled but didn't let it distract her from her focus.

Malcolm attacked again, his blows slicing through the air field of energy, faster and faster. While Claire could still read them, it became clear that she was nowhere near the warrior that Malcolm was and her skill was no match for his.

Bringing her staff up to block a blow from above, she allowed it to knock her backwards, exhausted. "I yield," she said from the ground.

"Holy shit." Desmond had entered the arena.

Claire opened her eyes and let the shadows fill her world again. Malcolm stood above her. She reached out a hand and Malcolm helped her to her feet.

"I've got to agree with Desmond," Malcolm said, "that was much better."

"What was your idea?" Everett and Desmond moved closer to form a square.

Claire got momentarily distracted by the pull she always felt when she was around them. "What? Oh, um, well..." she realized she had never told the Triad about her Energy Reader ability.

"Going off what Everett said about us placing too much emphasis on seeing, I tried something else which was basically trying to sense where the hits were."

"And how did you sense them? Your eyes were closed when I came in." Desmond said, confused.

Claire took a breath, they were her Triad so they should be exempt from the 'tell no one policy' Holly advised. "I read the air field's energy around Malcolm and used it to predict where the staff was going."

The Triad was silent.

"You can read energies?" Everett said quietly.

"Yes. I mean not well, but enough that it helped."

Claire could practically feel the looks the men exchanged. "What is it?"

"Who all knows about this?" Desmond asked first.

"Holly and I'm sure Professor Helene does as well. She gave me a book about it and is looking for another one for me."

"That's something at least," Malcolm told Desmond.

"Why? What is it?"

The shadows shimmered around them as Desmond threw up a privacy spell.

"What did Holly tell you about it?" He asked.

"She said to keep it a secret as not many people were able to do it."

"She's correct. Only the most powerful witches among us can do it. And the Fae."

"So what does that mean?"

"It means, little witch, that you are going to be very powerful. It makes me wonder who your parents are."

Claire rubbed her arms as she thought about it. This was the first real lead she had had about her parents. She tried to not get too excited about the thought after a lifetime of not knowing. "So what do we do?"

"You said Professor Helene was searching for another book?" At Claire's nod he continued, "I'll search my library as well and see if I can find anything. I can also go back and search my family's library if I can't find something here."

"Won't that alert your family?" Everett asked, "We should keep this quiet until Claire learns more. No need to create even more talk about her."

"It shouldn't. I'll blame it on a mastery paper if I need to."

"More talk?" Claire questioned.

Again, more looks were exchanged and Claire folded her arms, waiting them out.

"Due to the nature of our Triad and our families, word has leaked to outside the Academy that we have found our Fourth."

"Oh?" Outwardly, Claire was calm but internally she was panicking. What if their families didn't approve? Would they make the Triad leave her?

Everett wrapped an arm around her shoulders, "It's no big deal, our families are eager to meet you. We were trying to give you more time to adjust before including the entire Realm."

Claire's fears still swirled in her brain but she took a breath. "So what do we do?"

"Nothing," Malcolm was blunt, "they are all nosy bastards but they also know better than to come here and violate the

Academy's neutrality. When you are ready, we will take you to meet them."

"Until then, when people don't know the whole story, they speculate." Desmond waved a hand, "it's been a habit for these people that's as old as the realm. Don't worry about their words, little witch."

Claire wasn't all the way convinced but she let it go. She could always ask Holly or Bethany later.

The bell rang for breakfast and Malcolm took her staff to put it away. Everett handed her a towel to wipe her face with. The chill of the air usually prevented her from getting too sweaty that it was uncomfortable to sit through classes but she was going to have to shower before breakfast as the weather started changing in earnest for spring.

Malcolm and Desmond headed towards the door and Claire moved to follow. Desmond had already stolen her bag from her. Everett's hand on her arm stopped her.

"What is it?" She asked.

"Do you have any plans this weekend?"

Claire thought for a second. It was a weekend so no classes. She had promised to study with Cody for their History exam but that was it.

"No plans," she said.

"Could I take you on a date tomorrow?" He asked quietly.

Claire smiled, "I'd love that. What were you thinking?"

"A picnic?"

Claire stood on her tiptoes and kissed his cheek, "That sounds wonderful."

While she had gotten more comfortable with the men the last few months, they hadn't increased their physical affection more than hugs and kisses on her cheek. Claire didn't know if they were waiting on her to initiate something but she didn't know what to initiate. She would have to ask Holly or Bethany about it.

She looped her hand in Everett's elbow as they started the walk to the dining hall. "When do you want to go?"

"How does an early dinner tomorrow afternoon sound?"

"Sounds lovely."

They met Desmond and Malcolm at the base of the stairs to the dining hall and headed in. She couldn't wait to tell Holly and Bethany she had another date and pick their brains about how she could get the Triad to kiss her.

CHAPTER 22

As it turns out, Holly and Bethany had lots of ideas on how to get the Triad to kiss her. After they got over their initial shock it hadn't happened yet.

"I just still can't believe they haven't kissed you yet," Bethany was lying on Claire's bed as Holly sifted through Claire's clothes for a warm outfit to wear for the picnic date.

"I mean they've kissed me on the cheek," Claire said.

"That doesn't count." Bethany waved her hand, "grandmothers kiss people on the cheek. You all are mates."

"Everyone's relationship moves at different speeds," Holly said.

"I mean yes, but still. It's been what? Three or four months since you all have gotten together? They must have some iron will power?"

"What do you mean?" Claire asked

"I mean that usually mates are all over each other,"

Claire frowned, was there something wrong with her?

"There's nothing wrong with you," Holly read her face, "they were just giving you space and time to adjust. They likely didn't want to scare you off."

Bethany was quick to agree, "I didn't mean it as a bad thing. If anything, it's a sign of their devotion to you that they've been waiting for your lead."

"So how do I tell them I'm ready?"

Bethany shrugged, "I'm a big fan of action so I would just lay one on them."

"And if I'm not ready to do that?" Claire was a little intimidated at the idea.

"You could always just ask them." Holly said.

"And say what? 'Would you kiss me?'" Claire thought that sounded awkward as hell.

"Men like it for some reason," Bethany said, "your men would probably love it. Especially as they've been letting you take the lead."

"I don't think I'm ready for everything else after kissing."

"And you don't have to be." Holly came to sit next to Claire on the bed, "If you ask for a kiss, that's what they will give you. If they haven't pushed you so far, they won't push you for anything else until you are ready."

"Okay, so when does one usually ask for a kiss on a date?"

"If it's a first date, usually at the end. Is this your first date with Everett?"

Claire thought about it, "I guess officially? He sits with us at lunch and will come stay with me in the library as I study but this will be our first official date. So I ask at the end?"

"Yep," Bethany said.

"Okay, then what?"

"Then you come back and tell us how magical it was," Holly laughed.

Claire giggled with her, "Sounds like a plan. Now tell me what I'm wearing."

"I've got your fleece-lined leggings, a long-sleeve shirt and a green sweater over it with your cream scarf. It's actually starting to warm up a bit so this should keep you plenty warm."

"And if not," Bethany said, "you can always ask Everett to keep you warm."

The girls giggled and Claire ducked into the bathroom to get dressed.

Parting ways with Bethany and Holly at the end of the hallway, Claire headed downstairs and outside to the tree Everett said he would meet her under.

"Claire," he greeted warmly, "you look lovely."

"Thank you," she said shyly, still not used to the Triad's compliments.

Everett offered her an arm. His other arm had a square object hanging from it that Claire guessed was a basket. He led them past the dormitories and past the Combat Arena. Taking a left, they followed a dirt path through some trees for a few minutes to a small clearing. Claire looked around, feeling the energies of the massive trees standing steadfast like guardians around the clearing.

Everett, mistaking her curiosity for nervousness, reassured her, "These areas are heavily patrolled. You don't need to worry about anything in this section of the woods."

"Oh, I wasn't thinking about that," Claire said quickly, confident he wouldn't put her in any danger, "I was just admiring the trees, I can feel their energy."

"What does it feel like?" Everett asked as he let go of her hand to spread a blanket out at the base of one of them.

Claire lifted her hand to place it on the trunk of the tree feeling the energy around it, "Steadfast, ancient, watchful. It makes me wish that they could share the stories of the things they've seen."

She could feel Everett's eyes on her and she blushed, "Or at least that's what I think. I could be wrong."

"You're not." His quiet confidence in her warmed her more than their compliments on her appearance did.

"Come, sit." He invited as he pulled things out of the basket.

"We have an assortment of sandwiches and fruit to choose from."

As they ate, Everett told her stories of the forest and the beautiful and deadly things he's seen in them.

After they finished eating, Claire leaned back against the solid tree behind her, legs outstretched as Everett packed up the remainder back in the basket. Moving slowly, as if to give her time to protest, he crawled towards her and stretched out next to her, laying his head in her lap. His warm breath puffed over her stomach and Claire swore she could feel it through the layers of her clothes. Tentatively, she lifted one of her hands and ran it across his brow lightly, smoothing his hair back and then running her fingers through the short, soft locks. His sigh gave her confidence to do it again and they were silent for a few minutes, enjoying the moment.

"Tell me more about your childhood," she requested softly, wanting to know more about him.

Everett was silent for a moment before answering, "I faintly remember my mother holding me on her lap, my father behind her smelling of the pipe he liked to smoke at the end of the day. I can't remember their faces though. Even before the Great War culled our numbers, Gryphons without a colony were hunted. When the big colonies were wiped out, the remaining gryphons went into hiding."

"Malcolm's aunt and uncle found me wandering in dragon territory, dirty and cut-up looking like I'd survived an attack but just barely. Unable to have kids of their own, they took me in and raised me as their own. So in a way, I grew up with parents and lost parents."

"I'm sorry that happened to you." Claire said softly.

"It's shaped me to who I am today." Everett said simply, "They were the best parents I could have asked for and other than living next to my annoying dragon cousin Malcolm, it was a good childhood."

Claire smiled, "He couldn't have been that bad."

Everett laughed, the movement shifting his head on her lap slightly, "He was grumpy as you call him even as a child. Always going on about responsibility and duty. I like to think I had a part in pulling him out of his grumpiness but it wasn't until we were 12 and attending a Capitol event where we met Desmond that Malcolm softened."

"Oh really?" Claire wanted to know more and Everett obliged her.

"Yes, it was a few years after the Great War. Our parents and other high-ranking people across the Realm were meeting as part of the Council's peacemaking plan. Anyways, Desmond in his family's finery and with the air of superiority and mischievousness that only he can pull off marched over to the corner of the ballroom that Malcolm and I had found. He stuck his hand out, introduced himself, and told us we were going to become the best Triad the Realm had ever seen."

Claire laughed, "What did you say?"

"I didn't say anything," Everett said, "but Malcolm started on his grumpiness, hoping to scare him off but it didn't work on Desmond. He filled the conversation with enough words for all three of us and by the end of the evening something had just clicked into place.

"Anyone that came up to us got introduced to us as his Triad and eventually word made it back to all of our parents and the Council that there were three twelve-year old boys in the corner calling themselves a Triad. They came to investigate and when a Councilmember tried telling Desmond that the Council connected Triads, Desmond looked at him and said 'We've done you a favor and connected ourselves so you don't need to worry.'"

"He said that to the Council?" Claire was shocked. She knew Desmond spoke his mind but that was the Council, the ruling body of the Realm.

"He did. I don't know who was more shocked, our parents, the Councilmember or Malcolm and I. The Councilmember started forward towards us and Malcolm stepped in front of Desmond and growled 'you will not touch my Triad brother' and that was that."

"And they let you stay together?" Claire couldn't not imagine the Council taking their plans being circumvented well.

"I think they were hoping it was a fantasy of youth and we would fall apart naturally but we didn't. For the next four years, we traveled back and forth from Brandlevine and the Dragon Mountains, studying from tutors and getting into trouble that only teenage boys can seem to conjure."

"That sounds beautiful," Claire said wistfully.

Everett stilled on her lap, "I didn't mean to make you feel bad with my stories,"

She was quick to reassure him, "Oh no, Everett, I love hearing your stories. Especially the ones about the three of you. Like I told you all in the garden a few months ago, I had a good childhood. I couldn't have asked for a better one considering the situation."

Everett didn't seem completely convinced but he continued to tell her stories for the next few hours about growing up in the Dragon Mountains and the antics that the three of them would get into. When the shadows stretched longer, and the sun's rays began to get weaker, he rolled up onto his feet and packed the basket efficiently.

Extending a hand towards her, he gently helped her to her feet.

"So what happens now at the end of one's first date?" Claire asked and Everett stilled.

"This was your first date?" There was an odd note in his voice.

Claire blushed and looked down. "My second date. Actually,

I don't know if Malcolm counted our Market Square visit as a date." She rambled to fill the silence.

Everett was silent and Claire worried her admission had scared him in some way.

She began to speak but he placed a finger to her lips, surprising her into silence. "I cannot begin to tell you how honored I am to be your first date. I do wish you had told me and I would have made sure..."

It was Claire's turn to cut him off. "Everett, this was the most perfect date I could have asked for. I just don't want to mess it up by not knowing what to do on a date."

Everett took in a breath, "There are no expectations, Claire," he said softly, "if that's what you are asking."

Claire blushed and tried to figure out how to bring it up. Her conversation with Bethany and Holly lingering in her ears. "And what if I have one, an expectation I mean?"

Everett shifted closer, setting the basket on the ground at their feet, "And what expectation would that be?"

"I have been told," Claire began, trying to be bold for once and stepped closer to him, raising her hands to his chest, "that after a first date, there is a certain ritual that happens,"

"A ritual?" Everett was amused, his hands lifted to her hips, not pushing or using, just resting there, waiting. Waiting for her.

"Everett," Claire found it hard to breathe at his closeness, much less remember how to put sentences together. Part of it was the pull of energy she always felt around him and the Triad but part of it was all Everett, his scent and the heat of his body scrambling her brain.

"Yes, Claire?"

"Would you kiss me?"

That's when he moved, pulling her hips closer as he leaned down, the warm air from his lips brushed over hers, once, twice, three times. Just as she was about to ask again, he lowered his lips to hers.

When his lips touched hers, he let out a small groan, sweeping her closer with his arm around her lower back. He sipped from her lips, placing small soft kisses and then tugging at her bottom lip with his teeth briefly.

Claire couldn't think, could only feel. The warmth of his lips on hers, the delicious pressure as he tugged at her bottom lip. The heat of his chest under her hands and down her entire body as he pressed them closer together. His hand came up to where her shirt hem danced with her pants and the feeling of his thumb on her bare skin had her surging closer to him, pulling his head down so she could kiss him harder.

Breathing heavily, Everett broke the kiss, his lips a breath away from hers as they breathed the same air for a few moments. Claire could feel his lips part in a grin and she let out a small giggle, feeling giddy.

"How was that ritual?" Everett breathed, teasing her.

She giggled again "I think we nailed it but practice makes perfect, right?"

Groaning, he lowered his lips to hers again, and Claire surrendered to the feelings. After what seemed like no time at all, the bell rang in the distance, signaling dinner was in one hour.

Reluctantly they broke apart. Everett grabbed the basket with one hand and tucked Claire under his other arm. They walked down the path and Claire looked around at the trees, silently thanking them.

"We'll come back," Everett said, "this is our spot now."

Claire smiled, she liked that.

"Now usually at the end of a first date, the male would drop the female back off at her house to do this, but Malcolm wants to give you something so he asked if I could bring you by our suite. Is that okay?"

Claire let out a nervous laugh. That seemed like a big step, going to their suite and entering their space but it was probably past time and she did want to see Malcolm and Desmond. "That's fine."

Everett squeezed her shoulders slightly and adjusted their course towards a different dormitory. Speaking softly, he guided her up the eleven steps and through the double doors. The Triad Suites took up the top two floors of this building, he told her, and her Triad lived on the top floor.

When they reached the door at the end of the hallway, Everett pushed it open and stepped through. Claire hesitated on the threshold. She didn't know why he expected Everett to knock. He did live here after all.

"Malcolm," Everett called into the rooms, his voice echoing slightly on the stone walls which told Claire the room was much bigger than she thought.

"I'm here." His voice was distant, like he was eight paces away. His boots sounded on the floor until his shadow appeared in Claire's vision. "Claire, how are you?"

"I'm good," she said, feeling shy for some reason. Or maybe off-balance being in their space, "How are you? How was patrol?"

"Uneventful."

Claire nodded, "Everett said you asked to see me?"

"Yes," he stepped closer, "I have something to show you. Take my arm so you don't trip over the furniture."

As Claire took his arm, he continued, "Right now we are in the main room. There are a few couches and chairs in the middle. The wall right behind you has the door. The wall to your right has windows looking outside as our suite is on the corner of the building. Straight ahead are the bedrooms, to your left is the kitchen and the doors to Desmond's study and my space."

As he spoke, he guided her through the room towards the

door to his space as he called it. Everett disappeared in the direction of the kitchen to put away the remains of their picnic.

Malcolm pushed open the door to his space, the heavy wood creaking softly.

"This is your space?" She questioned as she stepped through. The air felt cool, the stone walls feeling almost like a cave.

"Yes. Every dragon has a hoard. In fact we usually carve our hoard into a special space in the Dragon Mountains. Each dragon chooses their own space and fiercely protects the contents and its privacy. While I'm at the Academy, this room acts like my hoard. We keep our weapons here and other resources."

"That's very neat that you each get to claim your own space in the mountains."

"I'll take you this summer."

He guided her over to the far wall, where a long table rested against the wall. Shadowy outlines of weapons laid on both the table and the wall above it. Malcolm studied the weapons, looking for something.

"What are you looking for?"

"You've improved so well in training in the last few months that I want to start training you with the daggers you liked."

"The wooden ones?" Claire asked, surely he wasn't going to give her daggers from his hoard.

Malcolm turned towards her, studying her face now with the same intensity he had been studying the weapons with earlier. His body heat radiated across the few feet that separated them. He took her hands with his. "I want to give you a gift." He said, "Your very own daggers. Yes we will train with the wooden ones to start with but having your own weapons will speed up the training."

"Malcolm," Claire breathed, "I can't take something from your hoard. It's your hoard." Even though information about the secretive dragons was rare one of the more prevalent rumors was how fiercely they protected their hoard.

"A dragon's hoard is meant to provide for their family, Claire," Malcolm's hand lifted from hers to cup her cheek, "My hoard provides for Desmond, Everett, and now you. My dragon wants to give you this gift."

Mutely, Claire nodded.

"Good, now that we've established it's a gift, I want to make it a bit more special. Will you wait outside in the living area so I can select it?"

Claire realized that he was going to slip the gift in as if it was a necessity but her stubbornness had insulted his dragon. "Yes, Malcolm. I'm sorry for being stubborn."

His thumb brushed across her cheek, "I like you stubborn. I'm just more stubborn."

Claire laughed, "We will see about that."

She crossed the room and pulled open the door.

"Claire?" Everett questioned from the center of the room.

"Malcolm asked me to wait out here so he can properly present his gift," Claire smiled.

"Ah, so the ruse about it being better for training is up?"

"You knew about it?" Claire asked as she carefully picked her way towards him. Moving around a small, low table, she settled into the couch behind it, falling next to him.

"He was worried you wouldn't accept his gift." Everett placed an arm around her shoulders and she snuggled in closer.

"He explained why it was important to him. Although accepting all of these gifts is hard for me, Everett."

"I know, but we want to spoil you. And nothing we give isn't given freely."

Claire felt slightly better at his words.

Malcolm entered the room, "I know I said this is a gift but I wanted to present you a few options. It's important that your weapon becomes an extension of you so pick the one that feels the most right."

Claire nodded, sitting up straight out from Everett's arm. She wouldn't be able to focus with his arm around her. Malcolm sat on the couch next to her, his thigh brushing hers and Claire sighed internally. She might have as well not moved as she wasn't going to be able to focus now with both of them touching her.

Malcolm placed the bundle in his arms on the low table in front of them and unwrapped it. "This first set of daggers is classically made. They'll give you a standard to measure the others by."

Claire accepted the daggers, the pommels resting comfortably in her palms. "Do the daggers always come as a set?"

"Yes, usually they are crafted by the same person. That allows them to be perfectly balanced and the most effective."

Claire nodded, "It's the same feeling as the wooden ones in the Arena. This is the weapon but these aren't the daggers that invoke that feeling of... knowing."

Malcolm grunted in agreement and took the daggers from her. He placed another set in her hands, "These are made by the Council's metalsmith. The blades are slightly curved,"

Claire held them in her hands, focusing on the weight of them and twirling her wrists experimentally, careful to keep her arms outstretched and away from her men. "They feel... heavy," she said, "I think the curve is making them feel awkward."

She held two more sets of daggers, neither set feeling quite right in her hands. After she put down the fourth set, she placed her hand on Malcolm's leg, worried he was thinking that she was rejecting his gift, "The first set was nice."

Malcolm covered her hand with his and squeezed lightly, "You won't offend me, little treasure, if you didn't like any of them. I stand by my first statement that these weapons need to become an extension of you and my dragon won't let you accept something subpar. If anything, it's a good challenge for him to find you a weapon that fits."

Claire nodded, but her thoughts were still troubled. Maybe she picked the wrong weapons.

Everett picked up on her thoughts, probably reading her face the way he did so well. "You didn't pick the wrong weapons. Hold fast to that feeling you had when you picked them. That was your magic telling you you made the right choice. Shifters call it instinct."

"Instinct," Malcolm mused.

He stood abruptly. "I have one other one to bring you." He gathered the weapons and disappeared into his hoard.

Not being able to read their faces the same way they could read hers, she settled back against Everett, waiting for Malcolm.

Malcolm appeared a few moments later. "This isn't part of a set," he warned, "so it might not be appropriate either, but when Everett said instinct it made me realize my dragon was pushing for this one."

He unwrapped it carefully on the table and Everett took in a breath, going rigid beside her. "What is it?" She questioned.

"It's a Fae dagger."

"A Fae dagger? I don't understand,"

"Fae-made weapons are highly sought after due to their craftsmanship and scarcity. The Fae rarely share their weapons with outsiders, their quality rivals the Elves' weapons. Occasionally, a Fae will give a weapon to an outsider as a gift for a large event or to repay a life debt."

Claire simultaneously drew back into the couch and yet wanted to lean forward, intrigued by the blade, "Malcolm, I can't take that from you."

Malcolm disagreed, "Yes, you can. This dagger was gifted to my family by a Fae warrior during the Great War as a symbol of an alliance after my father saved the warrior's life."

"I thought the dragons and Fae were on different sides in the

Great War?" Claire questioned remembering her history lessons.

"They were. Fae were always honorable in battle though." Malcolm agreed, "I don't know why my father spared this warrior, he won't speak of it but he did give me this dagger at my coming-of-age ceremony. Said it was a symbol of what could happen if the race worked together."

"Now I really can't take it," Claire said, "It's a part of your family history."

"My dragon is insisting this is the dagger for you."

"But it's not part of a set."

"It's not, and I'll still find you a set."

"Malcolm," Claire was exasperated. Why did they insist on all of these gifts? Everett's hand squeezed her arm and Claire cut off the rest of her sentence. Everett had said that everything they gave, they gave freely. If Malcolm ever wanted this dagger back, Claire would gladly give it to him.

"Why don't you hold it and see, before making any decisions," Everett suggested.

Claire sat up and reached for the dagger. She closed her fingers around it and her world exploded.

CHAPTER 23

The second she wrapped her fingers around the hilt of the dagger, heat emanated from the connection, shooting down her arm and into her center where it hit the dome surrounding her magic. Her magic reacted to the intrusion by splintering out of the dome and sending a shockwave through her body. It exploded out of her, sending the men flying back from her and the table sliding from the force of it.

Claire struggled to open her eyes, confused as to when she had closed them, and gasped. Her world was no longer filled with shadows. Instead, bright shades assaulted her eyes as she took in the room, clearly. So clearly. She closed her eyes as the images assaulted her brain, unused to the onslaught on her senses.

Her grip loosened and the dagger clattered to the floor. When she opened her eyes again, her world was back in the shadows but there was something different about them. Everett was kneeling in front of her, holding her wrists lightly and saying something but Claire was still recovering.

She took a deep gasping breath. And then another. Everett rubbed his thumbs over the pulse points on her wrists, waiting for her to come back. Malcolm was pacing the wall of windows, barking into an orb for Desmond.

One more breath. "Everett," she said quietly, "what the hell was that?"

Everett moved as she spoke, picking her up in his arms and sitting down on the couch with her in his lap, "I don't know, little mate, but it's okay, I've got you."

Claire could feel the slight shake in his arms and realized that she had probably just scared her men as much as she had scared herself. "I'm sorry,"

His arms tightened around her, "Don't. Don't apologize. That was not your fault."

"It was mine," Malcolm's voice was little more than a growl as he kneeled in front of her.

Claire realized what was different about the shadows now. She could make out more detail. Where before she could see the shape of her men's bodies, now she could make out their features and the clothes they wore.

She lifted a hand to Malcolm's cheek, he covered it with one of his own, as if he was scared she would take it back. "It wasn't your fault." She insisted. "I don't know what happened but I don't think any one of us was expecting that."

"Claire!" Desmond burst through the door of the suite and Claire realized the second difference. Whereas before she could only make out shadows three paces around her, now it seemed she could make out at least a six pace radius around her, the room coming into better focus as she watched Desmond race towards them.

"I'm okay," she reassured. Malcolm growled and Claire repeated it, "I'm okay. I don't know what happened but I'm okay."

"What the hell did happen?" Desmond demanded.

"It was my fault," Malcolm ignored Claire's earlier words.

"My dragon wanted to give her a gift and selected a Fae dagger that had to be booby-trapped or something."

"It wasn't your fault," Claire insisted, trying to wiggle out of Everett's lap with little success, he did let her turn so her back was to his chest but his arms stayed around her waist as if he couldn't let her go just yet.

"Booby-trapped?" Desmond questioned.

"It wasn't booby-trapped," Claire said, "I mean maybe it was but not in the way you think."

Malcolm ignored her, "Can you check her over? The magic that exuded from the dagger once she touched it threw Everett and I away from her and pushed the furniture back."

He took her hand off his cheek and gave it to Desmond who took her other hand as well.

"Desmond," she complained, "I'm fine, this is unnecessary."

"You might think so," Desmond said with forced cheer, "but Malcolm just scared the shit out of me with an emergency message that you had been hurt so humor us and let me check you over for any magical effects of that spell."

"Desmond," Claire was insistent, "I could see."

Desmond paused in his spell casting, "What?"

The men were quiet, "I could see." Claire said again, "For a brief moment, I think I could see color. And now, the shadows are much clearer to make out and I can see the shadows more than three paces."

Desmond was quiet and then spoke, "Let's start at the beginning,"

Claire started with her handling the first sets of daggers and not feeling a connection with any of them. Malcolm brought out the Fae dagger and something about it drew her towards it but she ignored the feeling initially because it was a family heirloom. When she held it, she described the feeling of heat that emanated from it and raced through her body. When she got to the part about the heat or magic attacking the dome where her magic sat, she saw Desmond and Malcolm exchange looks. She described how her magic had flowed out of her in response and the force of her magic had knocked the men back, not the Fae magic. She explained that for a brief moment she could see brighter shades but it was overwhelming so she had closed her eyes and when she opened them again, the color was gone but the shadows had changed.

When she finished, Desmond sat back on his heels, her hand still in his. "What is it?" She asked.

"What you just described," he rubbed his free hand across his face, "What you just described changes everything. This was the missing piece," he muttered the last part more to himself.

"Desmond," she said, sharper than she intended to, "what changes everything."

"What you just described wasn't a magical attack. At least not in the way we were initially thinking. It was an attack on the bindings of your power."

"Bindings?"

"That dome you are describing where your magic sits, that's not supposed to be there. Your magic is supposed to flow freely through your center. The dome means that someone bound your power. And being that it's all you've ever known, someone powerful had to have done it when you were very young."

"But… why?"

Malcolm answered her, "That's the priceless question. Why and who. I think I agree with Desmond's assertion in the Arena earlier this week. Your parents are powerful."

Claire's mind was swirling and she sagged back into Everett's chest. What did all of this mean?

She must have voiced the question out loud.

"It means," Desmond said, "that the bindings on your magic are loosening or have loosened. We will have to investigate and see where we can add to your training to prepare."

"Prepare for what?" Claire asked.

"If your magic was truly bound for that long, loosening the bindings now could unleash it faster than you are prepared for as it has built up for years."

Claire tensed and Everett hugged her tighter, "We will prepare you." he promised, "You won't be alone in this."

"Never," Desmond vowed as well, "I love a good puzzle and I will help you figure this out so we can be prepared."

Malcolm took one of her hands from Desmond. "I will as well. We will train you to defend yourself."

"With the dagger?" Claire questioned.

The men exchanged looks. "We'll see." Malcolm said.

Her magic protested at that, causing Claire to pause and realize that it was much more present in her center than before. "No, I need to." She said, "It's important."

"I don't want it to react to you like that again. Not until you can control it."

"It won't," Claire didn't know how she was so sure. "It won't. It did its job. Hand it to me."

The men hesitated and while Claire understood their hesitation she remained firm. "Hand it to me."

"Let me throw up a barrier spell so we don't take down the building by accident." Desmond said.

He quickly threw up the barrier and Malcolm retrieved the dagger from the floor where Claire had dropped it. He hesitated in handing it to her but Claire reached up and grabbed it.

Collectively, they all held their breath but nothing happened. The dagger warmed in her palm but there was none of the blinding heat from before. Instead, a sense of rightness fell over Claire, her magic reaching out through her hand to test the dagger, once her magic reached it, the dagger glowed lightly in her hand. The intakes of breath from her men indicated they saw it too.

Gently, Claire set the dagger back into Malcolm's hand. The glow faded as soon as she released it and Malcolm wrapped the dagger up in some cloth. Claire felt a weird pang of loss but pushed it down. "Now what?" She asked.

"Now we train you." Desmond said. "We train you for all the different scenarios that might happen when your bindings loosen. I'll teach you spells and how to send your magic to something and how to draw it to you."

"I'll continue teaching you combat. We will train with the daggers until you are proficient." Malcolm said.

"And I'll teach you to survive." Everett said, "Stealth and strategy."

Claire nodded. "What about classes?"

"We'll build off your classes when we can but if it gets too much, I'll speak to the Headmaster." Desmond said, "but I'd rather keep it between us now. Until we have more answers."

"What about my friends?" Claire asked.

Desmond hesitated, "I don't believe that they would use this information against you but remember their lives are not their own in a sense. Cody still answers to his father, the Alpha. Bethany is the same with her father, the Pride Leader. Holly still answers to my mother at Brandlevine and we've all seen the asshole that Zack answers to. I'm not saying they would intentionally hurt you or betray you but their lives are not their own yet."

Claire nodded, "I understand. I don't want any of them getting hurt over this. I'll try and keep it a secret but they'll know something is up."

"We can be vague about wanting to train you more but anything about your heritage or how the dagger reacts to you would be best kept a secret."

Claire nodded. "Will I be training with the dagger?"

Malcolm spoke, "Not until we have more answers about why it glows when you touch it."

"I think I can answer that one," Claire said, "it didn't glow until I let my magic soak into it."

"Claire," Desmond admonished lightly as Malcolm growled, "let's avoid sending magic into rare, sacred objects until we know the consequences. What if it reacted poorly?"

Claire winced, she could see their point, "Instinct?"

Everett chuckled lightly behind her, "Something that we will also cultivate during your training. I think it would be fine for her to work with the dagger in our morning sessions. As long as Desmond is there to put up a barrier spell."

Desmond groaned, "You're going to make me be a morning person, little witch?"

"You don't have to," Claire said quickly.

Malcolm slapped Desmond upside his head, "Quit making her feel bad!" He growled, "She doesn't need that shit. Start going to bed at a reasonable time."

"Fine." Desmond grouched but he squeezed Claire's hand to let her know he wasn't actually upset. "Now as exciting as this afternoon has been, we probably need to make our way to the dining hall if we want to avoid any additional questions about our tardiness."

The men stood, the dagger still wrapped in cloth in Malcolm's hands. He saw where her eyes had landed, "I'll get you a sheath to keep it in. You can't openly carry weapons around the school grounds unless it's during combat class but you can keep it in your bag for class."

Claire nodded and let Desmond help her to her feet off of Everett's lap. "Let's get to dinner, little witch, before we have another life-changing magic release from your hungry stomach."

CHAPTER 24

If Claire's weeks were busy before, it was nothing on what they looked like now. She still got up every morning and went to the Combat Arena for training. Malcolm, true to his word, pushed her hard. She was using the wooden daggers now, fighting him off with his own set as well as a staff to give her practice with swords. The weapons felt good in her hand and the training was paying off as her movements became more nimble. Being able to see the shadows a bit clearer helped but Malcolm also had her practice her energy reading abilities as well.

Class work was still intensive but Claire found that the little bit of magic that was loosened in her bindings made some of her class work much easier. Runes in particular was where she saw a lot of improvement with her control getting more and more refined as well as the force behind which she was able to wield the elements. Professor Andy announced that as the weather warmed up, they would take some classes in the Combat Arena in order to have the room for larger elemental wields.

Professor Benton was still grumpy as ever in Spells and

Potions but with Desmond there, he didn't say much to her directly. The class had moved on to the second half of the semester with spells and under Desmond's tutelage, Claire was excelling. During dinner, Desmond, Claire and Zack often lapsed into theoretical conversations about spells and their various uses.

History class didn't require magic but Claire soaked up all of the information she could on the different races and the histories of each. In Herbology, Professor Helene had pulled her aside and given her another book on energy reading, this one specific to Herbology and plants. She had also cautioned Claire to pull back on her magic use during class as apparently her and Bethany's garden plot was growing much better than the others. Some of Vivienne's friends in the class made snide remarks about her background that allowed her to grow a better garden but Claire ignored them.

Her lessons with Everett in the evening were the most interesting to Claire. They took walks in the woods and around the Academy as Everett taught her stealth and how to move unseen. When they did talk, they discussed strategy and sometimes recapped her history lesson with an added layer of why the races reacted the way they did based on their respective heritage.

All of the work was good and she soaked up the knowledge like a sponge but it seemed that this weekend she was hitting a wall. Closing the book on her lap, Claire rubbed her eyes. She was sitting on a couch in the Triad's suite with Desmond at one end. They were looking for more information on energy reading and Fae artifacts.

"Tired?" Desmond asked.

"Is it possible for one's brain to become stuffed with knowledge?"

Desmond laughed, the rich melodious sound a balm to her ears, "It is. We have been pushing you rather hard, little witch."

"It's been nice to spend time with you all," Claire said, "I just don't know if I can take any more studying."

Desmond closed his book as well, "What would you like to do instead?"

Claire set the book on the low table in front of the couch and stood. She studied the room around her, thinking back to the day she grabbed the dagger, only a short month ago. The late spring sunlight streamed through the windows as she recalled the bright shades that had assaulted her senses.

"I think I saw colors that day," she mused, "at least I think that's what they were. It was very bright, overwhelming actually."

"Have you ever seen color?" Desmond asked, standing as well.

"Not that I can remember." Claire said, walking around the table to trail her fingers on the opposite couch, "this color was more muted than the rest. So were the walls."

Desmond followed her, stepping up to her side. "This couch is brown," he explained softly, "like the soil but a bit lighter of a shade. Soil is a richer brown."

"What does brown feel like?" Claire didn't know if the question was silly or not but having spent most of her life navigating her world based on feeling, she struggled to connect Desmond's words to the color in her brain.

"Steady," he said, "warm sometimes, like when you have your hands buried in the soil in the garden on a sunny day. Cool when the day is cloudy."

Claire nodded and stepped away to trace her fingers over the stone wall, "And the walls?"

"Those are grey. Grey is a mixture of black and white."

Claire arched an eyebrow and Desmond cursed, "Which would not make any difference to you." He hummed as he thought, "Grey feels like the air on a cloudy day, it's dull, drab. It feels like.... sadness?"

Claire nodded, stepping back to his side and squeezing his hand. "What about this pillow?" She pointed to the pillow on the chair next to the brown couch.

"That's green, it's the color of plants and most leaves on the trees. It's a vibrant color, full of life and growth but also steady. A bit like brown in that way but reaching up towards the sun if that makes sense?" Desmond's voice was low, husky in a way that made Claire tingle a little as the pull strengthened between them. She realized she had not had many opportunities to be alone with Desmond over the last few months. At lunch or dinner they were always with people and same with Spells and Potions.

She tugged his hand over to a tapestry that hung on the wall between the kitchen and Desmond's study door.

"And what was this color?" Claire touched a tapestry that hung on the wall. It was a bold color from what she remembered.

Desmond stepped up close behind her, his chest to her back. His breath wafted across her neck, "That's red."

"Tell me about red?" Claire's voice was softer than she intended it to be. She cautiously leaned back into him.

Desmond's hands lifted to rest on her hips, and Claire shivered. Desmond groaned softly and pulled her back into him harder. His voice in her ear had her stomach clenching and her heart beating quicker.

"Red is a bold color, the color of a fiery sunset, the color of your cheeks when you blush, the color of passion and love." Desmond's thumbs stroked her hip bones, slipping slightly under her shirt.

"Is this what red feels like?" Claire's body heated as she pressed harder back into him, playing with something she didn't quite understand but enjoying the feeling all the same.

Desmond groaned and dropped his mouth to the bare skin on her neck. Claire inhaled as what felt like sparks pressed in her lower stomach. Pressing soft kisses along the exposed skin he trailed his lips up to her ear, "Yes, my little witch, this is what red feels like,"

His one hand left her hip to grasp her chin and turned it till his lips met hers. Claire sagged further into his grip while she also tried to turn in his grasp to capture his lips more fully. Groaning and nipping her bottom lip, Desmond allowed her to turn in his grip, his hands slipping from her waist to her lower back with one tracing up her back causing her to arch into his chest.

She captured his lips again, pressing harder and with a fervor that matched the ache she felt inside. One of his hands wrapped his fingers in her hair, angling her head so he could kiss her deeper. Pressing her back into the tapestry Claire smiled internally and thought to herself that she really liked the color red.

A knock broke them apart. "Desmond, I know you're in there." Holly's voice came through the door. "You all have hogged Claire all week so I'm here to rescue her."

Claire giggled softly as Desmond groaned. "One minute," he called but made no move to break away. Claire closed her eyes, the feel of him pressed against her body and the remnants of the kiss made it hard to think. Or want to move. He groaned again. "My cousin has impeccable timing."

Claire opened her eyes and smiled up at him. "She's right though, I haven't had a chance to hang out with her or any of them in a while."

"I know, that's why I'm not telling her to shove off so we can continue what you started."

"What I started?" She arched an eyebrow at his teasing, "I'm just the student here, you were teaching me colors."

Desmond groaned, "Don't tease me now or I'll continue your lesson." He stepped back reluctantly as if it caused him physical pain to do so. He held out a hand, unwilling to let her go completely, "Come on, let's get your bag."

Claire retrieved her bag sitting next to the couch and placed her books in it. Desmond opened the door. "Cousin," he greeted, "to what do we owe the rude interruption?"

"I'm rescuing Claire for a girl's night. You all have been suffocating her." Holly declared, striding past Desmond to stand by Claire. "Bethany is getting us snacks."

Claire laughed, "They haven't been that bad. I've enjoyed the suffocation."

"Still. I know you want to bring Claire up to speed as soon as possible to prepare her for the outside world," Holly went along with the excuse everyone had been given about the additional training, "but she needs breaks too so say goodbye for tonight so we can go stuff our faces and gossip."

Desmond huffed dramatically "You're lucky I love you for letting you steal my soul flame away from me."

Holly smiled, "If I truly stole her away, you would never find her."

Claire squeezed Holly's arm to stop the argument from going forward. There was a weird tension in the air that wasn't usually there. She stepped to Desmond and wrapped her arms around his tense body. He relaxed into her, his frame softening as his arms wrapped around her. He placed a sweet kiss on her forehead, such a difference from the passionate one they just shared against the wall. "I'll see you tomorrow," he promised.

"See you tomorrow."

Claire followed Holly out and waited until they were outside the building to ask, "what was that about?"

"What was what about?" Holly tried to play it off.

"Holly," Claire warned gently, "what was that weird tension?"

Holly grumbled but she explained, "They agreed they wouldn't overwhelm you and it seems like in the last month all they've done has been that."

"They are just trying to get me prepared for the Realm." Claire felt bad lying to her friend but it wasn't a total lie. "But I agree that it has been a little intense so let's compromise. Saturday nights are for friends only?"

Holly squeezed her arm, "You're too sweet, Claire. How about Saturday night is for the girls and Wednesday night is for the friends. Zack and Cody miss hanging out with you too."

"Sounds good to me. I'll let my Triad know."

"You said, 'My Triad'" Holly pointed out.

Claire smiled, "I did, didn't I?"

A warm feeling spread through her. A feeling that stayed with her though girl's night and well into next week. She was finally finding her place here.

CHAPTER 25

The late spring sun warmed the seats around the wall of the Combat Arena. It was the end of the semester and Malcolm had arranged their final to fall two weeks earlier than the rest of her classes. He had told the group that Combat's final would be two weeks earlier than the other classes to allow them the extra study time but he expected them to keep up their skills over the summer.

The final was structured like combat matches. Malcolm paired the students up and had them fight to show off their learned ability. It was the only time in the class that Malcolm let them use their magic or shifting abilities if they had them. He had carefully paired the students to have equal footing in the matches. The goal, he told the class, was to demonstrate to him that they had learned something, not knock out their classmates.

Claire ran her hand over the Fae dagger hanging at her hip. The warm metal of the handle, a comfort for her nerves. Malcolm had paired her with a shifter in her class that was proficient with the staff. Her match wasn't until later in the week, with three matches fighting per day. They were fighting with wooden weapons but Malcolm was letting her use the Fae dagger in case the shifter decided to use her wolf form. Claire could tell he wanted to ban the shifter from shifting but Claire had reminded him that he promised he wouldn't go easy on her.

The thwack of wood hitting wood brought her attention back to the match. Brent was fighting one of Vivienne's friends. Both were wielding the wooden staffs for the first part of their match. Many of the matches had started with weapons and devolved into magic wielding as the match went on. Watching the two move around the arena, using the space to land their blows or retreat, her magic became unsettled inside her.

Frowning, Claire tried to isolate what was causing her magic to flair. Over the last few months, Desmond's tutelage and Everett's meditation lessons had resulted in a much closer bond with her magic. She could feel the dome around it where the bindings still were but the magic that had been released had become an extension of herself. And now it danced nervously in her stomach. Sensing a threat that she could not see yet.

The Fae dagger at her hip warmed slightly through the finely crafted leather sheath that Malcolm had given her. She grasped the pommel with her left hand as she saw it happen. The match in front of her had devolved into magic shots. Brent and Vivienne's friend trading magical blows. Vivienne's friend moved so her back was to Claire's seat and Claire saw Brent focus over the girl's shoulder for a brief second at her before winding up his next shot.

A much bigger ball of magic then Claire had ever seen him conjure formed in his hands and he flung it in an easy throw at the girl who instead of absorbing or deflecting it as she had been, added her own magic to it and tossed it over her shoulder, straight at Claire.

She could hear Malcolm's roar and the other students cry out but she had a split second to react. Going off instinct, she drew the Fae dagger and held it in front of her body, rising from her seat and planting her feet to meet the magic head on. The ball of angry magic hit the dagger full on and Claire gritted her teeth under the pressure. Brent was a formidable fire witch and the girl had added her air power to the blast but when the blast hit the dagger, a field of energy rose through the dagger, drawing on her magic and using it to absorb the blast. Brent and the girl's magic coursed through the dagger as it absorbed the blast, filtering through her magic until her center was swarming with magic, making Claire drop to her knees as it beat on her insides, demanding to be unleashed.

"Claire," Desmond's voice seemed distant, when had he gotten here? She forced her eyes open to see him crouched about ten feet away, Holly next to him. "Claire," he said again and Claire strained to hear him through the feeling of her body lighting up, "you have to let the magic go. You have to redirect it."

Claire heard him but redirect it where? Even the barrier that Desmond was working to erect around her wouldn't hold under the onslaught, Claire knew that instinctively. She couldn't release it, it would hurt her Triad and the other students. A solid, steady energy called to her from beyond her magic's reach as she sagged back into the stone wall. The Academy. It could take the magic blast.

Turning, Claire slammed her free hand into the wall of the Combat Arena, demanding her magic release into the structure. Like a tidal wave, it blew out of her and into the wall. Instead of blasting the wall into smithereens, it absorbed the magic from her. For a brief moment she could feel the sentient Academy sending the magic outward from the arena and into the other buildings as the magic coursed through her. It was pulling too much now, the excess magic having flown out of her, the Academy was pulling on Claire's magic now which was hindered by the bindings. The Fae dagger heated in her other hand again, breaking the Academy's pull and allowing Claire to focus. Weakly, she pulled her hand off of the wall, pleading with her magic to retreat. As the world faded into black, she caught a glimpse of three shadowy figures running towards her.

* * *

"HEALER. NOW!" Desmond's heart was in his throat as he reached Claire, Everett and Malcolm on his heels.

Malcolm scooped Claire up in his arms, her limp body cradled against his chest.

"Make a hole," Holly's voice demanded and the students parted as the earth literally shoved them backwards.

The Triad raced towards the administrative building and the Healer's room.

Madam Pinney looked up as the men burst through the door, her sharp gaze landing on Claire. "Place her on the bed," she demanded, "and move back so I can see what I'm working with."

Malcolm growled but placed Claire on the bed gently. He didn't retreat but did move up to the head of the bed, his hand brushing Claire's hair from her face.

Desmond quickly recounted the events at the arena while Madam Pinney efficiently checked Claire over, her hands a cool white glow as her healing abilities checked Claire's body and magic.

Finishing her scan, she took a step back.

"Well?" Everett demanded.

"She's fine. Or she will be fine. She's extremely lucky. Her magic is drained but it's nothing that time and rest won't heal."

"So there's nothing you can do?" Malcolm growled.

Madam Pinney arched an eyebrow at him, "There's nothing to be done. She overextended her magic in self-defense and it's running on empty. Only time will replenish her magic."

"What about us? She's my soul flame and Malcolm and

Everett's mate." Both Everett and Malcolm growled at him but Desmond had known Madam Pinney a long time. She would keep their secret. To the Academy, Claire was Everett's mate and their Fourth

"Have you bonded?" Madam Pinney asked.

Desmond shook his head and she sighed. "Then I'm afraid there's nothing you can do either. If you had bonded, she would be able to pull on your bond slightly to restore her magic levels faster but she will recover. It would probably help if you kept her close but right now it's just a wait."

Desmond's heart sank but he nodded, "Is it okay for her to be moved? I want to bring her back to our suite."

Madam Pinney nodded. "Yes, she can be moved. I can inform Headmaster Dorian if you wish?" Her look asked him if Headmaster Dorian knew the whole story.

Desmond nodded, "That would be appreciated. Let him know we will speak to him later when Claire wakes up."

Madam Pinney left the room and Desmond stared down at Claire. She looked as if she was sleeping if it wasn't for the paleness of her skin.

"That was no accident," Everett growled.

Desmond and Malcolm whipped their heads from Claire to look at him. "What do you mean?" Desmond demanded.

"Brent and Cassie." Everett said, "I was watching. Cassie maneuvered her back to Claire and Brent looked over Cassie's shoulder before he fired that shot. Cassie deflected down and to the side for the entirety of that match except for that one shot."

Malcolm let loose a thunderous growl and Desmond's magic fought him for control. "They'll claim it was an accident," Desmond could appreciate the genius of their plan.

"I'll kill them!" Malcolm growled.

"You can't." Everett said. "It would take you away from Claire. But they will suffer."

He looked at Desmond who nodded, "They won't get away

with this, brother." Desmond clasped a hand on Malcolm's shoulder. "Let's get Claire out of here and back to the suite."

Malcolm lifted Claire into his arms again, cradling her gently to his chest. Everett sagged the blanket off the bed and tucked it around Claire. The Fae dagger hung at Claire's hip still and Desmond reached over her stomach to untie the sheath. Desmond wondered for a brief second how the dagger got back into the sheath but pushed that thought away for another day as they exited the building.

At the bottom of the steps, Claire's friends waited anxiously. "How is she?" Holly demanded.

"She'll be okay," Desmond said, "she's just exhausted her magic and it needs to replenish."

Bethany growled, "I'll kill them." She whirled away as if to go find them and Cody caught her arm.

"You can't kill them. You'll get kicked out of the Academy."

"Worth it." Bethany snarled at him, "You know as well as I do that Vivienne put them up to this."

"We have no proof of that," Zack was pale as he looked at Claire, "it will be your word against theirs just as they intended."

Bethany snarled again and Cody grabbed her face, "We'll find proof," he growled, "but going off half-cocked isn't helping Claire."

Bethany growled back at him but settled and Cody removed his hands, "We'll find out what we can," Holly promised, "take care of her." She looked at Desmond who nodded.

The Triad quickly made their way across the courtyard, ignoring the curious stares and whispers of students. Once in their suite, Desmond crossed the room to a rarely used door. Each Triad suite had a room for the Triad's Fourth. After they found Claire, Malcolm had visited Pinscer Street with Desmond and they had outfitted Claire's room to match her personality.

Malcolm gently laid her on the light blue sheets when Everett pulled back the cream comforter. Desmond pulled off her shoes and then toed off his own as he climbed up to her side. Malcolm slid in on her other side and Everett lifted her feet gently and placed them in his lap as he sat cross legged at the foot of the bed, staring at Claire.

Her face looked more peaceful now, the color slowly returning to her cheeks. Malcolm placed an arm around her hips and slid his other one under her head. Desmond placed a hand over her stomach, feeling the rise and fall of her breath underneath it. That motion finally calmed his heart to a reasonable rate as he felt the rise and fall and let that lure him into a light sleep.

CHAPTER 26

Claire was warm. So very, very warm. It was like when she fell asleep in front of the fire in the orphanage living area under a scratchy blanket. The kind of warmth that makes you a bit itchy from its presence.

She shifted restlessly to try to kick off her blankets. Her legs met warm bodies on either side and her eyes flew open.

"Easy, Claire," a voice started, "It's just us."

"Desmond?" Claire could hear the waver in her voice, her panic subsiding as her magic recognized the pull towards all three bodies. Her Triad. She frowned, usually she recognized the pull right away even at a distance. Exploring further, she found her magic was reacting sluggishly in her center.

"Yes, little witch, it's us."

"What happened? My magic..."

A strong, calloused hand ran across her legs. Everett. "What do you remember?"

Claire's face scrunched up as she tried to remember. Malcolm's smoke and cinnamon scent grew stronger as he shifted at her left side. "Don't stress yourself, little treasure, it'll come. What's the last thing you remember."

"We started Combat Finals today," Claire began slowly, "but my match wasn't today, was it?"

"No," Malcolm said, "it was later this week."

"Oh. Oh!" Claire started remembering in flashes. Brent and Cassie fighting. A large ball of magic. Pulling the Fae Dagger. Absorbing the magic then sending it into the Academy.

As she remembered, the shadows around her got clearer. "I remember. What happened?"

Desmond spoke, "You took in a blast of magic that should have killed you and sent it into the Academy. Unfortunately you sent too much and the Academy took not only the excess magic but also pulled on your magic till it dropped to dangerous levels. That's why you passed out."

"I drained my magic?" Claire panicked, half sitting up. She hadn't meant for that to happen.

Everett squeezed her feet, "Not permanently, little mate, it'll replenish. Think of it as a muscle that you just strained from overuse. It will recover."

Claire settled back in between Desmond and Malcolm. "How did I end up here?"

"We took you to Madam Pinney, the healer, and once she confirmed your magic levels were low but you were otherwise unharmed, we brought you here to recover." Malcolm said, his arm tightening across her hips, "You scared us, little treasure." His voice gruff.

"I'm sorry," Claire said, "I just reacted."

"And reacted well," Desmond soothed, "you did the absolute right thing reacting the way you did. If you had sent the magic blast anywhere else, it would have been a lot worse."

"I just wish… I wish we had more answers. About who I am or what I am. Why my magic is bound." Claire waved her hands in the air lazily. "All of it."

"We'll figure it out together." Everett said.

"You shouldn't have to," Claire's voice was small, "you all deserve a better Fourth. A better mate. One with more answers."

"Hey now." Desmond cupped her chin and turned her face towards him, her lack of magic making the shadows fuzzier than they had been in a while, "Where is this all coming from?"

"What if it's always like this?" Claire whispered, "What if I never figure it out. If my magic is always bound. You need a powerful Fourth."

"You are powerful," Malcolm growled from behind her, his voice heavy in her ear when Desmond refused to let go of her cheek.

"Like a loose cannon," Claire whispered.

"No one has control at first." Desmond said lowering his forehead to hers, "We all struggle in the beginning. But a Fourth doesn't make us more powerful, not at all. She gives us something to fight for. You give us something to fight for."

Everett broke in, "Everyone else wants something from us. Our status. Our power. Our wealth. A Fourth doesn't want any of that. She just wants us. Like you do." The last sentence was soft, like Everett wasn't sure how she would react, her insecurities must be affecting all of them.

"I'm sorry," Claire said, "I don't know where all these doubts are coming from."

"If I had to take a guess," Desmond's voice was wry, "it might have come from the near-death experience yesterday."

Claire smiled as Malcolm growled, clearly not appreciating the reminder. "Wait, yesterday?" Her eyes widened.

Everett started rubbing her feet as Malcolm's hand massaged her hip. At their touches, her heartbeat slowed and she relaxed back into Desmond's hold.

"Yes, yesterday." Desmond said lightly, "You've been resting since then while we monitored your magic levels. It's about dinner time now."

Claire's stomach growled at his words, as if recognizing it hadn't eaten in a full day.

The bed shook slightly as the men chuckled. "Let's get you fed." Malcolm said, placing a gentle kiss to her shoulder before rolling away and out of bed.

Everett squeezed her feet one last time and got up as well. Desmond released her but not before placing a light kiss on her lips that had Claire blushing. She swung her legs over the side of the bed, noting the massiveness of it. "Whose room is this?"

The men stilled briefly. "It's yours." Malcolm said firmly.

Claire arched her brow, "No it's not. This bed would take up the entire room if it was my room."

Desmond rounded the bed and interlaced his fingers with hers. "It's your room in the suite."

Claire was shocked, "In your suite?" She parroted.

"Yes." Malcolm's voice was firm, as if he was ready to argue with her about this, "Every Triad suite has four rooms, three for us and one for our Fourth. You."

Claire took a breath as her brain tried to process. Deciding it was a problem for another day once her magic returned and she could think clearly. "Okay," she nodded.

"Okay?" Desmond was understandably wary. All three men had tensed like she was going to argue.

"Okay." Claire repeated, smiling slightly at his confusion.

Everett broke their back and forth by approaching. "Here's some clothes you can change into." He led her to another door in the room, "This is the bathroom."

"Thank you, Everett." Claire smiled at him, kissing his cheek lightly as she passed through the door.

The sound that came out of his throat wasn't a growl but more like a purr?

Claire dressed quickly in clothes that she knew weren't hers but fit her perfectly. Malcolm. She shook her head with a smile. The growly dragon had probably filled her room after their first market trip but Claire discovered that she wasn't actually mad. Her brief moment of nerves earlier seemed to be fading as her magic slowly came back. She smoothed her hand down the silky, lightweight blouse. Short sleeves brushed midway down her arms and the pants cut off right under her knees.

Stepping outside, there was more than one throat clearing. Her men hadn't strayed far from the room. "Would you like to eat dinner here or go to the dining hall?" Malcolm asked.

"The dining hall, please," Claire said, "Holly and the others must be out of their mind."

"Holly came by this morning to check on you and she and the others came by last night as well." Desmond said.

Claire's center warmed at the words. Her friends were pretty great.

The Triad and her exited the suite and started down the hallway. She paused at the top of the stairs, the short walk down the hallway had her slightly out of breath. She squeaked as Everett picked her up off her feet. "Everett!"

"Let us spoil you, little mate." He nuzzled her hair as he carried her down the stairs

Claire made him put her down at the entrance to the dining hall. They were a little late to the regular dinner period but that meant all the students were still inside. She wanted to walk in on her own volition.

Claire held onto Everett's hand with one hand and Malcolm's with the other as Desmond got the door for them. As they entered, a hush fell over the students. Claire kept her chin up high as they made their way back to their regular table.

"Claire!" Holly cried before a shadow was flying their direction. Everett and Malcolm dropped their hands and Everett placed a hand on her lower back, providing support as Holly threw her arms around her. Claire hugged her back tight. Holly really gave great hugs.

"Okay, move out of the way." Bethany grumbled, "Don't hog her."

Holly reluctantly released her and Bethany hugged her so tight she could barely breathe. "I'm okay," she whispered in the lion shifter's ear.

Bethany squeezed tighter for a moment before releasing her. Cody and Zack gave her quick hugs as well, ignoring Malcolm's growls. They all took a seat around the table.

"How are you feeling?" Holly asked.

Claire smiled, "Good, all things considering. Hungry."

Holly laughed, "I would imagine. Did you just wake up?"

Claire nodded, "Probably not even a half hour ago."

"You scared the shit out of us." Bethany was blunt as always.

"You're not the only one," Claire confessed, "I scared myself a bit too."

Everett shifted a bit closer to her and laid a hand on her leg.

"Would any one of you happen to know why Brent and Cassie are sporting black eyes today?" Desmond's question had her friends stilling.

"No idea." Holly's voice was level.

"I see," Desmond's voice was amused, "and would you happen to know the reason Vivienne is not at lunch?"

Bethany growled, "Unfortunately, she was called home for a family affair yesterday afternoon."

"How disappointing," Desmond's answer had the table breaking into laughter.

"You aren't going to get in trouble?" Claire worried.

"They would have to know who attacked those poor students for anyone to be in trouble." Zack informed her.

"Well done," Malcolm grumbled.

They kept the topics light for the rest of dinner. Before it was over, Claire found her eyes going heavy which was odd as she had rested for a full day.

The Triad, deeply in tune to her needs it seemed, made their excuses. Claire made it out the dining hall doors before Malcolm swept her off her feet. She didn't protest, instead curling into his chest. She was asleep before they reached the suite.

CHAPTER 27

The next day Claire insisted on going to classes, wanting some normalcy back in her life. The men grumbled but relented with the compromise that they walk her to and from every class.

Professor Andy made a small fuss over her in Runes, telling her not to worry about making up the assignment and giving her notes from yesterday's lesson. She checked in with Claire about her magic levels and Claire told her that they were almost back to normal.

Professor Storm didn't make as big of a fuss in History but he did hold her back at the end of class asking about her health. It was hard to read the stoic professor but he seemed pleased she was okay and asked if she needed an extension on her final paper.

Professor Benton gave her the most normal reaction which was to ignore her. Claire didn't know if that was because he truly didn't care or that Desmond was shooting glares at the man over her shoulder. Either way, she kept her head down and copied the lesson.

Professor Helene didn't make a fuss in front of the class, it wasn't her way. But she did check in with Claire as she monitored the students transplanting seedlings from their garden into small pots.

Malcolm refused to let her take part in Combat Finals but allowed her to spar with Everett one day with Professor Andy present to give Claire her final grade.

And so the next two weeks passed by quickly. Her friends and her crammed for their finals but the last test came and went one morning and they were celebrating over lunch when the Headmaster's assistant approached the table.

"Instructor Malcolm, Captain Everett, Assistant Desmond, students," she addressed the table in greeting, "Headmaster Dorian requests your Triad's presence with your Fourth in his office."

"Thank you, Gwen," Desmond said, "what time does he wish to see us?"

"It was an urgent request."

"We will head that way shortly." Malcolm dismissed her.

The table was silent for a beat. "What do you think he wants?" Holly asked, worry threading through her voice.

"I'm sure it's nothing," Desmond said, "he probably wants to chat about our summer plans."

Holly had invited Claire back to Brandlevine with the Triad and Claire was considering her invitation. There was really no point in returning to Windshire but for some reason Claire felt a bit of loss leaving the Academy.

The men guided Claire out of the dining hall through the interior doors that spilled out into the hallway of the administrative building. Their steps were loud against the stone floor, the sound echoing against the walls. Claire knew it was strange but she could feel the Academy more since she pushed the magic into it a few weeks ago. She had heard some students discussing that the internal maintenance and things like laundry seemed to be happening much faster now. There was probably a connection there, she thought and made a mental note to ask Desmond later.

Walking past Gwen at her desk, Desmond strode to the doors of the Headmaster's office and knocked twice. Claire had a brief flash of deja vu from her first trip to this office after just arriving at the academy.

With her increased shadow ability, she took in the room noting the differences from the first time. With her increased distance of six paces, she could nearly make out the whole room while standing at the door. Six paces in front of her was the desk with two chairs in front of it and the Headmaster's chair behind it. The Headmaster was not sitting in the chair, however. He was standing at one of the windows framed by bookcases to the right of the room. While before, the room had been mostly encased in darkness, Claire could see the bookshelves that lined the other three walls and were filled to the brim.

Everett led her to one of the chairs in front of the Headmaster's desk as the Headmaster left the window and settled into his own chair. Everett took a seat on the arm of her chair while Desmond settled into the other on her left and Malcolm stood behind them, standing sentry.

"Thank you for coming so quickly." Headmaster Dorian began.

"Gwen made it sound urgent." Desmond replied easily but Claire could hear the slight tension in his voice.

"It is," the Headmaster's deep bass voice was steady.

Malcolm growled at the implication that there was a threat to Claire and the Triad.

"It's not what you are thinking." Headmaster Dorian said, "but it needs to be handled carefully."

"Sir, what is it?" Desmond asked, all pretense of lightness in his voice was gone.

"I received a missive today. From the Academy."

Claire sat back in her seat, from the Academy? The sentient Academy?

"Sir?" Desmond sounded as shocked as she felt.

"From your tone it's clear you recognize how rare that is."

"I don't understand," Claire said softly.

The Headmaster explained, "At its prime, the Academy was fully sentient and would often communicate with the Headmasters directly to provide council, not just influence admission decisions. Since the Great War, the magic in the Academy has faded. Some theorize this is because the Fae and Elven students are no longer present and thus the Academy is low on the extra magic it requires for those larger acts. This was the case up until two weeks ago."

The silence was long as everyone processed. Two weeks ago, Claire had sent a huge ball of magic into the Academy and now it was sending letters to the Headmaster.

"What did the missive say?" Claire asked softly.

Headmaster Dorian rubbed a hand over his face, looking tired for a moment before he straightened. "It warned of change coming, troubling change that was going to take every student here being at their best to protect the Academy and themselves."

"What else?" Desmond demanded.

Headmaster Dorian sighed and addressed Claire directly, "Claire, there's something you need to know. There was no mistake regarding your admission to the Academy. No one applied on your behalf. The Academy sent your invitation directly by itself. It shouldn't have had the magic to do that but the only thing I can think of is it held the magic necessary to do that in reserve until it sent it to you."

"How do you know that?" Everett asked.

"Because in this missive, the Academy told me why." Headmaster Dorian said, "It has named you, Claire, as a Champion."

"A Champion of the Academy?" Desmond asked, the familiarity in his tone told Claire this wasn't a new concept.

"No." The Headmaster paused. "A Champion of the Realm."

"What?" The growl exploded out of Malcolm. "That's impossible."

"It's not," the Headmaster held out a piece of paper, "read it for yourself. Claire has been chosen as a Champion of the Realm and the neutral Academy has pledged itself to her aid."

The impact of that statement was staggering. The room fell deathly still until Desmond reached forward and practically snatched the paper out of the Headmaster's hands.

While Desmond read the letter, the Headmaster continued explaining, "In the missive, the Academy asks that our best become available to train Claire in all areas and warns of trouble coming to the Realm. Unfortunately, it does not say what kind of trouble or when it is coming."

Desmond passed the letter back to Malcolm and leaned forward, placing his elbows on his knees. "We have been training her over the last few months extensively."

The Headmaster nodded, "We can review that plan and make adjustments as needed. You have the full weight of the Academy's resources behind you as well as my own."

Claire was still processing as the men began discussing a training plan for her. A Champion of the Realm? The Academy pledging itself to her aid? But against what? And why? Yes, the bindings on her magic were loosening but she was still nowhere near powerful enough to be a champion of anything, much less a realm. She had barely survived a direct magic attack from two students two weeks ago!

"There has to be some kind of mistake." Her soft whispered words halted the conversation.

Everett picked up one of her hands and squeezed it.

"There's been no mistake, Claire," the Headmaster said gently, "I know this is all very overwhelming but the Academy will help you through it."

"We will help you through it." Everett promised softly in her ear. Claire was grateful for her support but this was all still very overwhelming.

"Let's reconvene tomorrow." Malcolm said. "We can make plans then."

Headmaster Dorian agreed. "I know you were planning on spending the summer in Brandlevine but that might not be the best place for Claire now. I want to offer you all to stay at the Academy this summer."

"We will think about it." Desmond said, rising and helping Claire to her feet.

Her men guided her out of the door, talking over her head still about training and summer plans. She stopped walking, halting their conversation and forcing them to turn towards her. They were in the middle of the hallway heading back towards the dining hall. She couldn't think any more about this.

"I know we have to do all of this planning and I'll need more training," Claire said, "but can we wait on that for just a day? Today I want to celebrate the fact that I survived my first year here at an Academy that this time last year was just a dream. I want to enjoy my friends' company and I want to spend time with my Triad. Tomorrow we can worry and train, but not today. Please?"

The men were silent before Malcolm picked up her hand with his and threaded their fingers, "If that's what you want, little treasure, then that's what we will do."

"How about the Market?" Everett suggested. "We can use a portal to make the trip faster and be back in time for dinner with your friends."

Claire smiled, "That sounds lovely."

"I'll let Holly know where we are taking you so she doesn't worry and I'll let her know about dinner plans tonight."

Desmond continued down the hallway towards the dining hall as Malcolm and Everett guided her in the opposite direction.

"There are portals in a room next to the Headmaster's office," Everett informed her, "we just have to check-in with Gwen before we go."

They checked in with Gwen, letting her know of their plans as Desmond caught up to them. The portal was a weird experience. She held tightly to Desmond's hand as she felt the magic tug on her. One second she was in a small quiet room in the Academy and the other second her senses were bombarded as the portal dropped them across the street from the Market. Other people were stepping out of portals next to them and Desmond guided Claire away from the entrance so Malcolm and Everett didn't bump into them.

With her hand firmly in Desmond's elbow, they weaved through the noisy market, stopping to get sweet rolls and listening to the street musicians. Unlike last time, when Claire felt the pull towards the back section of the market, she led the men that way. She could feel Desmond's curious gaze on her but she hoped he wouldn't ask. Because she had no reason other than her gut feeling. A feeling, she was learning to trust more and more.

The market was quieter in this section. The sharp smell of iron filled the air. Ah, that made sense. Fewer people came to the marketplace for the weapons than they did for the revelries.

The spicy scent of jasmine wafted from one of the tent's darkened interiors. There. That's where she was being guided. She tugged Desmond's elbow towards the tent, intent on entering and pausing when Malcolm ducked in front of her. She gave a half smile at her dragon's protectiveness. When he moved further into the tent, she took it as an all clear. Using the shadows, she made out the shape of a few tables scattered through the tent and a lone figure at the back.

"Welcome Lady and Gentlemen," a woman's older warm voice flowed from the shadowy figure. "Are we looking for something in particular?"

"Just browsing." Everett's voice was crisp but polite. Some vendors could get pushy but Claire didn't sense that this woman would be.

Claire let go of Desmond's arm, drawn to a table on the left. She could see the shadowy outlines of daggers and let her hand out stretch, guided by the warm tug of her magic in her center. At the top left corner of the table, her palm heated and tingles stabbed into her fingers like mini needles.

It seemed as if the tent held its collective breath, all four pairs of eyes on her. She dropped her hand and grabbed the pommel of the dagger.

Unlike the heat of the Fae dagger, this dagger cooled drastically under her touch, the icy touch of it freezing her palm around the grip. The shadows lightened drastically until Claire could make out the script inlaid on the dagger's blade. She didn't recognize it but instinct told her this was Elven script. What was happening?

The Fae dagger at her hip heated unbearable and with a gasp she quickly grabbed it with her other hand. Magic shot out of her center through her hands into the daggers and they glowed. Claire panicked and called her magic back quickly, not wanting the same explosion to happen as the first time she grabbed the Fae dagger. If her magic exploded like that it would hurt her Triad again.

Her magic fought against her call to return. She dug her heels in her mind, Desmond's warning to not push magic into random magical objects repeating in her head. Her magic struggled a bit just as it reached the tip of both daggers. The tips gleamed brightly on both for a stomach-dropping second, like the brightest of jewels on a summer day and then the magic heeded her command.

Claire let out a breath of relief that quickly caught as she realized the new problem. Her magic retreated from the daggers with a ferocity as it rushed back towards the dome of bindings over her center. It hit the dome with a vengeance, forcing Claire to her knees under the pressure as the magic ate at the bindings until the dome looked like a patchwork quilt. Apparently eating all of the bindings it could, the magic settled at her center again.

"Claire," Desmond said softly.

She lifted her gaze, noting a glow fading around her like her magic had thrown up a protection dome without her telling it to.

She blinked rapidly at the assault on her senses as her eyes struggled to adjust. Her gaze landed on her Triad, all three kneeling around her, reaching for her. She sucked in a breath as she met their blue, green, and gold gazes, looking at them in color for the very first time.

She could see.

ACKNOWLEDGMENTS

A huge shoutout to everyone who helped introduce my first RH book to the world! To my best friends who are unerringly supportive in whatever I do, thanks for celebrating the small and large wins with me!

To Author Stella Brie, your advice, help, and support has been instrumental in getting this published. I could not have done this without you so a huge thank you!

To my beta readers who were some of the first eyes on this book, your comments and feedback helped make it the story it is today!

If you find a typo in the book despite my best efforts, please send me an email at sunnyhartauthor@gmail.com

Get book 2, With Her Sight, here!

OTHER BOOKS BY AUTHOR

Writing as Sunny Hart

Unitam Realm Series

By Her Sight

With Her Sight

Beyond Her Sight

All Her Feelings

Writing as Maddi Hart

Avoiding the Sack

ABOUT THE AUTHOR

Sunny Hart lives in the rolling hills of the Kentucky Bluegrass. She has spent her entire life expressing herself through writing and short stories until one NaNoWriMo she challenged herself to write a book to share with the world. By Her Sight is the first book Sunny has published but is one of many floating around in her head. When not writing, Sunny is spending time with her dogs and horse and working her 'day job' as a business strategy consultant.

For the latest news, updates, and giveaways, check out Sunny's Facebook group,
Sunny's Rays of Sunshine

To sign up for her newsletter and more, check out her website at authorsunnyhart.com

Printed in Dunstable, United Kingdom

83217037R00160